BY JOVE

Also by Marissa Doyle

Skin Deep

The Leland Sisters series:
Bewitching Season
Betraying Season
Courtship and Curses
Charles Bewitched

BY JOVE

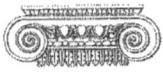

Marissa Doyle

BY JOVE

First Book View Café edition published 2017
Previously published by Entangled Publishing LLC 2014

Published by Book View Café
ISBN: 978-1-61138-667-7

Cover design by Dave Smeds
Cover art by SelfPubBookCovers/Shardel
Interior design by Marissa Doyle

Book View Café Publishing Cooperative
P.O. Box 1624
Cedar Crest, NM 87008-1624

www.bookviewcafe.com

For Scott, who understands

Part I

De rerum natura

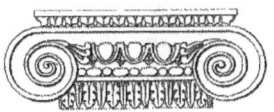

One

"COME IN, MISS FAIRCHILD," called the clear baritone voice from behind the closed door.

Theodora Fairchild blinked at her fist, raised to knock. Did Dr. d'Amboise have closed-circuit cameras trained on his doorway? She almost glanced behind her to search for hidden lenses, then gave herself a mental shake, straightened her skirt, and turned the polished brass doorknob.

A man with sleek silver hair looked up at her from a large mahogany desk, regarding her with interest and something suspiciously like amusement. Before she had time to wonder why, he'd risen and come forward to meet her. "*Salve, mea amica.* Welcome to John Winthrop University."

She shook his hand. "*Gratias, Magister d'Amboise. Hic gaudeo esse.*" Wow. Chairmen of Classical Language departments weren't supposed to be so attractive. He looked more like a wealthy polo player than head of one of the most distinguished classics departments outside of Europe. She couldn't help covertly admiring his broad shoulders and the easy grace of his movements. His blue button-down shirt, sleeves casually rolled up over tanned forearms, bore an expensive logo.

He laughed and held up one hand. "I'm afraid that exhausts my conversational Latin. Greek's my subject. Won't you sit down, Miss Fairchild? Do you prefer to be called Theodora?" He waved her into the leather wingback before the desk and resumed his own seat. On the linenfold-paneled wall behind him were shelves with red-figured Greek vases and fragments of stone statuary. They didn't look like copies. Wow again.

She tore her attention away from them. "Just Theo is fine. Fewer syllables."

"But Theodora is a beautiful name. 'Beloved of the god.'" He leaned back in his chair and gazed at her.

Theo shifted uncomfortably. His turquoise eyes were disquieting; they were slightly prominent, which might account for her feeling that they saw everything about her. "I hope I'm not disturbing you," she said to fill the silence.

"Hmm? Oh, not at all. I did request new students to stop by. Now, let's see..." He picked up a pen and tapped it on the blotter. "Double major in Latin and history, with interests in historiography and, ah the Republic-to-Empire transition? Three years teaching middle school Latin?"

How did he know all that without looking it up? "You have an amazing memory, Dr. d'Amboise."

He smiled again. "Please call me Julian. I imagine it might be difficult to go back to living like a student again. You're in the graduate student residence hall, yes? Finding decent affordable apartments in Boston is a nightmare, but maybe next year something better will turn up. Di always seems to be looking for roommates in that house of hers. Professor Hunter, that is. She teaches Greek and coaches field hockey." He examined her, head to one side, and his eyes narrowed once more. "Though you may not fit in with that crowd. It will be interesting to see."

2

This wasn't going quite as she had expected. There was a subtext running through Dr. d'Amboise's conversation that she couldn't quite read. She felt as if she were being assessed and measured for—for what? She reached for her notebook to cover her confusion.

"I've got my course list here," she said, flipping it open. Anything to evade those all-knowing eyes. "Dr. Waterman suggested I take his Advanced Latin Rhetoric and Composition and Dr. Forge-Smythe's Pre-Roman Italy. And maybe the course on Roman Religious Thought and Philosophy that's being offered in the Philosophy Department."

"Ah. Are you interested in religion?" Dr. d'Amboise—how could she call this elegant, self-assured man by his first name?—leaned forward.

"I'm interested in anything Roman. But religion was in as much turmoil as politics at end of the Republican era."

"It was indeed." He sighed. "Will you be studying early Christianity as well?"

"It's beyond my period. Besides, I find pagans more intriguing."

"Do you?" Dr. d'Amboise rose and passed behind Theo's chair to one of the tall windows. He pushed aside the heavy draperies. Late August sun flooded the room.

"What do you find intriguing about pagans?" He leaned against the sill, watching her.

She turned in her chair and squinted up at him, silhouetted in the glowing window. "In the case of the Romans, how religion reflected their cultural attitudes. It was highly practical. Their gods had roles and duties that they were expected to perform in exchange for worship and sacrifice. Christianity was nothing like that. Though the Roman gods were in many ways just reflections of the Greek pantheon."

"And does your interest extend to them as well?" There was

a smile in his voice though she couldn't see his face.

"How can it not?" She hesitated, then said in a rush, "I grew up on the stories of the gods. My father's an amateur classics scholar and read me Ovid's *Metamorphoses* instead of fairy tales. I'll take Zeus and Athena over St. Paul any day. And—well, this will sound silly, I'm sure, but there's a story in my family that we're descended from a child Emperor Constantine had with a native woman when he was with the army in Britain. Dad always says that Constantine was a complete spoilsport because he ended official worship of the old gods and it was up to us to keep alive the old stories that our ancestor tried to smother." She gave him what she hoped was a self-deprecating smile.

Dr. d'Amboise was silent, watching her from within his halo of light. Damn. Had she sounded like a silly schoolgirl, rattling on about mythology and Daddy's crazy story?

"My *dear* Theodora," he said at last. No laughter edged his words. "I can see we chose this year's students well."

He left the window and prowled gracefully toward her, seating himself on the edge of his desk in front of her. "Are you sure I can't interest you in studying Greek with me? If you love Ovid, you'd also love Hesiod and Homer. I'd be happy to tutor you myself."

His smile was wide and charming. Theo began to feel oddly warm. Hmm, Greek. She'd never had time or opportunity to explore Greek. It had always been Latin for her. But maybe it was time to expand her horizons a little—

"She'll be busy enough with her required classes, Julian."

The deep, disapproving voice hit her like a splash of cold water. She looked back over the top of her chair. Dr. Arthur Waterman, senior professor of Latin, stood with crossed arms in the doorway, his eyes grim above his full salt-and-pepper beard. The stern expression on his face contrasted sharply with his exuberantly flowered blue-and-red Hawaiian shirt.

"Hello, Arthur. Nice shirt. Didn't hear you knock," said Dr. d'Amboise cheerfully. He didn't move from his perch next to Theo.

"That's because I didn't. Good afternoon, Theo."

"Hello, Dr. Waterman." She started to rise. Dr. d'Amboise glanced at her and she sat down again. His look had felt like hands pushing her back into her chair.

"I think Theodora has much potential, Arthur. Surely a working knowledge of ancient Greek will enhance her Latin scholarship." Dr. d'Amboise smiled down at her.

"Her schedule will be full both semesters this year." Dr. Waterman came to stand next to Theo's chair.

"Oh, you and your required courses. After three years of teaching Latin, I doubt she needs a course in rhetoric—"

Dr. Waterman ignored him. "Stop by my office tomorrow morning around eight, Theo. I'll go to registration with you."

"Oh, you don't have to do that—"

"Yes, I do." His face was stern. "I'll see you at eight."

Theo got the hint and stood up. She was relieved to find that this time she could. "Yes, Dr. Waterman. Thank you for meeting with me, Dr. d'Amboise."

"*Julian*, my dear. We're not formal in this department. At least, some of us aren't." He rose and extended his hand again, holding hers a fraction of a second too long. "I look forward to seeing you tomorrow at the department dinner."

"Thank you, Dr. d'Amb—Julian. Good-bye." Theo nodded at Dr. Waterman as she passed him. He smiled back, but his eyes were somber.

She slipped out the door, shutting it behind her, then leaned against the wall next to it and closed her eyes with a sigh. Obviously there was bad blood between the two professors who just happened to be her degree advisor and her department head. Would she be drawn into it too? *This* was why she'd been nervous about returning to school for her doctorate—the politics, the turf issues and squabbles over issues real or imaginary. But it was too late now. She was committed—

"Was it that bad?"

People walked too quietly on these thick carpets. Theo opened her eyes.

A man stood before her, smiling companionably as if they'd just shared a joke. She couldn't help smiling back into his deep-set gray eyes, then got caught by the small dimples that punctuated the corners of his mouth. They contrasted with the stern brows and thin ascetic face framed by high cheekbones that reminded her of a painting of an early Christian martyr. He seemed too old to be a student despite his longish dark hair, but not self-important enough to be a faculty member. Whoever he was, those dimples were wreaking havoc in her midsection.

"I don't know yet. I hope not," she replied.

He nodded. "I can understand that. Julian's a law unto himself. Always has been." The dimples vanished, sweetness subsumed in a bitter curl of his lips. "You must be one of the new students."

Theo wished she could think of something to say to make him smile again. "I'm Theodora Fairchild. And I *am* new," was all she managed. Familiar heat suffused her cheeks. Why had she buried herself in the library all summer? At least if she'd spent some time getting a tan her habit of blushing might not be so obvious. Her eighth graders at Sneed teased her unmercifully about it whenever they translated Catullus's love poetry in class.

"Greek or Latin?" the man asked, brows drawn again.

"Latin."

His brow smoothed. "That should help. Grant Proctor." He held out a hand. "Visiting fellow."

She shook his hand and began to feel better. "Visiting from where?"

"No place you've heard of. It's a small research institute in New Hampshire. We share the property with a lot of moose."

"Do they speak Latin or Greek?" she asked. He seemed like he might have a sense of humor...

"Both, by the time we're through with them. Their enunciation is dreadful, though."

Theo laughed, and her anxiety eased a little. Maybe the year wouldn't be so bad if there were others in the department as nice as this man. Not that Dr. Waterman or Dr. d'Amboise—darn it, would she ever be able to bring herself to call him Julian?—hadn't been nice enough. But as she'd left the office it had felt like thunderstorms and earthquakes were imminent, so palpable was the tension between them.

A rumble of thunder startled her. She glanced toward the nearby window and saw that dark blue-gray thunderheads loomed in the late summer sky, blotting out the day's earlier sunshine. The university clock tower stood outlined against them in vivid contrast.

Grant Proctor looked up too. "Maybe I should come back later. I doubt Julian will be in a very good mood by the time he's ready to see me."

"Do you already know him?"

"We've met." His tone was curiously flat.

But before she could question him, the door opened again, and both Julian and Dr. Waterman stepped out. Dr. Waterman's face was still somber, but he managed a smile at her and a nod to Grant as he walked by. She stole a peek at Julian, who was frowning at Dr. Waterman's retreating back. Then he recollected himself and turned to her.

"So stubborn. But I'll have you studying Greek yet." He glanced at Grant Proctor next to her. An expression of puzzlement flitted across his face, replaced at once by his usual charming smile. "Good afternoon. May I help you?"

"Grant Proctor." Grant nodded pleasantly but did not offer his hand.

Neither did Julian. He continued to regard Grant appraisingly. "Ah. The visiting fellow. You seem familiar but I don't quite place the name. You're from—"

"The Eleusinian Institute." Grant's voice was cool.

"Indeed? Are you sure we haven't met? You've lured a few of our faculty there over the years. How's Olivia?"

Theo began to feel superfluous. "I should get back to the dorm before it rains. Nice to meet you both."

Grant glanced at Julian before replying. "Nice to meet you too, Theo. See you later."

"Till tomorrow, Theodora." Julian nodded at her, his eyes warm turquoise as they moved over her, then darkening to match the clouds outside as he turned to the other man. "Won't you come in?" he asked Grant politely.

She hurried down the paneled hall to the stairs, dark now with the storm hovering outside. Rats. If Julian's door hadn't opened just then, she had been thinking about inviting the very interesting Grant Proctor to go for a beer at the graduate student lounge. By the expression in his eyes, she got the feeling he might have said yes.

Promptly at eight the next morning Theo ascended the stairs in Hamilton Hall. Julian's door was still closed, but Dr. Waterman was standing by his. His shirt today was purple and orange, swirling with curiously tame-looking sharks. He looked relieved when he saw her approaching.

"Come in while I get a few things together." He waved her past him.

She walked in, then stopped short. "Oh," she breathed.

Built into the walls of the office were three enormous fish tanks, softly lit and teeming with a myriad of exotic fish. They turned the dark-paneled office into a kaleidoscope of moving colors and shapes.

"It's my hobby," said Dr. Waterman from behind her, sounding a little apologetic. "I've got more at home. They remind me of—that there's more than just the University in the world."

"They're amazing!" Theo bent to peer into the nearest one. This was not what she'd expected. Dr. Waterman had seemed so stern yesterday, despite his funky shirt. "Are they fresh or salt water?"

"Salt. It's a little trickier to keep them happy, but I flatter myself that I've done all right by them." He pulled out a handkerchief and polished a spot on a tank wall with a proprietorial smile.

The fish moved serenely around the crystalline water, their scales bright and glossy. Plants swayed in the current generated by the aerators.

"I should say so—oh, is that a sea horse?"

"It is. Would you like feed them for me while I get organized?" He stepped back to his desk, opened a drawer, and handed her a plastic tub.

Theo pulled the top off. A clean, sweet odor wafted upwards from the bowl, subtle yet strong. The sunlight filtering in the east window seemed brighter all of a sudden, and the fish more colorful. A warm tingling sensation spread from her nose down to her toes.

"This is fish food?" she asked, lifting the tub to her nose and sniffing. It smelled of hyacinth and lilies and something else too, something indefinable, but rich and deep.

"Oh...er, yes. My own blend." Dr. Waterman hastened over and took it from her. "Here, I'll show you." He folded back the cover from the tank and sprinkled some of the silvery flakes onto the surface of the water from a small silver spoon. The fish darted upward, scratching at the food.

"You do the others. Not too much in each." He held the tub and spoon out to her and watched as she shook flakes onto the water. Fish circled and lunged. "Oh, good, they like you. Maybe you wouldn't mind taking care of them occasionally when I'm with—when I'm at conferences." He whisked the fish food from her hands and slipped it into a desk drawer.

"I'd be happy to. Do you go to many?" She turned away from him as if to study the fish and surreptitiously smelled her fingers where a flake or two clung. The tingle surged through her again and she shivered with pleasure. What was Dr. Waterman feeding his fish? They were darned lucky, whatever it was.

"A fair number." He gave her a sharp glance as she turned back toward him. "Shall we go?"

The Graduate Student Union was still quiet at this hour. Only a few students stood waiting in line to register, most clutching Starbucks cups and looking dazed. Theo and Dr. Waterman joined the queue.

"Why, good morning," said a pleasant baritone voice.

Dr. Waterman stiffened. Theo turned.

Julian d'Amboise stood behind them, a cup of coffee in one hand. "What a nice surprise," he continued, smiling. "You're here early, Arthur."

"So are you," growled Dr. Waterman. The building seemed to tremble around them.

"I'd just stopped in for a cup of coffee and thought I'd see how registration was going. How nice of you to help Theodora. I'm happy to wait with her if you'd like to run out for your tea."

"No thank you, Julian." Dr. Waterman's bushy gray brows were drawn.

"Next!" said the bored-looking woman at the desk. Theo and Dr. Waterman walked over to her, trailed by a humming Julian.

"Is your form filled out?" The woman eyed Julian's coffee with such a yearning expression that Theo was tempted to go get her a venti espresso at the kiosk downstairs.

"Yes." Theo opened her portfolio. She stared. The paper had vanished. She looked up, frowning. "But it was right here this morning when I—"

"Is this what you were looking for?" Julian waved a piece of paper at her. "It was on the floor behind you. Must have slipped out." He held the document out to the woman behind the table, but Dr. Waterman snatched it out of his fingers.

"Nice try, Julian," he said. Frowning, he read it, shook his head, then blew across the paper and looked at it again. "That's better." He handed the form to Theo with a nod of approval.

She took the paper from him with a quick glance at Julian, who wore an expression of pained boredom on his handsome face. This was starting to get more than a little weird. She looked down at the paper. It was her registration form all right, neatly filled out in black ink in her tidy teacher printing. So what had all that been about? She gave the form to the woman, who tapped on her computer keyboard for a moment, then nodded curtly.

"You're all set. Next!"

Julian nodded to Theo. "Till later, my dear." Ignoring his colleague, he strolled to the door. Dr. Waterman watched him with the same somber expression he had worn yesterday.

"Dr. Waterman? Is everything all right?" Theo asked. Julian's posture as he strode from the room all but screamed annoyance. At her, or at Dr. Waterman? "That was… er…a little strange." Strange didn't begin to cover it, but how else could she politely word it?

"It's nothing to do with you, Theo. I'm sorry you had to see that. Please don't let our...er, discussions color your impression of us too much. Julian and I have known each other a long time. Sometimes we disagree on things."

"But what—"

"He has his own ideas about what classes you ought to be taking. He gets excited when promising students arrive. He'll settle down shortly. He really is an extraordinary teacher. His students worship him." His mouth quirked.

Something about his evasive tone bothered her but she couldn't say why. "Thank you for coming with me, Dr. Waterman."

"It was nothing. I'll see you at the department dinner." He nodded and followed Julian out the door.

"I'm not sure coming here was such a good idea after all."

"But you were miserable at Sneed, darling," Mom replied. "Remember?"

"I know. But sometimes the misery you know is less miserable than the one you don't."

Theo lay on her bed in her room in Graves Hall, the graduate residence, talking to her mother on the phone as she stared at the ceiling. There was a crack spanning it that reminded her absurdly of a map of the Via Appia in the textbook she'd used to teach her seventh graders last year. A faint clinking sound on the other end of the phone told her that Mom was probably on her chaise on the porch sipping a gin and tonic, the way they often had together this summer. A sudden homesickness surged through her. "Where are you, Mom?"

"Is the connection bad? I'm on the porch, but I can—"

"No, it's fine. I'm just picturing you there and missing you.

How's my small furry beast?"

Leaving Dido, her Abyssinian cat, with Mom and Dad had been the hardest thing she'd had to do, worse than giving up the lease on her adored apartment or leaving her few faculty friends at Sneed. She missed Dido's sleek golden head butting against her legs when she worked in her kitchen, her seismic purr as they sat together while Theo corrected homework, even her maddening ability to find and lie down on whatever part of the Sunday newspaper Theo happened to be reading.

"Dido's fine. She's taken to sitting on your father at every opportunity. He grumbles but won't move a muscle if she falls asleep on him. Is it that bad, honey? Haven't you met any nice people?" Mom's voice was sympathetic.

"Oh, yes. Very nice." Theo had a memory of deep-set gray eyes.

"What about the faculty? You liked Dr. Waterman."

She didn't want to tell Mom about Professor d'Amb—*Julian's*—slightly strange behavior. Mom sometimes forgot that she was an adult now. "I still do. They're fine, too—the ones I've met."

"You don't sound convinced."

"Well, I've only met a couple of them—"

"Give it a chance, honey. You know that if you were back at Sneed, you'd be sighing that if only you had your doctorate you wouldn't have to deal with those adolescent monsters and could spend your time teaching college students who actually want to learn Latin."

"I know. You're right." Theo flung an arm across her forehead and hissed in pain.

"What was that?" demanded Mom.

Theo stopped cursing under her breath and got up to peer into her mirror. "It was me being dumb. I stayed up till two-thirty last night reading. Then I was up at seven to register, and then this afternoon I decided to lie out in the sun and get a little color so I didn't look too much like the Elgin marbles at the dinner tonight. I fell asleep, of course. I hope they're not serving lobster or they might mistake me for the main course."

"Oh, Theo." Mom sighed. "You know you have to be careful with the sun. You have such fair skin."

"It's not that bad. I just look red, that's all. It's embarrassing, but at least no one will be able to see if I blush."

"They will, too. You'll turn purple," said a new voice.

"Lionel!" said her mother. "Get off the extension!"

"Oh, hi, Dad. Thanks for the vote of confidence."

Dad chuckled. "I'm sorry, sweetheart. I'm sure you'll be fine. Send me your reading lists when you get them. I want to be able to quiz you when you come home."

Theo groaned. "I think I'll be getting enough quizzing here. I'll e-mail them when I can. Classes start tomorrow. Be nice to my cat, you hear?"

"Hmmph. She's a spoiled brat, but I suppose I will. *Vale, cara rufula filia.*"

"Are you referring to my red skin or hair? *Vale, stercoreus senex. Amo te.*"

"Ah." Dad chuckled again. "Nice alliteration. Love you, too. *Vale.*" There was the beep of a phone being switched off.

"Theo, stop calling your father bad names in Latin," Mom scolded. "Yes, I know you called him a nasty old man."

"He called me 'little red child' first. And anyway, he loves it when I come up with new Latin insults. Um, I've got to go get ready for the dinner."

"Please wear your hair down and not screwed up in that tight little knob you used to wear it in at Sneed. You're so pretty when you let yourself be."

"Okay, Mom."

"Promise?"

"Yes, I promise."

Theo hung up and gathered her toiletries, then headed down the hall to shower in the communal bathroom. It *was* hard to go back to being a student after three years of paid working life and her own apartment. But she'd dreamed of coming here, dreamed of spending her time discussing the finer points of historical prose and making convoluted Latin puns over glasses of Chianti at department gatherings. Most of all, she'd dreamed of being with people who under-stood her love of the past, who would share her enthusiasm and speak her language, in all senses of the word.

Gray eyes and unexpected dimples flashed across her mind's eye again. Not everyone she had met was that bad. Surely Grant Proctor would be at the dinner tonight.

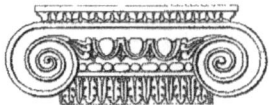

Two

An hour later Theo stood in the Great Room at Hamilton Hall, clutching a glass of wine and exchanging nervous smiles with the other new grad students. Dozens of candles glowed on the long linen-covered table set in the center of the room. Undergrads in white tunics and garlands of ivy circulated with platters of stuffed mushrooms and smoked salmon canapés. She turned to the student standing next to her. He studied the scene before him with such a lack of surprise that she guessed he was in his second year.

"Are department gatherings always this, er, elaborate?" she ventured.

The young man shrugged. "This is how Julian likes it." He grabbed at the tray of a passing server. "'Least he feeds us well," he said around a mouthful of goat cheese crostini. "New here?"

"Yes." Theo self-consciously sipped from her glass.

"You ought to see the *real* department dinners. The symposia. You'll get to one if you're lucky. The faculty has them every month, but they're by invitation only. I've been *twice*," he added with smug emphasis. "They're the real thing. We eat reclining on couches, and drink from silver cups, and tell riddles and play Greek and Latin drinking games."

"Wow. Really?" Not that it was terribly surprising. She could just picture Julian in a toga, looking autocratic and handsome in snowy white, like a statue of an Olympian god.

A tall woman in a gauzy, peacock-blue dress walked by. The student next to Theo bobbed his head respectfully. "Hello, Ms. Cadwallader. Nice to see you."

"Hello, Andrew," replied the woman. She glanced at Theo with eyes as dark and sharp as flint and kept walking.

"I can't picture her at one of those dinners," Theo murmured. Those eyes had given her a chill all the way down to her toes.

"Oh, she's there. That's June Cadwallader. Julian's secretary. More or less runs the department. Don't get on her bad side. She can make life miserable if she doesn't like you. You're probably already screwed, though. She doesn't like female students."

"Why not—oh, who's that?" She nodded toward a couple who had just entered.

The man, dark and bearded, leaned on a pair of crutches. His upper body appeared massive in contrast to his wasted legs. His much younger companion fussed and patted his arm when he paused.

Theo nearly gasped aloud; she had never seen such an exquisitely beautiful woman outside of a fashion magazine. Long blonde hair tumbled over her shoulders, framing a face so symmetrical, so perfect, so pink and ivory and gold that Theo felt like one of the gargoyles carved on the building's exterior in comparison.

"Dr. Forge-Smythe! Mrs. Frothington-Forge-Smythe!" breathed Andrew. He shoved his wineglass at Theo and hurried over to them.

"Frothington-Forge-Smythe? That's a mouthful," Theo murmured, watching the pair greet the student. Dr. Forge-Smythe's manner was warm enough as he shifted his crutches to shake Andrew's hand, but his wife's smile lit up the space around them like a klieg light. Andrew swayed as if he were going to faint under its impact.

"She never did have a sense of proportion," murmured someone behind her. Theo turned to see Grant Proctor watching the professor and his wife.

"She doesn't have to, looking like that." Theo shook her head in admiration, then turned to him. Yup, just as good-looking as he'd been this morning. "I was hoping you'd be here. I want to hear more about your erudite moose." She handed her and Andrew's wineglasses to a wandering toga-ed server.

He nodded. "They're good, but they're nothing compared to the porcupines. We've trained them to do the choruses in Aeschylus and Euripides. Their diction is better than the moose's, but they do tend to overact shamelessly."

She giggled, and he smiled with her. "I'd love to see them."

"It's very funny, especially when their quills get tangled. I'd like to switch them to comedies but they're too in love with doing the *Oresteiad* every fall before they hibernate." He shrugged.

"You might read Aristophanes to them in their sleep over the winter. Subliminal suggestion might work," she said, matching his serious tone.

"That's a very good idea. I'll have to try it. Though I think they're a little too touchy to deal with satire well. The moose have a much better innate grasp of comedy." He leaned a little closer to her. "Mind you, we might get the bears back if we did comedies. They marched out last year and swore they wouldn't come back until we promised not to make them do *Trojan Women* in drag again."

She laughed out loud. The sound attracted the attention of the trio standing nearby. Mrs. Frothington-Forge-Smythe looked at them in surprise. When she saw Grant, her eyes widened. She walked over to them, followed by Dr. Forge-Smythe and Andrew.

"Hello, Renee," said Grant as the woman glided up, her megawatt smile trained on him.

Theo felt even more awkward. Renee Frothington-Forge-Smythe was inches shorter than she, but so well proportioned that Theo amended her comparison: now she felt like a gargoyle on a ladder.

"Hello," the woman purred back at him. "Do my eyes deceive me? Is it——?"

"Grant Proctor." He nodded to her.

Theo watched him from the corner of her eyes and held her breath, waiting to see if he would be transformed into a fawning puddle like Andrew. But his expression of polite interest didn't change.

"Pro—ah, yes, of course. How lovely to see you after all these years. What brings you here?" The woman's violet-blue eyes raked over him, a speculative gleam lurking in their depths. She leaned toward him with a sinuous movement, and Theo saw Andrew swallow hard.

"A visiting fellowship. I'm looking forward to working with my new colleagues." He smiled at Theo. She felt her heart beat faster. Did he—could it be that he—that he liked her better than this elegant beauty?

Renee caught the smile and frowned. She moved closer to her husband and took his arm. "Dear Henry. Do you remember, uh, Mr. Proctor?"

Dr. Forge-Smythe peered at him uncertainly. "Hmm? No, can't say I do. Pleased to meet you, though. And you are...?" he continued, turning to Theo.

"Theodora Fairchild. I'm pleased to meet you, Dr. Forge-Smythe."

"Ah, yes. You're in my Pre-Roman class. Renee, dear, this is one of my new students."

Renee turned to Theo. Her glance was dismissive. "How nice to meet you. Dear me, child, is that a sunburn? Is it as painful as it looks?"

Theo felt herself flush at Renee's tone, silky and edged all at once. She'd forgotten her blazing cheeks and nose during Grant's cheerful conversation. Now she remembered her father's dire prediction. *Another correction*, she thought: *bright red gargoyle on a rickety crimson ladder.*

A sudden movement at her side caught her attention. "I'm sure it's uncomfortable, Renee, but certainly not as bad as you make it out to be." Julian had materialized next to her, his voice chilly as he surveyed them. He'd changed into another crisp button-down, white this time, and looked even more tanned and suave.

Theo felt her blushes redouble. Why hadn't she just stayed in her room and hidden under the bed?

"Evening, Julian," said Dr. Forge-Smythe. "Nice party."

"Thank you, Henry. Hello, Mr. Proctor. Welcome back, Andrew. My dear Theodora." Julian smiled at each of them, pointedly passing over Renee. Theo saw her pout but hold her tongue. Odd. Why wasn't she turning her feminine magnetism from 'stun' to 'kill'? Surely Julian, handsome as he was, would be a prime candidate in her eyes?

"Now, my dear, let me see that sunburn." Julian's voice interrupted her musings.

"Oh, it's nothing, real—" Before she could finish, he'd tilted her chin toward him and fastened that blue gaze on her, then brushed his fingertips over her forehead. A blessed coolness quenched the fire in her skin as he touched her.

Julian smiled in satisfaction. "Not bad at all. Can I get you another glass of wine, Theodora? You really ought to wear your hair down like that all the time. That golden red is stunning."

"You look tired, my pet. Let's find you a chair, shall we?" cooed Renee, tugging on her husband's arm. She ignored Theo and gave Juliar a reproachful frown. He smiled and shook his head at her as she and Dr. Forge-Smythe moved toward the table, still trailed by the eager Andrew.

Theo wished she could run off to the ladies' room and have a quick look in the mirror. What had Julian done? She glanced beside her at Grant and saw that his face was carefully blank as he looked at Julian. But then he met her eyes, and she felt her confusion and discomfort fade.

Julian waved his hand negligently in the air. One of the garlanded undergraduates appeared at his side, holding a tray of full glasses. He handed one to her. "You mustn't mind Renee. She's quite devoted to Henry, so we tolerate her. But she doesn't like competition."

"I can't imagine she ever has any. She's gorgeous."

"Not frequently." He looked at Theo and said softly, "But it does happen."

A loud *clang* directly behind her made her jump. June Cadwallader stood there, holding a small bronze gong and looking grim.

"Ah, June," said Julian with a bright smile. "Have you met Theodora yet? My dear, this is June Cadwallader, chief prop and mainstay of the department. We'd all be in desperate trouble without her firm hand on the wheel."

"You generally are, even with it," said Ms. Cadwallader. She scrutinized Theo, her expression stony and her lips pursed. "It's time for dinner."

"Dear me, is it really? Well, I'll let you get on with the summoning." Julian turned from her and held out a hand to

Theo. "Won't you join me?"

Grant cleared his throat beside her. "I'll just—"

Theo turned to him and put a hand on his arm. "But you were about to tell me about the bears in drag. Please don't go." Why did their conversations always seem to be interrupted? And why wouldn't June and Julian and everyone else just go away?

Julian's smile dimmed as he and Grant exchanged glances. "Indeed? I would like to hear about that too." He gestured politely that they should precede him to the table, seating himself at the table's head and placing Theo at his right hand. To her delight, Grant seated himself next to her, ignoring Julian's gesture at the chair across the table. Julian scowled.

Theo saw Dr. Waterman sit a few chairs down on the other side of the table next to a sturdily built young woman with short hair and a deep tan. She was chatting with a handsome man with shoulder-length blond hair and delicate features.

"We've definitely got a shot at the Division title this year," Theo heard her say. "We're into our second week of practice and it's really coming together. We'll bring that trophy down yet, you'll see. They're a dedicated group of women."

"Not bad-looking, too, if you'd ever let them out of uniform," drawled the man. He toyed with a bread knife, stroking its flared blade with long, slender fingers.

"You keep your hands off 'em, you. Those are my girls, and I want them focused on hockey, not hormones."

"You're such a single-minded bore," returned the man amiably, throwing a piece of roll at her. He missed. She nipped it up and landed it squarely on his nose.

"I never miss, remember? Don't get into a bunfight with me or you might regret it," she said, wiping the butter off his nose with her napkin and grinning at him.

"Children," sighed Julian. He turned to Theo. "That irresponsible pair are Diana Hunter and Paul Harriman, and they teach Greek when they're not squabbling. Diana also coaches women's field hockey, and Paul dabbles in early music."

"I beg your pardon, Julian. I don't call a two-album recording contract *squabbling*," sniffed Paul. He looked at Theo and his expression altered. "Hello," he said, turning a sunny smile on her.

Julian frowned. "Behave, Paul."

"Yeah, behave, Paul," said Diana. She punched him in the arm.

The gong sounded again, this time from the foot of the table where Ms. Cadwallader was seated. She stared at Diana and Paul until they joined in the general quiet.

Julian rose. "Welcome, my new and returning colleagues, to the start of a new academic year. I am delighted to see all of you here and ask that you join me in drinking to our continued prosperity here at the university."

Theo turned to Grant and held her glass of wine out to him. He smiled and touched his own to hers. "To Latin," he said.

"To Latin," she echoed. "May your moose improve their mastery of it." Was there a Latin word for moose?

"I'll settle for my undergrads mastering it for now," he said lightly. "But I'll work on the moose when I get back."

Theo waited while their salads were served, making a list of small-talk topics in her head that would hopefully draw him out. "You're teaching this year?"

"Just one class. I enjoy teaching, and it'll give Dr. Waterman a break from First Year Latin."

Theo shuddered. "You like teaching First Year Latin? Try it with twelve-year-olds for a while, and I'll ask you again how you feel. Unless you like being a martyr."

Several expressions seemed to cross his face: pain, defiance, then a glimpse of self-deprecating humor. He stared at his salad for a moment then looked up at her. "I suppose you could say that I'm used to it. What about you? Are you running away from twelve-year-olds?"

Theo hesitated. Did he really want to know, or was he just making polite conversation? She took a deep breath. "Running away from them? No. Well, maybe a little. It's disheartening when they're required to take your class and ninety-five percent of them don't want to be there. I love Latin. I always have, even when *I* was one of those twelve-year-olds. Is there anything more satisfying than reading Vergil or any of the poets and seeing how they used meter and sound to make you *feel* as well as understand their words? To have that connection with them across two millennia? It gives me goosebumps sometimes to read them and know that I'm sharing the thoughts of someone so distant from me in so many ways, yet also alike. I love it, and I want my students to love it. I thought maybe..." she looked down at her plate and crumbled a crouton with her fork. "Maybe if I came back for my doctorate, I'd be more able to help them see the wonder of it. If I can make myself better, I'll make them better too." She looked up from her plate.

Grant was watching her, his gray eyes intent on her face. She reached for her wine and took a long drink to cover her embarrassment. "I'm sorry. That was a little earnest, wasn't it?"

"No, it wasn't. What good is our knowledge, if we don't share it with others and light their way?" he replied, still looking at her. She could feel his regard like a touch on her face. Her hand moved of its own accord to her cheek.

A loud laugh rolled across the table, tearing the fragile web of quiet their words had woven around them. Another rumbled toward them, so jolly and heartfelt that she had to smile.

Grant chuckled. "It's just Marlowe," he said, inclining his head.

A tall, bearded young man, dark of hair and red of face, was teasing the girl seated next to him, waving a cherry tomato impaled on a fork in front of her. She obligingly snapped at it and he roared once more.

"Who?"

"Marlowe Vine. Of all the perpetual students I've met, he's the most perpetual. Accumulates fellowships like barnacles. You can guess what his major course of study is."

Theo watched him drain his wineglass and refill it to overflowing, then wave the be-tomatoed fork in front of the girl once more. "Fluid dynamics?"

"More or less. He's harmless, though, even when thoroughly in his cups. He spent a year up in New Hampshire with us, in fact. We're still recovering." Grant smiled at him once again, and turned back to Theo. "You'll have to come visit us up there some day. I think you'd fit right in."

"Thank you," she said simply, afraid to say more. Some of the other faculty at Sneed—the young, male ones, alas—had been mystified when they found out what she taught. 'Are you a nun?' one had blurted at a faculty cocktail last year. Somehow they had equated her with the ancient language she taught, had assumed she too was dusty, dry, and dead. As a result the last three years had been very lonely ones. And now to find this man who *understood*...

Dinner arrived, served by the garlanded students. Theo drank and ate but scarcely noticed what was on her plate. All her attention was on Grant: his words, his spare motions, the way his too-long dark hair curled on the back of his neck, the way those dimples appeared when he smiled just so. And the way he listened to her, so focused and intent that she almost felt that she could stop talking and just *think*, and he would hear.

"You never finished telling me about the bears," she said to him as tiny cups of espresso and plates of baklava were served after dinner.

"Oh, there's not much to tell. Given a choice of moose,

porcupines, or bears wearing gauze veils and silk robes while playing a group of women, which would you pick? Our costume designer put her foot down on that issue, so bears it was. They're the least pointy."

Theo giggled. His smile widened as he watched her. "Having a bear play Cassandra was never satisfactory, though. I suppose the bears felt the same way. My only concern is if we give in and let them do comedies, will they be upset if we do *The Wasps*?"

She laughed again. Grant leaned forward and touched her arm. His eyes were filled with a strange yearning. She stared at him in surprise.

"I'm sorry. I didn't mean to startle you. It's just...your laugh. I want—I want to keep hearing it. It makes me feel that maybe I—" he broke off and looked down at his plate.

Theo's skin tingled where he had touched her. "I can't help it. You make me happy when you talk."

He stared at her. "I do? Really?" He looked as though she had handed him a gem of great price.

It was the wine. It had to be. The student servers had been silently efficient; their glasses were never empty all through the meal, no matter how often they had drunk from them. And they had drunk from them a great deal. But Theo didn't care; she was too busy enjoying the way his look and words were making her feel. "Really," she whispered.

He leaned toward her again and she waited, hardly daring to breathe. A loud *clang*, this time close enough to hurt her ears, made her jump in her seat.

Julian was holding Ms. Cadwallader's gong and frowning at Grant. When he met Theo's eyes, the frown vanished. He rose and addressed the seated diners, "If you would care to finish your coffee, Paul Harriman and his colleagues from the Music Department have agreed to entertain us with selections from their upcoming album of ancient Greek instrumental music."

"I didn't know they'd found enough transcribed music from that time to fill an album," Theo said shakily to Julian, who held out a hand to lead her from the table.

"Oh, Paul's indefatigable when it comes to tracking down his music. Yes, Arthur, what is it now?" he snapped at Dr. Waterman, standing at his elbow.

Under cover of Dr. Waterman's interruption, Grant escorted Theo to the semi-circle of chairs that had been set up at the other end of the hall and found them seats in the back row. Julian glowered again when he had finished with Dr. Waterman and saw her there, and seated himself in the front row. Ms. Cadwallader claimed the empty seat next to him with an air of proprietary self-assurance just as the musicians lifted their instruments.

Theo relaxed in her chair and let the soft, unfamiliar music wash over her. The lack of sleep and all that wine at dinner were starting to catch up with her. If she weren't careful, she'd doze off right here, start snoring, and insult Dr. Harriman.

She looked down at the floor and realized that the entire room was paved in mosaics, thousands of tiny shards of glass and stone forming elaborate scenes and pictures. Partly covered by the chair in front of her she could see a bird, a vulture or maybe an eagle, picked out in brown and black with a cruel hooked beak and enormous, ragged wings. An iridescent scrap of glass formed the raptor's eye, giving it a savagely life-like gleam. It was poised in a stoop, beak open in a silent scream of triumph, claws extended to rend and tear.

She moved her foot aside, trying to see what the bird was glaring at with such rapacious glee. Her chair covered most of the rest of the image, but she could just see something long and light beige. She blinked sleepily, and the long beige something resolved itself into the naked torso of a man.

Next to her, Grant began applauding and she looked up,

startled. The first piece had ended. She sat up and clapped too, the mosaic forgotten, and did her best to stay awake for the rest of the evening.

She almost succeeded. A little later she felt a touch on her arm.

"I've never seen anyone sleep sitting bolt upright with wide open eyes before," Grant murmured to her under cover of the final applause.

"You've never sat through weekly faculty meetings, then," she whispered back.

He grinned. "Meet me for coffee in the Faculty Lounge tomorrow afternoon. A little caffeine might help."

Theo thought fleetingly of coffee right now, but feared she'd fall face-first into her cup and drown. "That sounds nice," she agreed as they joined the group congratulating the musicians.

"G'night, Theo." He looked at her for a moment, his gray eyes soft and thoughtful, and then he was gone.

Theo made her way to the door of the Great Room. As she waited with the exiting crowd she glanced in the large gilded mirror beside the door. Her reflection looked back at her, her hair curling flamboyantly around her face in the evening's warm, humid air. She pushed it back from her forehead then stopped and stared in confusion into the mirror at the pale oval of her face. The angry red sunburn that Renee had smirked at was gone. Theo remembered the tingling sensation of Julian's fingertips on her skin and, despite the heat, shivered.

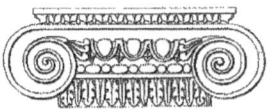

Three

BREATHE, STROKE, STROKE, STROKE. Breathe, stroke, stroke, stroke. C'mon, girl, keep the rhythm. Don't let those legs lag—

Theo was swimming laps in the pool at the university gym. She'd been amused to see that most of the people there for early morning swims were all older, university faculty and staff. Including Dr. Waterman, who was over in the far-left lane, swimming as if his life depended on it. It seemed that undergrads didn't have the discipline to get up at 6:30 to swim. Then again, she almost hadn't.

But entry-level teachers at Sneed hadn't been paid enough to afford memberships at expensive gyms with pools. She was going to take advantage of the university's facilities and maybe get rid of a little of the softness around her hips and thighs.

She'd expected to feel far worse this morning after all the wine she'd drunk the night before. But to her surprise, she'd felt just fine. Downright perky, in fact, once she was vertical, which was unusual—she was never perky in the morning.

Her goggles were fogging up again. She finished the lap and

clung to the tiled side of the pool to pull them off. As she disentangled her hair from the strap a pair of bare feet came to a halt next to her. She found herself looking up at Grant Proctor.

"I thought it was you," he said, squatting beside her and reaching down to help free her goggles. "If I'd known you were a swimmer we could have met." He handed them to her.

"Thanks. I didn't expect to be up to it after last night. But I felt great this morning. No, er, adverse symptoms." Theo pulled herself up out of the water onto the edge of the pool, wishing she'd worn her green bathing suit and that her thighs were thinner.

"I think you'll find that's the case with all department parties here," he said, looking out at the pool. "How's the water?"

"A little cool but fine once you get moving. I—I hope I didn't say anything embarrassing last night," she blurted.

He shook his head. "Not a thing. I had as much or more to drink than you anyway. I should be apologizing to you because I'm much more used to it."

"Apologize for what?"

"We're even, then." He hesitated. "Julian has...unusual tastes in wine. It's powerful but has little residual effect, fortunately."

"Fortunately," she echoed. "You seem to know him well."

"We were colleagues many years ago."

"Colleagues? But you must be almost half his age." Though his face was somewhat lined, his hair was untouched by gray and his body young and strong. In fact she'd been acutely aware of it for the last few minutes as she sat dripping next to him, stealing looks at his broad shoulders and smoothly muscled chest.

"I'm older than you might think," he said, then smiled. "But I'm not getting any younger sitting here." He rose and flipped his towel off his shoulder and onto the starting block above them. "Share the lane?"

"Well, I should—oh!" Theo stared up at his side. A long, jagged scar twisted across the lower right side of his torso, along the edge of his ribcage.

Grant jerked as if he had been burned and slid into the water. "It's nothing."

She impulsively reached down and touched his shoulder. "I'm sorry. I didn't mean to stare. Was it an accident?"

"Sort of," he said shortly, and ducked under the surface.

Theo felt like slipping back into the pool and not coming up. How could she have been so tactless? But the scar writhing across his side like an agonized snake looked painful even now, though the wound that created it was obviously old and well healed. She had almost felt a pain in her own vitals, just looking at it.

And now he would not meet her eyes, which was even worse. Why couldn't she just tell him straight out that the scar, horrible as it was, didn't matter?

"I need to go shower if I'm going to make it to Dr. Waterman's first class," she said. "What time do you want to meet for coffee? Around four?"

Grant looked at her, his face carefully blank. "Are you sure you still want to?"

She touched his shoulder again, a lingering touch this time, and felt shocked at her boldness. "Yes, I want to. Very much."

He gazed at her a moment longer then smiled wryly. "I'm sorry. I'm a little hypersensitive about my scar. Most people look disgusted and turn away, but it doesn't matter. I don't care if it revolts them. But you..."

"Apart from being sorry that you must have suffered dreadfully at some time—"

"You might say so," he muttered.

"—apart from that, it doesn't matter." She added softly, not caring for once if she blushed, "There's certainly nothing wrong with the rest of you."

His eyes widened. "If that was a sexist comment, then I thank you. Four it is."

Theo found herself slipping back into the routine of being a student with surprising ease. Her classes were absorbing, and some were downright fun. In her Rhetoric and Composition class Dr. Waterman set everyone to translating famous passages of English literature and poetry into Latin, to try to reproduce their tone and emotion.

Theo wrestled joyously with her translations of passages of Poe's *The Cask of Amontillado* and Twain's *Huckleberry Finn*...and taking her courage in her hands, persuaded Grant to try his hand at it as well. She told herself it was in order to expand her educational boundaries as they compared notes. But mostly it was to guarantee that they would meet for coffee or a post-swim breakfast or lunch several days of the week.

Grant quickly became as immersed as she in Dr. Waterman's exercises and seemed to enjoy their amicably fierce debates over the subtleties of verbs and grammatical structures as much as she did. The fencing with words, the thrust and parry of his conversation, was exhilarating. The fact that her partner in these verbal bouts had dimples to die for was even more so.

"Translating Jane Austen into Latin was an interesting experience," she said as they met for lunch during the second week of classes. Dr. Waterman had given them parts of *Persuasion* to translate. She'd been absorbed by the task of fitting early nineteenth-century prose with Latin vocabulary and grammatical structures that gave it a slight touch of formality without becoming too stuffy. But it had been enormous fun as well. *Persuasion* was her favorite Austen book; not even Colin Firth— er, *Pride and Prejudice*—could budge it from first place.

"I hadn't read it before," Grant said, frowning at his notes.

"Hadn't read *Persuasion*?!" Theo pretended to faint in her chair. "I am shocked—positively shocked!—to hear that."

He looked up at her in consternation, then relaxed and smiled. "Actually, I haven't read much modern fiction in general."

Theo hesitated. Oh dear. He wasn't one of those people who thought reading fiction was a waste of time because it wasn't "true," was he? She hadn't gotten that impression—not after the moose and the porcupines...and since when was Jane Austen modern fiction? "Um...why not?"

He sat back in his chair, thinking. "I'm not sure," he said slowly. "Other things always seemed to get my attention first. Do you think I should read more?"

"Well, what did you think of *Persuasion*? Did you enjoy it?"

"I did enjoy it. I liked..." he thought for a minute, eyes narrowed. "I liked Anne's and Captain Wentworth's constancy most of all, I think."

"Captain Wentworth wasn't always so constant. What about his flirting with Louisa right in front of poor Anne at Lyme?"

"But he didn't really care about Louisa. He just didn't know his own mind. As soon as he came to his senses, he remember- ed whom he truly cared about. 'You pierce my soul,' he wrote in his note to Anne," he said quietly, musingly. "It sounds as if it should be painful, doesn't it? And yet that pain was incredibly sweet. *Pungis animum meum*," he repeated softly then fell silent, gazing off into space as if caught in his own thoughts.

Theo watched him. "That line has always given me the shivers," she agreed. "But in a good way."

He smiled suddenly, but there was a touch of sadness about

it. "Has your soul ever been pierced?"

Theo took a breath. "No, it hasn't."

But she lied. That smile, both sweet and sad, had given her a new and very immediate understanding of just what it felt like to have one's soul pierced. She met his eyes, and blushed.

They looked at each other for a long moment. Then he cleared his throat and turned back down at his notes, but not before Theo thought she might have seen an answering flush in his own cheeks.

Despite her classes and Grant, though, she couldn't help feeling that there was something missing in her life. A few days later, she figured out what it was.

She was sitting in Dr. Herman's Roman Historiography class in one of Hamilton Hall's luxurious seminar rooms. Dr. Herman was, as usual, pacing around the table in his blindingly white Nikes as he spoke, hands behind his back. His curly brown hair bounced above his narrow, beautiful face with every step.

"By the middle of the first century BCE the word *historia* was used to indicate a narrative history, while *fasti* took the meaning of calendar, or a list of historical dates. The term *commentarius*, however, had gained an interesting new—oh, hello Arthur."

Theo sat up straighter. Dr. Waterman had slipped into the room. He looked toward her and smiled.

"Sorry to interrupt, Freddy, but I need to borrow Miss Fairchild for a few moments. Theo?"

She swallowed her surprise and nodded. "Excuse me, please."

In the hallway Dr. Waterman gestured her toward his office.

"I'm sorry to pull you out of class, but we wanted to talk to you right away."

"We?"

"Grant and I." He held his office door for her.

Grant stood by a fish tank, staring at a large and gaudy belted angelfish. He looked up eagerly as they entered the room. "Did you ask her yet, Arthur?"

Smiling, Dr. Waterman held up a hand. "I just got her out of class. Give me a moment." He waved her into a chair. Grant perched on the arm of the chair next to it, looking impatient.

"Theo, we hope you can help us with a slight problem," Dr. Waterman began.

"It's not a problem," Grant interrupted.

She raised an eyebrow at him. "All right. So what's the non-problem you need my help with?"

"What Grant means is that our problem is an opportunity for you. Our first-year Latin class is overenrolled and has to be split into two sections. We wondered if you'd like to take over teaching one of them."

She felt a trickle of shock, followed by a wave of excitement. "Me? Really?"

"There's no one better qualified. None of even the second-year students have your teaching experience. Julian's given us the okay pending administration approval. We can't pay much, but you could take payment in the form of reduced tuition next semester. The curriculum's already in place. What do you think? I don't want to press, but we'd like to be able to divide the class as of Monday morning. Think it over, and let me know tomorrow."

"She doesn't have to think it over. C'mon, Theo. Say yes." Grant's foot tapped impatiently.

"I told you teaching First Year Latin was no picnic. Tired of martyrdom already?" she teased.

Dr. Waterman started to speak, then stopped. He stared at Grant piercingly for a few seconds, sitting back in his chair. She thought she heard him murmur, "Oh, my," under his breath, but it was drowned out by Grant's snort of irritation.

"Twelve-year-olds were too much for you, huh? Afraid of freshmen?" he said, looking down his nose at her.

"Is that a challenge?"

"Well? Can you do it?" He crossed his arms.

"Better than you can!"

"Hah. Bet you dinner at the University Club that my students get better grades than yours on the midterm exam."

"Better go make the reservations now, and save yourself the bother later," she said with a sweet smile.

He grinned. "Good. Then I take it I'll see you Monday morning at nine in the classroom next to mine?"

Dr. Waterman chuckled. "I'll sweeten the pot with a bottle of Veuve Clicquot to the winner, provided she—or he," he added, holding up an apologetic hand at Grant's protest, "shares it with the loser."

She frowned for a second, then laughed too. "You're dreadful, you know," she said to Grant. "I was going to say yes anyway, so don't think you pulled one on me."

"I know you were. But it's more fun this way." He smiled down her.

And Theo realized, when she walked into the class-room next to his the following Monday and greeted her class of freshmen, what it was that she'd been missing. She had her class of interested students at last.

It was Friday. Four-thirty on Friday, which was even better. Theo stretched luxuriously in her seat in the Graduate Student

Lounge. She loved her classes, loved her new life at college, loved teaching again now that her students were in her class because they wanted to learn Latin. But she'd never outgrown the exultation of Friday afternoons.

She finished her stretch and looked out the window for Grant. This was what she loved most of all—her time with him, sparring happily or finishing each other's sentences when they were done disagreeing. When she was with him she forgot that she was supposed to be shy, uptight Miss Fairchild. It was intoxicating.

But Grant wasn't moving down the sidewalk to the building in that purposeful gliding stalk of his that she'd described as half tiger, half heron, much to his amusement. Disappointed, she sat back in her chair. Then she sensed someone standing over her, and looked up with a welcoming smile.

But it was Paul Harriman, not Grant, who stood there.

"Hello, Theo Fairchild," he purred. There was a feline quality about Paul. Or at least a great deal of tomcat.

"Hello, Dr. Harriman," she replied politely.

"Oh, spare me the Doctor business, please. You make me feel about eighty when you do that."

He slid into the seat opposite her and tossed his head of shining gold hair. "All alone? How nice to have a chance to talk with you. I take it you're a Latin scholar, since I haven't seen you in any of my or Di's classes. Such a shame. But I suppose we must keep Arthur and Henry and Freddy in students as well."

"Er, yes, I suppose so." What could she possibly have to say to this Abercrombie model-turned-Greek professor? "Um...I enjoyed your music at the dinner the other night."

"Why, thank you. It's rather a hobby of mine—well, more than a hobby, now that we're recording." He let his gaze travel over her. "I understand that you're a teacher. Enjoying coming back and playing student again? I'm sure we have lots we could teach you. At least," his voice dropped, "I know I have."

Theo wiped her palms on her jeans and glanced around to see if Grant was anywhere in sight yet. All she could see were two tables of female graduate students, their attention riveted on her and Paul. Or at least on Paul. A few of them had their mouths hanging open.

"We're a close-knit group in the department," Paul continued, leaning a little closer. "Very close knit. We spend most of our leisure as well as professional time together. I should get my claim in now for the pleasure of your company at the next symposium. If you're teaching in the department, you'll be invited. It's where we let our hair down, so to speak." His voice lowered. "I would love to see your hair down. Spread over a pillow, perhaps."

Theo was glad that she hadn't ordered a drink yet or she might have choked...or more likely, thrown it at him. Then to her relief she felt a pair of warm hands on her shoulders, and Grant's voice said, "Hello, darling. I'm sorry I'm late. Arthur kept me talking."

Darling? Theo twisted in her seat and stared up at him. Had he just called her darling?

"Do join us, Grant." Paul waved at the table. "Theo and I were just having a lovely chat."

Grant muttered something under his breath and pulled a chair from another table, bringing it close to Theo.

"We were discussing music," Paul said. "You'll have to come over and see my instruments some time, Theo. I've got two lyres and a kithara based on ones found—"

"Uh huh," Grant interrupted in a bored tone. Theo stared at him in open surprise. He glanced at her and rested his arm along the back of her chair so that it just touched her shoulders. "Great concert the other night, by the way. Your ensemble was almost professional-sounding. I was astonished."

Theo darted a glance at Paul, sure he would be outraged at Grant's rudeness. Instead, he smiled.

"I expect I should be running along," he said. "Very nice talking to you, Theo. Maybe another time? Bon appétit, Grant." He rose, and with another dazzling smile at Theo, left them.

Theo watched as he drew near the first of the tables. One girl, quicker of thought than her tablemates, dropped a pen directly in Paul's path so that he was forced to stop and retrieve it for her. The other table of female students looked daggers at her; one actually hissed. Judging from his wide grin as he handed the girl her pen and accepted her invitation to join them, Paul didn't seem too put off by his conversation with Grant.

Theo turned back to the culprit who still sat next to her, now looking slightly dazed. "Um...Paul's not a friend of yours, I take it?" she asked tentatively.

"Actually, he is. Known him forever." Grant shook his head once more. "I can't believe I did that."

"Well, now that you mention it—"

"No, Theo, you don't understand. I saw him sitting there across from you, undressing you with his eyes, and I wanted to put my fist through his face. I was jealous."

She caught her breath. Jealous? "Er, should I take this as formal notification that you're interested in me as something other than a teaching colleague?"

"Hmm? Well, yes, of course I am. I just never thought it would hit me that way. Jealous," he said, with a wondering sigh. "Me, jealous."

Theo laughed. "Don't you think you've got it a little backward?"

"What?" Grant looked startled.

"Well, when most people start falling in—um, I mean feeling interested in someone else in a—er, romantic sense, they don't spend a lot of time thinking about how they're feeling. They just do it "

He frowned. "What do you mean?"

"I mean that maybe you should spend a little more time feeling and a little less analyzing." Was she really having a discussion with him about how to fall in love?

"Oh. I see." Grant studied her for a moment. "Uh, Theo? I think I'm starting to feel considerably more than mere friendship for you."

"Oh, Grant." She shook her head. "Haven't you ever been in love with anyone? Ever had a serious girlfriend? With your looks, I can't believe you haven't."

"My...really? I mean, yes, of course I have." He looked down and brushed a thread from his sleeve.

She cleared her throat and raised an eyebrow at him.

He flushed slightly. "I've just never met anyone like you. Do you—" he paused, then said quickly, "Do you think you feel something more than friendship for me?"

Theo wanted to laugh again, but didn't. She took his hand instead, moving carefully as if he were a wild creature she was trying to tame. "Yes, Grant, I am feeling something considerably more than friendship for you too."

"Oh. That's good." He smiled radiantly and held her hand in both of his. "So...what do we do next?"

Try as she might, she could not restrain a smile. "Why don't we just try to relax and see what happens? Get to know each other better?"

"That sounds like a good plan. I'm enjoying knowing you, Theo." He exhaled. "I guess I can start talking to Paul again, then. So long as he doesn't keep trying to get to know you better than I do."

Speaking of Paul... "What have you heard about these symposia that the department holds? Paul said we'll be invited."

"I've heard about them." Grant grimaced. "We have to come in appropriate Greek or Roman attire. Guess I'll have to get my toga sent down from Eleusinian."

Visions of toga-ed bears declaiming in a pine forest, Grant patiently correcting their grammar, flitted through Theo's head. "And I'll have to get my mom to send me one of her costumes that she wears to Dad's Classical Club dinners, except that she's married and wears the *stola*, not the toga. Dad made her do all kinds of research on Roman clothing."

"I bet I'd like your Dad. I hope I get to meet him some time."

An extra surge of happiness caught her. Men didn't say things like that lightly, usually. "I hope you do, too."

After that, their relationship did not change radically: outwardly they were still simply friends and colleagues. But Theo could sense something in the way Grant stared at her over their stacks of Latin quizzes when he thought she wasn't paying attention or over the drinks or pizza that frequently followed. She swallowed her eagerness and waited for him to make the first move; it was like pretending to be a statue, waiting to see if the shy wild bird would light on her hand.

One afternoon in early October they lay on the west-facing hillside behind Hamilton Hall. Theo had diverted them from their usual afternoon go-over-homework-and-class-assignments meeting to enjoy the Indian summer weather.

"Oh, what a day!" she sighed as she stared up at the cloudless blue sky. "Just breathe that air."

"I am breathing," said Grant seriously. "I usually do."

Oh, Grant. "No—I mean really breathe. Isn't it wonderful? It makes me want to flap my arms and follow those geese up there." She pointed with her chin at a V-formation that passed overhead. "And look at those maples over there, just starting to show color around the edges—incredible."

He squinted at the trees. "They're, um, very nice."

She let her arm fall to cover her face. This was the way he was, and it never failed to amuse her: so cynically observant about some things, and utterly clueless about others. Especially about anything that involved the senses. One day a few weeks ago he'd found her in one of the seminar rooms with her shoes off, blissfully burying her toes in the silk Kerman rug. He'd been mystified, even when she made him do the same.

Now he rolled over in the grass to regard her. She reached up and brushed aside his hair. "Just checking your ears," she said with a grin.

"My ears? Why?"

"To see if you're a Vulcan. Honestly, can't you feel what a glorious day it is? Don't you want to roll in the grass like a colt and be glad you're alive?"

"I'm very grateful to be alive," he said, looking down at the grass, then up at her again. "But thank you," he added in the same quiet tone.

"For what?"

"For teaching me to be human."

"Wait a minute. Let me see those ears again." She reached for his hair. He captured her hand and held it.

"You have no idea what being with you is like for me," he said, looking earnestly into her eyes. "You are so here, so in the minute, seeing and feeling and knowing."

"Aren't you here? Don't you see and feel and know?"

"Not in the way you do. I see that the sky is blue and that the leaves are changing colors because it's fall. But they've done that for millennia. They just are. Only man can look at them and see the passing beauty in them. Maybe it's their mortality that gives men the ability to appreciate the things that don't last."

"So you admit it—you are a Vulcan." She grinned at him again. "But those things do last. I'll always remember lying here on a perfect October day with you."

"Someday that memory will die with you." He squeezed her hand, then held it against his cheek. She held her breath. "But I don't want to think about that."

"Then don't think about it." She stroked his cheek. "I know we all have to die someday. But until we're dead, we're alive. They say that where there's life, there's hope."

"Hope," he said, with a tight, humorless laugh. "You talk to me of hope?"

What had happened to Grant that he was this way? "Why not? That's what it means to be alive. To live in the hope of another perfect fall day. Can't you see that?"

He studied her face as if looking for some hint of irony, and she felt the tension slowly leave him.

"Theo," he said, his voice hoarse. "You make me see that." He bent his head toward her.

A flutter of excitement ran through her at his closeness. She slid the hand that still rested on his cheek around to entwine in his hair, as soft and dark as mink, and pulled him down to her.

He touched his mouth to hers carefully, delicately, like the brush of a feather. She felt him tremble, and with a rush of tenderness held herself in check and let him set the pace of their kiss, closing her eyes and keeping her lips soft and yielding as he explored them. Time stretched and slowed.

But after a brief eternity she couldn't hold back any longer. With a little sigh she let her lips part and brushed her tongue across his lips.

"Theo!" he gasped, and gripped her shoulder.

She murmured into his mouth, "I want you to taste me, Grant. Please."

"Taste you…oh, god, Theo…" Now it was her heart pounding as the slow honeyed seconds flew by. He may have had little practice, but the sheer emotion—the passion, the longing—in that kiss was making her—

"Oh, really," said a disapproving voice above them.

"You're just jealous, Di," came the cheerful reply. "I know I am."

"Jealous? I don't think so. Kissing is so—unsanitary!"

Grant sat up as if jerked by a string. Theo made a small, anguished sound, and her dismay threatened to choke her. Past Grant's shoulder she saw Diana Hunter and Paul Harriman standing over them. Di looked disgusted, but Paul regarded them with interest.

"That looked like fun," he said, turning his smile on Theo. "You never told me you were such a good kisser. Or offered to show me, for that matter."

Theo closed her eyes for a second, trying to gather her scattered wits and conjure some answer that wasn't too irritable. She said politely, without sitting up, "Lovely afternoon, isn't it?"

Grant glanced at her. A hint of a twinkle showed in his eyes.

"Well, it was," said Di. "C'mon, Paul. Let's walk somewhere else." She cast one further dark look at them and flounced away. Paul blew Theo a kiss and followed.

Grant collapsed on his back, eyes closed, and began to shake.

Theo glowered at the retreating pair and muttered, "Damn them anyway." When she looked back at Grant she was relieved to see that his shaking was actually muffled laughter.

"I'm glad you think it was funny. I thought it was singularly poor timing," she said in an aggrieved tone, then pushed herself up on one elbow. "I'm sorry if I startled you—I mean, if you didn't want…"

Grant's laughter ceased. He opened his eyes, and now his

expression was gentle and wondering. "Theo, you don't know how much I did—do—want it. I've never—"

"I guessed." She touched his cheek.

He stiffened, then relaxed as her fingertips brushed his skin. A rueful smile tugged at his mouth. "Really? Am I that transparent?"

Yes. "No. And anyway, it doesn't matter." She touched his lips with one finger.

"Theo. My beautiful, warm Theo, let me explain—"

"You don't need to explain anything to me."

"But I do. All my life I have worked and watched...and suffered. But I have never loved. No, that's not true. I've always loved people but in a theoretical sort of way. Never singly, never just one at a time, like this. Like you. Now it's happening to me, and I'm terrified. Excited and eager and exhilarated and scared nearly witless. I don't know if I'm doing it right, and I live in fear that I'll make a stupid mistake and drive you from me."

"You won't, but even if you did, don't you think I'd forgive you?" She reached out to stroke his cheek again.

"Be patient with me while I learn to love you, Theo. Please. It's all so new to me." He swallowed, and asked, "Was it—all right, to kiss me? Did I do it right?"

She smothered the smile that his earnest expression evoked. "It was more than all right. Why do you think I was so annoyed at the intrusion?"

"Oh. I thought so. Your expression was remarkably eloquent when you looked at Paul and Di. You were right. Damn them anyway."

They both laughed and Theo nestled against him, head on his shoulder, rejoicing to herself as his arms went around her. "You did it very well," she whispered in his ear. "But further practice is always a good idea, you know, if you want to perfect your technique."

His embrace tightened. "I'll remember that, thank you."

Theo thought of something. "Grant?" she asked softly.

"Hmm?"

"When we kissed—were you there? Were you in the moment then?"

He pulled back and smiled down at her, the pale, serious El Greco face transformed. "I was, Theo. I was there, I think."

She kissed his nose. "That was your first class in Being Human 101. Congratulations, Mr. Spock.

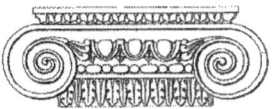

Four

THE FOLLOWING FRIDAY DR. Waterman asked Theo to fish-sit while he went away for the weekend. She drove that afternoon out to his house, a handsome colonial on a low cliff overlooking Massachusetts Bay.

Following him from room to room, Theo marveled at the tanks of fish everywhere. Fortunately their care was simple.

"A teaspoon in each tank, every morning," said Dr. Waterman, tapping a large plastic container. "That's all you have to do."

"I thought tropical fish were more labor intensive. Changing the water and testing it and so on," she said, staring at a majestic pair of blue and purple angelfish that swept in tandem around one tank.

"Yes, well, there is a lot of that. But nothing you need to worry about for just a weekend. Feed them and they'll be happy." He smiled and nodded at her.

She picked up the tub and shook it gently. "Is it the same as what you use at school?"

She often stopped by his office in the early morning to gaze at the rainbow of fish, and more often than not he would let her feed them. She would carefully sprinkle the silvery flakes of food from the little silver spoon into the tanks, trying not to inhale, but it was impossible not to smell the ineffable sweet floral scent that made her nose tingle and her other senses heighten delightfully.

"Yes, it is. But please be careful with it, Theo. Breathing it in or otherwise ingesting it is...unwise. I don't often trust anyone else to take care of my fish, but I feel that they're in good hands with you." He gave her a fatherly pat on the shoulder and glanced at his massive diving watch. "I'd better get going if I'm to arrive in time for the dinner. You have my cell number if you need me, yes?"

Theo returned to school for her last class after assuring Dr. Waterman that she and his fish would be fine while he was gone. After class was over she stopped in his office to give the fish there an extra feeding to carry them through Saturday, then wandered down to the Great Room.

It had become her favorite place to study, its beauty in sharp contrast to her dreary room in Graves. More polished linenfold paneling covered the walls, pierced at regular intervals with diamond-paned windows. Small groups of couches and chairs were scattered on the mosaic floor, and it was in one of these that Theo generally spent a few hours after dinner each evening, reading or working on her laptop or sparring happily with Grant.

Just now, late afternoon sun illuminated the floor with rich golden light, making the mosaics glow on their creamy background. There was Apollo reaching toward a girl whose bare legs were being swallowed in gray bark and her long hair scattered with green leaves: the transformation of Daphne. And there was a magnificent winged horse, its neck a proud arch, eyeing a youth who held a golden bridle in one hand and in the other an apple to tempt the fey creature. Where was the cruelly magnificent bird she had seen as she dozed on the night of the department dinner? She glanced around, trying to estimate where the chairs had been set up, and saw Julian leaning against one of the Doric columns by the far door, smiling.

"They're something, aren't they?" he said. Walking up to her, he gazed down at Pegasus and Bellerophon, hands clasped behind his back. "I like to do just what you're doing, sometimes, when I need distraction."

She glanced at him cautiously but he stood still and looked down at the images with a pensive expression. He had made her nervous in her first few days here, and she had avoided him as much as she could after the department dinner. To her relief she'd seen little of him since then, and her attention had been caught up in her teaching and in—as he jokingly called them— her humanities classes with Grant.

But Julian seemed different this afternoon. His manner, though friendly, was easier. Less—well, predatory. "I love it in here. It's my favorite place for studying," she confessed, and could have bitten her tongue. Was that a wise thing to have told him?

But he merely smiled and nodded. "I can understand that. It's the most beautiful place on campus, in my opinion." He looked around the room, still smiling, then looked back at her. "Actually, I'm glad to find someone here. Do you have a minute? I could use a hand."

Theo thought quickly. *Someone*, he had said. Not *you*. "Sure. What can I do?"

"Come upstairs and help me find something. I'm working on a paper for a conference next spring and can't find a reference I need. A fresh pair of eyes would be useful."

Theo followed him up the stairs to the department library

and museum on the third floor. To her surprise he bypassed the library, another paneled room lined with shelves holding thousands of books and monographs, and led her into the museum.

If the library was impressive, the museum was astounding. Theo knew that art museums from all over the world constantly requested the loan of items from it: Andrew Barnes often worked with June Cadwallader on processing loan requests, and had told her about it. Its strength was less in the size of its collection than in its rarity and condition: from exquisite Greek jewelry and rare Roman glass beakers to near-perfectly preserved documents. State-of-the-art cases held the pieces on rotating display and kept the rest in storage in optimal conditions.

But despite the splendor of the place, Theo had visited it only once. The museum's curator, Dr. Bellow, had frightened her nearly out of her wits when she had gone up to see it in the first week of classes. He was a tall, somber man who gave an impression of overall grayness: his hair, his clothes, even his skin seemed to have an ashen tinge. Only his eyes were alive: they were black and glittering, like obsidian, and as sharp.

She had been admiring an elegantly wrought silver drinking cup, set in a case at eye level to enable viewers to appreciate its workmanship, when those eyes had appeared on the other side of the case, staring at her. She had nearly shouted in surprise. Nor had she been captivated by Dr. Bellow's small gray dog, which sniffed at her ankles and growled softly. It looked up at her with eyes as flat and remorseless as its master's.

"No, Kirby! Heel!" Dr. Bellow had said sternly, and tried to smile at her. He had chatted quite pleasantly after that, but she could not erase the memory of the terror she had felt when she glanced up from the dancing nymphs and satyrs on the cup into those gleaming pools of blackness that seemed to lead into eternity.

"I don't see Dr. Bellow anywhere," she said nervously to Julian as he unlocked the door and flicked on the lights. "Or Kirby."

"It's after regular museum hours. He's probably down in his office by now," Julian replied carelessly.

"His office isn't up here? I don't remember seeing it near the other faculty offices."

"It's not. It's in the basement. Don't ask me why; he seems to like it down there. And I don't care for Kirby any more than you do. I'm just as happy he's there and not here." Julian motioned her toward a case set against one wall.

The top of the case, set on rows of drawers, held a display of carved gems from different parts of Greece, once set in rings and used to seal documents and letters. They were tiny works of art, carved from colorful banded jasper and agate and quartz.

Julian waved a hand at the drawers. "I'm looking for a specific seal and can't find it in the museum index. As I re-call, it depicts a male figure holding a cup out to a reclining woman."

He handed her a small lump, and Theo saw that it was some type of plasticine clay. "Start with that drawer and I'll start over here. Look at each one and if it looks promising, press it on the clay. That helps make the image more identifiable if the stone matrix is striped." He pulled a couple of chairs up to the case and unlocked the drawers.

Theo held the clay in her hand to warm it as she surveyed the first row of seals, each in its own cushioned compartment. She sat stiffly at first but relaxed as she examined the exquisite little carvings, some of stylized trees and vegetation, others of gods and men. One depicting a pair of geese in flight reminded her of lying on the hillside with Grant. And there was one with a leaping dolphin. The sight of it made her smile. Good thing Dr. Waterman didn't keep any of those in his tanks.

She rubbed her nose to conceal her expression and felt a

tingle, accompanied by a rush of pleasurable wooziness. Dr. Waterman's fish food! Theo looked at the back of her hand and saw a few silvery flakes still clinging to it. Some of the food must have stuck to her hand when she'd fed them just now. She'd tried to be careful, really she had. She hadn't meant to...

A wave of euphoria surged through her. The seals glowed more brightly in their drab protective foam, and she stared at them in delight for a moment before shutting the drawer and opening another.

"Any luck?" said Julian from his chair.

"No. But they're so beautiful," she sighed. "I could look at them all day." She gazed around the room and drank in its contents. "All of it. So, so beautiful."

Julian glanced up at her, and his eyes widened slightly. "Is everything all right, Theodora?" He shut the drawer he had been searching and pulled his chair closer to hers.

"I'm fine. I love all this—love it here. It's everything I'd hoped it would be." She smiled at him. Julian was being so *nice* today—not at all alarming, really. He was awfully attractive, wasn't he? Those turquoise eyes were mesmerizing, and the tanned face was youthful and unlined despite the silver-gray hair.

"And what did you hope it would be?" he asked with a slight smile.

Tingles coursed through her; it felt like her blood had been replaced with champagne. "A place where everyone loves the same things I do, and where we can talk and laugh and even argue for hours, and still understand each other perfectly."

"Didn't you have that before where you taught?"

"No. Never." She shook her head earnestly and felt dizzy. "Even though I was teaching what I loved, no one cared about it. Or about me."

"No one?" His voice was warm and sympathetic.

"They were *afraid* of me. They all assumed I was an escapee from a convent because I taught Latin. My best friend was my cat. I do miss her an awful lot," she added with a sigh.

"Poor Theodora. So do you think you'll find your true home here with us?"

"I hope so. You are all so kind and so..." What was it she wanted to say? Beautiful glittering words danced away in her head as she reached for them.

"*Simpatico*, as the Romans would put it today?"

"Yes! That's it exactly." Oh, it was so nice to be understood. She smiled into his eyes. Just now they were an even deeper turquoise than usual.

"And are we all *simpatico*, or are some of us more so than others?" he asked playfully. But there was a note somewhere in his tone that required an answer. Even in her giddiness she could hear it.

"Oh, I like all of you. Dr. Waterman has been so kind, and so have Dr. Forge-Smythe and Dr. Herman and Dr. Zeno in the Philosophy Department."

"And?"

"And...well, Paul Harriman can be a bit difficult."

"I can imagine." Julian smiled wryly.

"I'm not sure about Dr. Hunter. I thought she liked me at first, but maybe not so much since she saw me kiss Grant a few weeks ago."

She saw the turquoise in his eyes fade to a grayer shade. Was she saying too much? But he wanted to know, and for some reason she wanted to tell him.

"Grant Proctor," he said slowly. "You're teaching with him, I believe. How is that going?"

Warm happiness flooded her. "It's wonderful. *He's* wonderful. He's so...I don't know. Funny and wise one minute, strange and vulnerable the next. But he loves to teach. I've watched him when we've combined our classes for special lectures."

Julian gazed at her and tapped a finger on his lips. She stared dreamily at his hands; they were well formed, the fingers long and supple. And his mouth...the lips were chiseled and smooth. She had to clench her hand into a fist to keep from reaching out to touch his beautiful mouth.

"Well, *eme phile* Theodora. I'm glad you're happy here," he said at last. "We try very hard to find the right people for the department each year. I'm more delighted than you can know that we did so well in finding you." He smiled and leaned forward. "You didn't have too much, did you? It was Arthur's fish food, I assume. Are you feeling quite well?"

"Hmm?" She tore her attention away from contemplation of his lips and blinked owlishly. "Oh, I'm fine. I feel wonderful."

"Good. That's very good. Not everyone can tolerate it so well. Very interesting, my dear. I think...ah, yes. I've remembered." He rose and pulled out the drawer she had been about to open, and pointed to a seal carved from deep blue lapis lazuli, flecked with gold.

Theo picked it up and stared at it raptly. Yes, there was the reclining woman, reaching up to take something—a cup?—from the man standing by her couch. Geologic chance and the carver's whimsy had made it so that the man's head was surrounded by a halo of gold flecks. "It's beautiful," she whispered.

"It is indeed. Thank you for your help, my dear," he said, taking the seal from her and looking at it with satisfaction. "You don't know how interesting this has been. Here." He took the forgotten lump of clay still warming in Theo's hand, smoothed it with his fingers, and pressed the seal into it. "For you," he added, handing the impression to her.

"Ahem." The polite cough startled Theo, sounding

unnaturally loud to her heightened sense of hearing. She turned. June Cadwallader stood in the doorway, arms folded on her chest.

"Yes, June?" sighed Julian.

"If you're going to make it for dinner with the President, you'd better get going now. It's nearly four-thirty." Theo's euphoria receded under the woman's basilisk stare.

"Thank you. I'll be right down. You can go home now," Julian replied.

"What about locking up the Museum?" June persisted.

"I am perfectly capable of doing it myself. I *am* the head of the department. Please remember that." He nodded coldly at her and turned back to Theo. "Thank you for your help. I enjoyed having a chance to talk—"

"Dr. Bellow wanted me to lock—"

"*Apeche, gunai! Epilanthanei tina to sou despoten einai?*" he shouted. "*Aperchome!*"

"My master?" June's voice dripped derision. "Once, maybe. But not now, if you recall. You can't have it both ways. Not even you. And I'm going, don't worry." She gave him one last baleful look and left.

Julian closed his eyes for a moment. His face was stiff with anger.

"Uh—" Theo rose from her chair. What had that been about...and what had he just said to June? Did she speak classical Greek too?

Julian's anger seemed to evaporate. His eyes were again warm, almost caressing, when he opened them and looked at her. "I'm sorry, Theodora. June is an excellent secretary, but she does try to run my life sometimes. Please pay us no mind." He took her chair and put it away, then put the lapis seal in an envelope, leaving a note in its place in the drawer. "That will do for up here. Are you all right?"

"I think so." A rosy curl of giddiness swirled through her brain and faded. She'd inhaled some of Dr. Waterman's fish food, hadn't she? And Julian had been so charming and easy to talk to until...what had they talked about? Something to do with her liking it here, maybe? "Yes, I'm fine."

"Of course you are." He locked the cases and motioned her through the museum's doors, locking them as well before he followed her down the stairs. On the landing outside the second floor he paused. "Well, I'll see you Monday, Theodora. Have a nice weekend."

Theo went back to the Great Room where she had left her book bag and suddenly remembered the little wad of clay in her hand. She stopped to look at the image impressed in it. Julian had been nice—she hadn't dreamed that. She could vaguely remember his face as he had handed it to her, intent on hers. But not frightening. As she walked back to her car and thought about going back to Dr. Waterman's quiet house, she actually found herself wishing that they could have chatted a little longer.

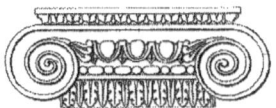

Five

"YOU'RE NOT GOING TO believe this, I'm afraid," said Dr. Waterman with a smile, stroking his beard.

It was the Friday before Halloween, and down in the Great Room the undergraduate Classics majors were preparing for their annual Halloween toga party. Sounds of moving furniture and shrill laughter could be heard even up here, but did nothing to dispel the intent atmosphere in the room. Midterms were over, and Grant and Theo had turned their grades in to Dr. Waterman. Now they were waiting to find out who had won the bet Grant had made with her in September.

Theo grimaced as the sound of a couch being dragged across the floor below grated against her ears. If those kids hurt the mosaics...

Grant patted her hand reassuringly. "We'll go down there and supervise after Arthur tells us I've won."

"Well, I hate to disappoint you, Grant," Dr. Waterman began.

Theo laughed and tapped Grant's arm. "I told you so!"

"Not so fast, Theo," cautioned the professor.

"What?" Both Theo and Grant stared at him. Then Grant laughed.

"It isn't," he said, shaking his head. "It can't be."

"It is, my friends. Your classes tied. I couldn't quite believe it myself, but I did the math twice. You make a fine teaching team."

Theo laughed as well. "And I was looking forward to your taking me to the University Club, too," she said to Grant.

"You think I wasn't looking forward to the same thing?"

"Wait, wait!" Laughing, Dr. Waterman held up one hand. "In view of your excellent work with the First Year Latin students—and to thank you for giving me a year off from them—I would like for both of you to be my guests at dinner on Saturday at the club. Will honor be satisfied?"

"Well..." Grant began, looking sideways at her.

She reached a foot out and stepped lightly on his toes. "We'd be delighted, Dr. Waterman. Thank you very much."

In the hallway Grant still chuckled and shook his head. She pulled him toward the end of the hall, her amusement gone. Dr. Waterman's invitation to dinner was very nice, but she hadn't really thought until now about how much she had looked forward to an excuse for a potentially romantic evening alone with Grant. Any time alone with him, come to think of it, where the only interruptions would be by impersonal wait staff.

Their few quiet moments alone together over the last weeks had always been spoiled by the arrival of someone wanting to chat, generally someone like Dr. Herman or Dr. Forge-Smythe who couldn't be given a polite brush-off, and it was getting on her nerves. But she didn't want to invite him to her dreary room in Graves, which was as romantic as a newsstand. Nor had he invited her to his apartment off-campus, despite her hopeful hints.

"C'mon, comedian," she said, smiling unwillingly at his

hilarity.

"Why, Theo. Don't you think it's funny?" They started down the stairs.

"Yes, but..."

"But what?"

"But this." At the stairwell landing she pulled him into a corner, slipped an arm around him, and pulled his face down to hers.

His hands moved to her waist, and he made a small sound in his throat as their lips met. Ah, *yes*...

With a jerk of his head, Grant suddenly broke the kiss and turned his face away. "I'm sorry, Theo," he said tonelessly.

She bit back an exclamation of dismay. "You don't want me to kiss you?"

His grip tightened. "Yes, I do! I do...but..."

"But what?" She leaned back to look into his face. All traces of laughter were gone from it. "I'm with you almost every day, and no five minutes of it go by without my wanting to reach out to stroke your hair, or hold your hand, or feel your arms around me." Her mouth felt dry, and she swallowed.

"I never thought I would be an object of desire," he said, avoiding her gaze. "My body—I'm damaged goods, remember."

She lifted his chin. "You're not *just* the object of my desire. Bodies are just tools, another way for me to tell you that I love you." She stopped and closed her eyes. She hadn't meant to say that. Not yet.

"You...love me?" he whispered. "Me?"

"No, that bust of Octavian over there." She disentangled her arms from him and wrapped them around herself. This wasn't going at all as she'd planned. "Yes, I love you. I wouldn't be so desperate for a simple kiss if I didn't. I've spent these last few weeks talking and laughing and working with someone more wonderful than I'd ever dreamed of meeting. How could I not fall in love with you?" she said, more to herself than to him.

"Theo—"

"I thought you were starting to feel it too. Sometimes I see you look at me, and there's something in your eyes that makes me think—" she broke off to steady her breath. "Maybe I've imagined it. Maybe it's just been wishful thinking on my part. I'm sorry if I've misjudged...this. Us." She edged away from him. Shrieks of laughter from the Great Room below grated on her ears.

"I love you too, Theo."

That stopped her. "What?"

Grant stood outlined in light from the high stairwell windows. His hands clenched, but his voice was steady. His eyes were steady, too, as he met hers. "I said, I love you. Maybe I should say it to Octavian. His ears might work better." A faint dimple appeared in one corner of his mouth, and he closed the distance between them and put his arms around her. She leaned her head on his shoulder, feeling like she had inhaled a full teaspoon of Dr. Waterman's fish flakes.

"I do feel those things that you describe," he murmured. "If I stare at you, it's because I have so many things I long to do and say but don't know how to. Oh, Theo, if you only knew—"

"Then tell me. You don't have to be afraid of me." She reached up to stroke his hair.

A slight laugh shook him. "Courage is not something I generally have a problem with."

"Then what is it?"

"I'm sorry. Maybe I'm not as brilliant as you think I am. I guess I'm not progressing in my humanities studies like I should, even though I have the best teacher I could hope for. I'm trying to be more human, really I am." His voice reached for flippant but missed.

"Grant, why haven't you ever been in love? Why don't you

know how to respond, even though you say that you love me?" She touched his face.

"I can't explain it to you yet. Not in terms that I think you'd understand."

"Try me. I'm a bright girl."

"That's not what I meant. I don't think I can explain it because I can't find the words. Be patient, Theo. I hate to keep asking that of you, but I must. Someday I'll be able to tell you." He kissed her hand again, then held her away to look at her with a wry smile. "I must be getting a little better, if I was able to tell you that I love you. But wouldn't it all be easier if we could be like him over there," he nodded toward the marble bust, "and just live a life of the mind, and *know* that we loved each other?"

She shook her head. "You're being a Vulcan again. True love is of the mind, yes, when it comes down to it. But we need our bodies and senses as well as our minds to express it. It's just the way we humans are." She pulled him close again, ran her hands up and down his back, then leaned forward and nibbled his earlobe. He shivered and his arms tightened around her.

"See? Didn't that feel good? Could Octavian over there feel that love, without having flesh? Could words alone do that? Love is physical as well as in the mind. Listen to yourself. Listen to what your body tells you." She bent and softly kissed his neck.

"Flesh is weak," he persisted though his eyes had closed in enjoyment. "It can betray us. It can lie."

"It can also tell the truth. And words can lie and betray as well as flesh can. There are no guarantees. Hoping is human, remember? So is taking chances. There's no reason to hope if you don't." Her lips brushed against the skin of his throat as she spoke, and she felt his hands start to move on her.

A crash from below, followed by more shrieks of laughter, startled them apart.

"That didn't sound good," said Grant. He let go of her and turned toward the stairs. Theo sighed and followed him.

In the Great Room a swarm of undergrads, some already draped in bed sheet togas, tugged furniture this way and that. Most of the floor space had been emptied for dancing, but a few of the Second Year Latin students who had actually been paying attention in class were trying to arrange the room's couches into something approximating a Roman *triclinium*, or dining room, for the refreshments. Grant hurried over to them.

"No, no, couches only on three sides of the table," he said, motioning them toward him. "You'll just have to make a couple of these if more people want to join in."

Theo shook her head and smiled as she walked away, but her heart was sore. Just when she and Grant had been getting somewhere, they were interrupted once more. Would she ever have more than a few minutes alone—really alone—with him? It was beginning to feel like some vast conspiracy of the gods against her.

A pair of toga-ed people ran by her, giggling madly, and then another. The second pair, a plump girl with curly brown hair and a man wrapped in a SpongeBob Square-pants bed sheet, nearly collided with her.

"Whoa!" said the man. He stopped and peered at her uncertainly. "Why, hello there, Theo. Coming to join us tonight?"

It was Marlowe Vine. He had occasionally joined her and Grant for drinks in the college pub and had only been asked to leave twice by the manager for excessive rowdiness. But despite his copious drinking Theo couldn't help liking him; he was unfailingly cheerful and treated her with jovial courtesy. "Nice toga, Marlowe."

"Isn't it? Allie here let me borrow it. It belongs to her little brother, but he manfully gave it up for the weekend. I may need to get my own, though. I think it makes quite a fashion state-ment." He swayed and caught himself on the girl's shoulder. She giggled.

"You could say that."

Marlowe leaned closer. "You don't look very happy, you know. Where's Grant?"

Was she that obvious? But no. It was true she and Grant were frequently together, what with the teaching. She lifted her chin and nodded back toward the couches. "Over there, helping with the banquet room."

"Is that what they're doing? Excellent! A symposium! Some-thing else to look forward to tonight, eh?" He squeezed the girl's arm and she giggled again.

"But I thought this was an undergraduate party," Theo said. "You know, no alcohol?"

"It is, mostly. And I'm a chaperone, sort of. But we don't need wine to be joyous, do we? Not much, anyway. Run along and make sure they're doing it right over there, love." He gave the girl a gentle push toward Grant and the others, and turned back to Theo.

"Now, why so sad? I hate seeing sad people around. It's so—saddening."

She smiled in spite of herself. "I'll be all right. I don't know how you got the idea I'm down."

"Ah, I always know these things. Ask Grant. Life's not meant for sadness. Tell you what, though. It's time you and he came to one of the proper symposia. No room for long faces there. I'm sure Julian will be happy to invite you to November's. In fact, I'm sure he was planning to."

"Thanks, Marlowe. That sounds like fun."

"Mean that when you say it, sweetheart," he said in a bad Bogart voice.

"Mean what?" Grant had come to stand with them.

"Ho there, Grant. I was just telling Theo that it was time you two made it to a symposium. Get some pink in her cheeks and some starch out of your shirt. I livened things up a little for you up in New Hampshire, didn't I? And to think you'd never tried cow-tipping." He shook his head incredulously. "By the way, how's our beauteous Olivia? Has she forgiven me yet? Now there's someone who needs a few more symposia under her belt. Far too solemn for such a handsome girl, don't you think? Then again, she always was too serious. You need to work on her more, Grant."

Theo pressed her lips together and looked down at her feet. She'd forgotten that Marlowe had spent a year at Grant's Institute and knew all his colleagues and friends up there. Like this beauteous Olivia. Julian had asked Grant about an Olivia as well, hadn't he? A small green snake hissed *'very interessssting'* in her mind's ear.

"Olivia's fine. I spoke with her a few days ago." From the corner of her eye she saw Grant glance at her as he spoke, but she would not look up from the floor.

"Fabulous. Send her my love, won't you? Tell her she has to come down for a visit here. It'll be like old times, eh?" Marlowe clapped Grant on the back, then made a grab for his sheet as it started to slide. "Whoops. I say, Theo, what's so fascinating about that floor?"

She was still staring down at her feet, but now from interest rather than from pique. "It's the bird I saw at the department dinner. I've been looking for it ever since then, but I guess there was furniture over it. Look." She took their arms and pulled the two men back a few steps.

There indeed was the sinister bird with its glinting eye, whether an eagle or a vulture she couldn't say, stretched in its exultant dive toward—toward—she stepped back further.

Yes, there it was, at her feet: a naked man, bound hand and

foot to a stained rock on the craggy side of a mountain, the granite beneath him worn smooth by his body's agonized thrashing. A long, jagged wound gaped across his torso, bleeding freely. It was his blood that had stained the rock below him. Looking more closely, she could see that the bird's beak was stained rusty red as well, and a fragment of purple flesh was still caught in it. It was mesmerizing and horrible.

"It's Prometheus. Prometheus and the vulture. I should have remembered," she said softly, staring down at it.

"Why, so it is. Didn't Olivia write an interesting little monograph on Prometheus for you, Grant?" Marlowe came around to peer down at the floor next to her. "You said you'd preferred Aeschylus's handling—"

A sudden movement silenced Marlowe and made her look up. Without a word, Grant turned on his heels and strode out the door.

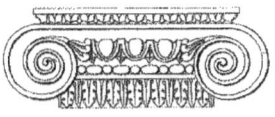

Six

SOME DAYS LATER THEO was walking down the hall after Dr. Herman's seminar when she saw Julian's secretary striding toward her. She hastily stepped to one side and tentatively said, "Hello, Ms Cadwallader."

To her surprise, the woman stopped in front of her. "Here," she said shortly, and shoved a small scroll of thick cream-colored paper, tied with a gold ribbon, at Theo.

"Thank you," said Theo, but June was already stalking back down the hallway to her office. When she got to it, she slammed the door behind her.

"You have a nice day too," Theo said under her breath, and let her backpack slide to the ground as she untied the scroll. Unrolling it, she read:

TUA PRAESENTIA
PETITUR
AD SYMPOSIUM DEPARTMENTI
IDIBUS NOVEMBRIS

HORA OCTAVA POST MEDIRIEM
VESTIS IDONEA REQUIRITUR

So she'd been invited to the next department symposium. Marlowe had been as good as his word. *Idibus Novembris*...that would be the, uh...

"November fifteenth?" said Grant, looking over her shoulder.

Theo jumped but maintained her composure. "Thirteenth. This Saturday. The Ides are on the fifteenth only in certain months, remember? What are you teaching your class, anyway?" She stepped a pace or two from him.

He didn't seem to notice. "I was saving the Roman calendar until right before Thanksgiving, when their attention span is short and we need something non-essential to learn about. I haven't reviewed them in a while."

"Hmmph. *Vestis idonea requiritur*. I wonder what 'proper attire' is for one of these? Maybe I'll borrow Marlowe's SpongeBob sheets for my toga."

"Hey, I was going to ask him. No fair."

"So you're going, too?" She hoped she didn't sound too pleased.

He waved his scroll at her. "I hadn't opened it yet, but I assume it's the same. Not the standard form for departmental mail, is it?"

"No, I guess not. Thank you." She accepted her backpack from Grant as he handed it to her, but avoided the touch of his hand. "No RSVP, I notice," she said as they continued down the hall.

"I don't think attendance is optional, knowing Julian."

Grant's voice was heavy with irony. Theo wondered why but let it pass. "No, I guess not. I hope Mom can get my toga done by then.'

"What? You didn't wear one teaching at your school?"

"And really freak everyone out? I don't think so. Toga parties went out of fashion decades ago, anyway."

"Not here."

"No, not here. What about up at your place? Do you have department symposia as well?" Before she could stop herself, she had pictured a beautiful woman, bearing a remarkable resemblance to Renee Frothington-Forge-Smythe, wearing a floaty pale pink toga and a gold ankle bracelet with a large diamond "O" on it, reclining on a couch next to Grant and batting her eyelashes at him.

"No, not generally. Not unless Marlowe's visiting. It upsets the moose too much."

"Ah, yes, the moose." Theo did not smile. "Well, I really need to be going, Grant. See you later."

Grant looked at her and frowned. "It's nearly quarter of five. Let's go have a drink and some dinner. It seems like I've hardly seen you lately."

She *had* avoided him since Halloween. Well, maybe not quite avoided him. Not really. Oh, all right. Maybe she had.

She couldn't help it. She had told the man, actually *told* him, that she loved him. And he had said he loved her too. So why had he run from her that Friday afternoon? Why hadn't she seen him for the entire weekend after that? She'd practically *lived* in the Great Room, waiting for him to come, wanting to finish their interrupted talk. She'd emailed and texted him, then incessantly checked her phone for a response.

But he hadn't called or showed up. By Sunday afternoon she'd finished her reading for her Roman Historiography class through a haze of tears. Had he spent the weekend in his apartment regretting those three words he had said to her?

Since then she had scraped up the remains of her pride and reassembled them into a fragile casing around her—a casing she'd hoped never have to use again after leaving her teaching job at Sneed. She had been cordial but distant when she couldn't avoid him. At dinner with him and Dr. Waterman just this Saturday to celebrate their midterm tie she had been as chatty and social as she knew how to be, but it had been a brittle sort of conviviality He had watched her with a puzzled frown in his eyes all evening, which just upset her further. How did he expect her to behave, after what had happened?

Now she reached for that casing again and drew it more tightly around her. "You see me every day. And we have our class meetings just as always."

He glowered at her. "You know what I mean, Theo. Come on. I need to talk to you."

They were standing by the stairwell again, Theo noticed. She tried not to remember their last encounter near here. "Oh, about the class term papers. Yeah, we do need to talk about them. Dr. Waterman said seven to ten pages, which seems reasonable for a first year class—"

"That's not what I meant! I...I need to tell you I'm sorry." He looked straight at her as he spoke, and she had to admire his courage. But the ache was still too recent.

"Sorry for what?" she asked, her voice high and sincere.

"I'm sorry I ran away last weekend when it all became too much for me."

"Oh, that. Well, it's...it's not a big deal. I understand if you—"

He rubbed his chin and stared at her, and she wished she weren't standing with her back to the wall.

"You understand if I what?" There was an odd bleakness in his eyes.

"If you don't want—you know." She began to sidle toward the stairwell door. "If you don't want me to—to love you. I shouldn't have said it that afternoon. It put you on the spot."

He gripped her shoulders and pulled her close. "No. You're not running away. You were brave enough last time to talk. Now you'll have to be brave enough to listen, before this gets any worse."

"Not here!" Not in front of everyone's offices. She pushed against him.

He let go of her reluctantly. "All right, not here." He took her arm and shoved the stairwell door open, then froze. Julian stood there looking startled, his outstretched hand still reaching for the door handle. He blinked at them, then smiled.

"Perfect! I was just looking for you, Theodora. Hello, Grant. Mind if I talk with Miss Fairchild here for a few minutes?" He looked at their faces. "Of course, if this is a bad time..."

"No, Julian, it's not." Theo fought to steady her pounding heart. "I'll talk to you later," she said quietly to Grant.

His mouth opened, then closed. With a nod, he pushed past them down the stairs.

Julian was silent as he led her to his office, for which she was grateful. There were no windows in the stairwell doors, thank heavens, and the doors were thick, so he couldn't have seen or heard any of their conversation. That would have been too embarrassing.

"Drink, Theodora?"

"Hmm?" She snapped her attention back to Julian.

"I said, would you like a drink? Sun's over the yardarm—what sun there is, this time of year—and I for one could do with a bracer." He opened a cabinet behind his desk and waved a glass at her.

A bracer. That sounded like what she needed too. "Yes, thank you."

He opened another door in the cabinet, and she was amused to see a wine refrigerator behind it. "I'll bet that's not standard university equipment, even for department heads."

He smiled as he pulled out a bottle and uncorked it. "No, it's not. It's my own addition. We classicists are a thirsty lot. Surely you'd noticed?" He poured two glasses of light golden liquid and brought them around the desk. He handed her one, then held his out in salute. She touched hers to it.

"To scholarship," he said.

"To scholarship," she echoed.

"And to my scholars—the best of them," he said with a smile, then drank.

Theo felt herself flush once more and took a sip. It was similar to the wine he'd served at the department dinner, deep and fruity and potent. She breathed its bouquet through her open mouth and felt a tingle not unlike that of Dr. Waterman's fish food. Strange—but welcome just now. "It's wonderful. Where is it from?"

"Do you like it? It's—well, I don't like to brag. I happen to have a small property in southern Rhode Island that's mostly given over to vines, and—"

"It's your own wine? You grew it?"

"Well, yes." He shrugged modestly.

"Wow. University professor and a vintner too." The wine was having an effect already, leeching the tension caused by her encounter with Grant from her bones like magic. She breathed its bouquet once more, then drank.

Julian nodded approval. "I think you needed it too. You looked a little upset when I saw you in the hallway just now. That's why I asked you up here, if you'll pardon my subterfuge. Is everything all right between you and Grant Proctor? Sometimes teaching in such close tandem with another person can be difficult." He sat back in his chair, watching her.

For a moment she hesitated, remembering their strange first meeting in this room. But the wine was relaxing, and god knew she could use a sympathetic ear just now. "Not entirely well. Things of a personal nature have been, er, cropping up."

"I'm sorry to hear that. It seemed such a good arrangement, giving Arthur a little break and you some valuable experience. Well, you know that as an enrolled student in my department, you are more important to me than Mr. Proctor. If having him here is distressing to you, he can be asked to leave at the semester's end."

"Oh, no! I mean, it's not like that. Not that bad," she amended. "I'm sure we'll work it out. Dr. Waterman says he's quite happy with our work."

"So am I. But I'm also concerned for the well-being and happiness of my students. Please let me know if you need my help with Mr. Proctor, and I shall be more than happy to give it to you, my dear."

"Thank you," Theo almost whispered, a lump rising in her throat. She had been wrong about Julian. It was comforting to know that he was looking out for her.

"You're more than welcome, Theodora. Now, onto to happier topics." He leaned over to refill her glass. "You received your invitation to the symposium?"

"Yes, just now. Thank you very much. I'm looking forward to it."

"Excelle—just now? You just got it today?" He frowned.

"Um, yes. Ms Cadwallader just gave it to me." Theo did not add that the secretary had looked as if she would rather have stuffed it up Theo's nose than hand it to her.

"I see." He was still frowning. "You should have received it days ago. We try to give first-comers plenty of notice to get ready. June sometimes—but never mind that. This doesn't give you much time to prepare appropriate garb. It's all quite silly, but we do like to 'do it proper', as it were. Morale building for the department, I suppose."

"Don't worry. I'm sure my mother can help me with something. She's made my father several costumes for his Classical Club events."

"Has she? I'm sure you'll outshine us all, then. Tell me about your father. Ancient languages are an unusual hobby in this day and age."

He kept her talking, quietly refilling her glass, nodding and asking more questions about her family. She didn't know how late it was until he glanced at his watch and said, "Oh, no. I'm keeping you from your dinner. Well, we must do this again, Theodora. I haven't had such pleasant conversation in a long time."

Theo rose. The wine seemed to surge into her head like a fountain, sparkling yet enervating, making her sway slightly. She remembered the glass in her hand and held it out to him. "Thank you very much," she managed to say.

He leaned forward, hand extended to take the glass from her. He seemed taller and broader all of a sudden, making her feel small and vulnerable. An image streaked across her mind, of a crowned figure reaching out to a reclining woman. That lapis seal in the Museum...but then her head cleared. Julian was standing where he had been, looking like his usual self, setting her glass down. He came around the desk, smiling his usual charming smile.

"Good night, Theodora," he said at the door.

"Good night, Julian," she replied, and left.

As she walked carefully down the stairs, Theo avoided looking at Octavian's bust when she came to the landing. Julian had been right; she *had* needed to step away from Grant for a minute. She felt better now. Far better than she had when she had entered Julian's office, if a little sleepy.

At the entrance to the Great Room she halted. Only a few lamps in the sitting areas had been lit, and most of the room was in shadow. But she didn't need their feeble glow to see the expression on Grant's face as he paused in mid-stride not ten feet away. He had obviously been waiting for her, pacing the length of the room. Any thoughts of sleep fled.

"Are you still here?" she said as he walked up to her.

She saw his nostrils flare. "I wait over two hours in this room to abase myself at your feet while Julian tries to get you drunk on his wine, and that's all you can say?"

Theo's chin went up. "Don't be silly, Grant. I'm not drunk and Julian had no intention of doing any such thing. I'm sorry, I didn't realize it was so late. But I couldn't just run out on him. And I didn't think you'd be waiting, either."

"What else could I do? Leave you to Julian to pursue his fancy unchallenged? I don't think so."

"Stop that!" she snapped. "He has zero interest in me that way. He's the head of an important department at a prestigious university, and oh by the way I *am* an adult and quite capable of taking care of myself. What's your problem with him all of a sudden?"

"All of a sudden?" Grant laughed. "Oh, Theo. If you only knew."

"Well, I won't, unless you tell me. Look, it's getting late. Why don't we have this discussion tomorrow?" She started to walk past him. He grasped her arm and pulled her around to face him.

"No. Now. You don't see his eyes on you as you walk down the hallway. Don't trust him, Theo. I *know* him."

She shook off his grasp. He let go and, to her shock, dropped to his knees in front of her and took both her hands.

She tried snatch them away. "Grant, I said stop. You're

being ridiculous."

"I have to be. How else can I get you to see that I'm serious?" He gazed up at her imploringly. "I'm sorry, Theo. None of this is easy for me. There are things you don't know about me that make it harder for me to—to properly show you that I love you. I wish I could just take you back to Eleusinian with me. Maybe I could explain it better there."

Theo finally succeeded in extracting her hands from his. "Oh, yes, Eleusinian. Don't you think it would be little awkward trying to explain me to your other girlfriend?"

"My what?" He looked up at her, confused.

"The Olivia I've heard so much about."

"Olivia?" To her amazement, Grant sat back and started to chuckle, then guffaw. "My *girlfriend*? Oh, wait till she hears that! She'll have a fit."

"I'm not sure what you find so funny," she said stiffly.

"Oh, Theo." Grant pulled her down to the floor beside him, still chortling. "Olivia's not my girlfriend. Really, she's not. Oh—" He shook his head.

"Everyone else seems to think it's a reasonable assumption to make."

"Who, Marlowe? You're going to take *Marlowe's* word for anything?"

"He's a very nice person."

"Yes, he is. He should also know better. Olivia's my friend, yes, and one of my very best ones. But a lover? No, never. Theo—" He leaned forward and took her hands. "Listen to me. I love you. You have no idea what you mean to me. When I see Julian watching you—"

"Now it's my turn. Julian is not and never will be anything more than my friend. But I *don't* know what I mean to you— you're right about that. Because when I told you that I loved you at Halloween, you disappeared for two days. How do you think that made me feel?"

He shook his head. "But that wasn't why I ran away. That wasn't it at all."

"No? Then what was it?"

"It was..." His mouth opened, then closed. "I can't explain it," he said at last, looking away.

To her mortification, a tear slipped down her cheek, then another. "Grant, I can't love you if you run away from me as soon as I get too close."

"Theo..." Grant leaned forward to touch her face, then stared in wonder at the moisture on his fingers. Abruptly he bent and scooped her into his arms, holding her close to his chest. She leaned her head against him and sobbed harder as he cradled her and murmured endearments.

"Why does this have to happen? Why does love have to hurt like this?" he whispered, when her tears had subsided.

"It's not the love that hurts. It's the doubt that sometimes comes with it," she croaked into his neck.

"But I have no doubt. I know that I love you."

"But if I'm not sure that you love me, I do."

He sighed. "I can understand that. I'm sorry, Theo. So I'll tell you now. Never doubt that I love you. No matter what. Because I do. I just can't seem to get the hang of showing it." He blotted her cheeks with his sleeve. "Now, come on. This floor is cold, and I'm starving. We're going to go have some dinner, and then we're going to come back here so I can do my best to convince you that I love you."

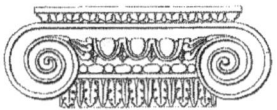

Seven

ON THE DAY BEFORE the symposium Theo was curled up on a sofa in the Great Room, reading a translation of Apicius's *de re Coquinaria*, a treatise on ancient Roman cookery. She turned the pages and hoped dinner tomorrow night wouldn't be *too* authentic.

"Apicius, eh? Studying for the symposium, Theodora?" Julian had come in, noiselessly as always, and smiled down at her.

"Why not? It's pretty interesting reading. I thought I'd give my students copies of the more bizarre recipes to bring home for Thanksgiving. Hmm, stuffed dormice with sardine sauce. I doubt you'll be serving them tomorrow."

"Oh, we have our sources."

She looked up at him in alarm. "You *are* joking, right?"

He laughed. "Of course I'm joking. We try for the spirit of authenticity, not the letter." He sat down on the couch next to her and stretched out his long, khaki-clad legs. "Any luck with your costume?"

"Oh, you'll see."

"Now you've got me wondering. Not Marlowe's SpongeBob toga, is it?"

"No. I doubt I could wheedle it out of him, anyway. I think you'll be pleased with mine, though."

"I'm sure I will." He sighed. "These things are a lot of work. But we do enjoy them. I think they help us remember why we teach—to bring the ancient world back to life, if only for a little while. Sometimes as we drink and talk, I feel as if I should expect our old friends Herakles or Theseus to wander in and demand a cup of wine."

"Or Jason? Or Achilles?" Theo smiled at the fancy. It was something she had often dreamed of as a child, reading and rereading the Greek myths: wondering what would happen if Herakles showed up at the door. Daddy had often compared her brothers' rooms to the Augean stables, so it wouldn't have been too surprising—

"Please, not Jason. He was a dreadful boor. Manners of a Thracian and breath like a wild pig. And Achilles was spoiled, no matter how good he was. And he *was* good. But he knew it, and that made him even worse."

She laughed in delight. "And surely Herakles couldn't have been the most polished dinner guest."

Julian crossed his arms behind his head and gazed up at the ceiling. "That's true. He wasn't the brightest lad, but his intentions were good. He had the biggest, saddest brown eyes you've ever seen, rather like a spaniel's. They were probably at least as effective as his muscles in many situations."

"And Theseus?"

"Ah. My favorite, despite his occasional cheekiness. But a gentleman nonetheless, in a time when the concept of gentleman had yet to be thought of. He stuttered, though. Did you know that? I've always thought it was the source of his compassion for others. It's also why he didn't last as long as he should have as King of Athens after his adventures. Good oratory was too necessary a skill for a ruler then and there."

She shook her head in admiration. "That's wonderful, Julian. You should write your own mythology book."

"Maybe when I retire. Who knows? I may just dedicate myself to my vines. I'm not sure the world would be ready for the real stories of the Greek legends." He rose and stretched. "I'm off to finish up the last-minute details. Oh, what kind of wreath would you prefer, oak or laurel?"

"Wreath?

He patted his sleek gray hair. "Crown. Garland. For your head. It's traditional at a symposium."

"Oh." Theo thought of Paul Harriman and his lyre. Definitely not laurel. "Oak, I think."

"Ah." His turquoise eyes gleamed. "Excellent choice. Till tomorrow, *philotate* Theodora."

"What? No Disney princess sheets? You disappoint me, Theo."

Marlowe was taking coats in the entry to the Great Room and hanging them on the coat rack there. After he hung hers up he took her hand and looked her up and down. "Well, all right. I'll forgive you. You're stunning in that. Shoes over here, please. I'm afraid our shoe-slave has the night off, so you'll have to remove your own."

Theo smiled as she slipped off her sandals. Mom had been as good as her word and sent not the *tunica* and *stola* that she as a married woman wore to Dad's Latin dinners, but a brand new *toga praetexta* with a deep purple edging stripe as befit Theo's unmarried status. She had even gotten the length right. "Thanks,

Marlowe. So where's Sponge-Bob?"

"I had to return him to Allie's little brother. I'm going to look for a set of sheets next time I'm at the mall, though I'm not sure I'll be able to find them in king size. But you don't wear SpongeBob to a symposium."

"Not even you?"

For once he did not smile. "Not even me. Oh, hello, Grant."

She turned to see Grant standing in the doorway, wrapped in a cloak. "Theo," he said, his eyes riveted on her.

"Do you like it?" She smoothed the shimmering folds of fabric over one arm. Mom had splurged and bought yards and yards of creamy white linen for her toga. She was in agony at the thought of staining its whiteness with food or drink, but the sheer luxury of being robed in so much linen was irresistible. She had put her hair up in a simple knot, not tight and strained as she had once worn it but soft and loose. Grant came forward now and brushed an escaped tendril from her cheek.

"Yes," was all he said, but the expression on his face was enough.

Marlowe cleared his throat. "You're holding up traffic, you two. Are you going to go in or just stare at each other?"

Grant stepped back and reached for a coat hanger, still looking at her. Marlowe snorted and put one into his hand. Then, as Grant unfastened his cloak, it was her turn to stare. She had always been drawn by the handsome melancholy of his deep-set eyes and narrow cheeks. But the impeccably arranged folds and sweep of his snowy white *toga virilis* accentuated the austere beauty of his face.

"It's a good thing you don't always wear that," she murmured as she took his arm and moved toward the door of the Great Room. Behind them she could hear Di Hunter slap Marlowe exuberantly on the back as she greeted him.

"Why not?"

"Because none of the girls in your Latin class would be able to keep their minds on their grammar. I can barely keep mine on walking, right now."

He held the door open for her. "We could always skip this and go somewhere else," he said, smiling into her eyes.

Theo felt her heart beat a little faster. Thoughts of unwrapping him from his toga, running her hands over the strong chest while she kissed him, intruded on her attention. Only when Grant stopped a few paces into the room and murmured, "What have we here?" did she take full notice of her surroundings.

The room was lit by candles. Only candles. All the usual lamps in the room had been banished, and the chandeliers were off. The linenfold paneling on the walls reflected the candlelight with a soft apricot glow that made the mosaics of the floor look subtly three-dimensional, as if the figures were straining to rise. The usual squashy chairs and couches had vanished as well, and in the center of the room was a great circle of cushion-covered divans, each with a small table by it. So they would eat reclining, just as the Greeks and Romans had. Larger tables outside the circle were set up as serving tables and a bar. On the tables small covered braziers emitted thin streams of smoke. Theo guessed they were incense burners, and sniffed the air. A faint scent, flowery but pungent, made her nose tingle slightly, and she was reminded of Dr. Waterman's fish flakes.

Undergraduates clad in tunics passed plates of hors d'oeuvres and wine. As she accepted a cup of wine Theo recognized Allie, whose little brother had lent his sheets to Marlowe for the Halloween party. Savory smells trailed behind another server holding a tray of puffy little meatballs; she caught hints of bay leaf and cumin as the boy passed by. Paul Harriman sat in a corner, quietly playing one of his lyres, watched by Dr.

Herman and a green-eyed girl from Historiography class.

"I hope I can manage to eat dinner lying down. It doesn't seem like the best position in which to digest anything," she said to Grant.

"It's all what you're used to," he replied absently, watching Paul. "In the old days we—they ate more slowly than do people today, so it evens out, I think. Besides," he turned back to her and grinned, "eating in that position is much friendlier, if you happen to have a congenial dinner companion." He squeezed her arm.

"Theodora, my dear! You were right. I *am* pleased with your costume. The toga becomes you."

Julian had appeared at her side, his eyes warm and glittering as an Aegean bay. Instead of a toga he wore a Greek *chiton* and *himation*, less bulky than the Latin costume. Its graceful sportiness suited him, and she couldn't help once more admiring his trim, muscular figure. He held out a hand to her, and she was forced to release Grant's arm.

"But where is your garland? Here." He reached up and took off his own crown of oak leaves, placed it on her head, and surveyed her with satisfaction. "There. Much better. Don't you think, Proctor?"

"Myrtle would be more becoming," said Grant pleasantly, but Theo caught an edge in his voice.

"But Theodora requested oak. Didn't you, my dear?" He brought her hand to his lips. "Enjoy yourselves. That's why we're here." He glided away, still smiling.

Di came in then, looking like an ancient Greek field hockey player in a short tunic kilted up around her knees, followed by Dr. Forge-Smythe and his wife. A toga suited the professor, covering his wasted legs and making his crutches less obvious. Renee was so beautiful in a lavender *tunica* and *stola* edged in gold and a crown of real violets that Theo could hardly, to her surprise, find it in her heart to hate her. At least Renee couldn't find fault with her appearance tonight.

"Good evening, Theo, Grant." Perched on the edge of one of the dining couches, Dr. Waterman greeted them with a cheerful wave as they approached. June Cadwallader, wearing Greek dress and a veil on her head, sat with him.

"You managed to find something to wear," she said, surveying Theo coolly.

"I did, thank you." Theo pressed her lips together to keep from laughing.

"At least I'm decently covered," she added as she and Grant moved past the pair. "Check *her* out." She nodded toward another graduate student, in short attire similar to Di's that seemed in imminent danger of complete disarray. Marlowe had finished his cloakroom duties and now stood with her, looking up to no good. As they watched, the girl threw her arms around his neck and stole his garland, put it on her own head and darted away, laughing back over her shoulder at him in clear invitation to give chase.

"It seems the wine's been flowing for a while, doesn't it?" Grant smiled. "You see why I say we're still recovering from Marlowe's time with us at the Institute." He halted and turned Theo to face him. "Speaking of garlands, take that thing off. You're more beautiful without it."

Theo put her hand up to touch the crown of oak leaves. "I can't. It would be an insult to Julian."

"Even better, then."

"Stop it, Grant. Not now."

He glowered but held his tongue.

"More wine!" roared Marlowe. Theo jumped; he had come to stand right behind her. "Ho, Theo. Don't you know it's bad manners to take measly little sips of wine at a department symposium? You too, Grant. You should know better." He refilled their cups from the bottle he carried, then touched his cup to hers for an instant before emptying it in one swallow.

She laughed. "I have to match that, huh?"

"As well as you can, anyway. I understand that you might not have my expertise."

"Or your hollow leg." She raised her cup to him and took a long drink. "Julian's wine," she said with relish as a heady shiver rippled through her.

"Of course." Marlowe turned to Grant. "C'mon, dude. Your turn."

His jaw tightened, but then he relaxed and nodded. However, Theo saw that he took the barest of sips. What was wrong with him tonight? This was fun—the elegant classical costumes, the candlelight, Julian's wine, Paul's mu-sic. No wonder it was considered an honor to be invited.

"Don't you like it?" she asked, watching him set his cup down on a table after Marlowe had wandered off.

"No, I don't," he said shortly, glancing at his cup with a frown.

"Because you don't like the wine, or because you don't like Julian?"

"Stop being so perceptive, please."

"Just behave yourself. We're guests, remember? Now come on, admit that the wine is good and relax and let me admire you in your finery. Marlowe!" She gestured at him, and he hurried over with a fresh bottle and grinned his approval as she took another deep drink. The golden syrupy tingle seemed to spread clear down to her toes.

"Careful, Theo," said Grant. "I might have to carry you home to bed if you keep that up."

She looked at him sideways. "Would that be such a bad thing?"

He frowned. "When I carry you home to bed some night, I

2222222

don't want you drunk on Julian's wine."

Theo's insides quivered at the intensity in his voice. Grant's scholarship of humanities had improved this past week. He was learning the joys of physical closeness: of holding hands under the table in the university coffee shop, of neck massages during late-night study sessions in the Great Room, of kissing with slow heat or swift ardor. That was as far as she'd taken it so far, until he seemed ready for more intimate contact. Not that she hadn't thought about more. Had thought about it frequently, in fact. But she was waiting for a cue from him. Was this one?

But no. He was still frowning at his cup. She sighed to herself and rubbed her toes on the floor. The tiny *tessellae* that made up the mosaic's surface were of different materials— stone, glass, ceramic—and all differed subtly in texture under her bare feet. She had expected that the floor would be cold, but instead found that it was oddly warm—yet another delight to the senses tonight. She thought about pointing it out to Grant but his expression was still too forbidding.

So she wandered from his side, enjoying the feeling of the floor under her feet as she walked, and joined the small throng that had gathered around one of the couches. As she peered past Di Hunter's shoulder she could see that Drs. Herman and Forge-Smythe were the focus of attention. They were playing some kind of game involving dice. As she watched, Dr. Herman threw the dice and groaned; then, while everyone laughed and cheered, he held out his hand for the large beaker of wine Marlowe brought him. Evidently he had lost his toss and had to pay a penalty. While everyone else clapped rhythmically, he drained the cup in one long draught. Cheers erupted as he flourished the empty cup and bowed.

"Again?" Dr. Forge-Smythe scooped up the dice, a mischievous gleam in his eyes.

"Not I. Not for a few minutes, anyway. I don't think I

could manage to lose again just yet." Dr. Herman stumbled back to the side of the green-eyed girl and slid a casual arm over her shoulder. She looked both delighted and nervous at the contact.

"I'll have a go, sir." Andrew Barnes, in a sloppily draped toga, took Dr Herman's place. The audience cheered him in turn and Ms. Cadwallader came to stand behind him, keeping a stern eye fixed on Dr. Forge-Smythe.

"He'd better watch it. Henry rarely loses," said Grant in her ear. Theo looked up at him and he offered her a contrite smile. "I'm sorry. I'll try to behave myself." To her surprise he held his cup up to her in salute, then drained it.

A server approached the edge of the crowd with a large tray of hors d'oeuvres. Grant chose a tiny stuffed fig and held it to Theo's lips. "Will you forgive me if I feed you?"

She accepted the fig, stuffed with sweet cheese and chopped dates, and looked up into his face, glowing in the candlelight. Then, before he could move his hand away, she delicately nibbled the end of his finger and drew it into her mouth for a delicious few seconds. Though the people around them were laughing and cheering again he didn't seem to hear them, but closed his eyes as she released him.

"I'm sorry, was that too much?" she murmured to him around the sweetness of the fig. It nearly had been, for her.

"You are not sorry. You enjoyed every second of that," he accused, eyes still closed.

"Yes, I did. Didn't you?"

"The least you could've done is warn me."

"What would the point be if I warned you? Consider that your punishment for being a spoilsport earlier."

He opened his eyes. "Punishment? Are you trying to encourage misbehavior?"

"Some kinds of it, anyway."

"'Scuse me," mumbled a voice. Andrew pushed past them,

looking both green and red at the same time, still clutching the cup he had evidently just been forced to drink. Before the crowd flowed back, Theo saw Ms. Cadwallader seat herself on the couch and pick up the dice, fixing Dr. Forge-Smythe with her gimlet eyes.

"Dear me, we need to teach that lad a few things." Marlowe had materialized next to Grant. He refilled Theo's cup, squinted at the bottle, then upended it over his mouth. "He'll never graduate if he doesn't learn to hold his wine," he added, wiping his mouth after he finished. A loop of golden ribbon suddenly descended around his shoulders and jerked him backwards. "Whoops! Hey cowgirl, be careful! You could've spilled something!" he cried, and turned in pursuit of a giggling, fleeing girl.

The group around the dice game cheered once more, and Renee Frothington-Forge-Smythe pushed her way through it, violet crown askew, and came to stand protectively by her husband.

"No! You know too much wine upsets his stomach!" she scolded June Cadwallader, who was holding a cup out to him with a grim smile.

"Now, now!' Julian swept through the crowd and held up one hand. "Time to find our dinner partners." He nodded to Renee, who took the cup of wine and drained it herself, then handed it back to June with a disdainful sniff. Someone whistled in admiration as she moved to another couch and patted it in invitation to her husband, who smiled sheepishly and pulled himself up to join her. Dr. Herman murmured to the green-eyed girl and led her to one of the dining couches.

Grant's hands circled Theo's waist, and his breath tickled her ear as he opened his mouth to speak. At that moment, Julian appeared next to her.

"My dear Theodora! You must dine with me and tell me how you are liking your first symposium." He held his hand out to her with an inviting smile.

But Grant's firm grip on her waist held her back. "Sorry, Julian. I've claimed Theo for the evening." The pressure of his hands belied his light tone.

Julian regarded him, head to one side, then smiled. "I see. But there will be other symposia. Surely you don't wish to deny me the pleasure of honoring my friend at her first one?"

Grant shrugged and maintained his grip. "As you say, there will be others."

The two men stared at each other, unblinking gray eyes meeting turquoise. Theo shivered as the temperature seemed to drop and the room to shift around her. But then Julian laughed. "You do not yield? Well then—a contest! You and I—and the winner may claim Theodora as his dinner partner."

This was too much. All of Theo's latent feminist instincts came to indignant life. "Excuse me, but do I get any say in—" she began, wriggling under Grant's implacable hands.

"Very well," said Grant. He released her and stepped toward Julian. "What do you propose?"

Julian examined him, brow creased in a frown. Around them the faculty and students fell silent. Dr. Forge-Smythe on his couch shook his head and buried his nose in a wine-cup, but Renee sat up, her eyes darting avidly from Julian to Grant and back again. Marlowe stood watching, the little braids someone had plaited into his beard bristling comically in stark contrast to his sober expression. Dr. Waterman stepped forward, frowning, but halted at a glance from Julian. The implacable turquoise gaze fell on the dice abandoned by Dr. Forge-Smythe. "*Tessellae*," he replied.

Theo looked wildly down at her feet. What were they going to do to the floor? Then she realized that she'd misheard him. Not *tessellae*, but *tesserae*—dice. They were going to play a game of dice for the privilege of sitting with her at dinner. This was utterly crazy. She wanted to laugh, to tell them just how ridiculous they were being, to call back the cheerful silliness that dressing up in costumes and drinking excellent wine had engendered.

But another look at their faces quelled that impulse. Julian's eyes were now more steel than turquoise as he seated himself in Dr. Forge-Smythe's place, and Grant looked more than ever like a figure from an El Greco painting, his face somber and unreadable.

Julian held up one hand, and a student leapt forward to hand him a cup of wine. He drained it, handed it back, and nodded at Grant. "One throw? I imagine everyone is eager to start their meal. I know I am." He glanced at Theo.

"One throw," Grant agreed shortly. He took the three dice that Julian handed to him with exaggerated courtesy, and surveyed them for a moment.

Theo felt Dr. Waterman sidle over to her and was grateful for the silent comfort of his presence. "This is nuts—" she whispered to him, but he shook his head and held a finger to his lips.

Just then Grant's hand flashed, and the cubes with their inked dots fell through the air and onto the couch. Theo had a moment to register the expression of concentration on his face before it relaxed into a satisfied smile.

"Seventeen," he said, and heads craned to see the three dice, two sixes and a five, resting on the linen-covered cushion. Theo exhaled, and realized she had been holding her breath.

Julian did not smile back. He scooped the dice up and weighed them in one hand for a moment, as if lost in thought. The gold edging of his cloak caught the candlelight as he lifted the dice and breathed across them. Next to Theo Dr. Waterman stirred but remained silent.

Then Julian's hand shot out, and the dice tumbled through

the air. Theo saw them fall as if in slow motion. Two fell swiftly and landed, six dots up on both, but the third bounced and rolled, following a declivity in the cushion. As it lost momentum it seemed to hover on edge for a moment.

Julian smiled triumphantly. "Eighteen!" he proclaimed as the die started to settle back, six dots upmost. But then, as if nudged by an invisible finger, it toppled once more. Two dots, like tiny baleful eyes, stared up at them from the stilled cube.

The room was silent. Even the candles seemed to stop flickering for a moment. Then Julian looked up from the die and into Grant's calm pale face. His eyes burned not turquoise or steel, but pure electric blue. "*Who are you?*" he snarled.

Grant smiled. "Don't you know yet?" He stood up and shook out the folds of his toga in a theatrical gesture, then turned towards Theo.

"You were right, Julian," Dr. Waterman declared in a loud voice. "We *are* starving. So I'm claiming my student here as my dinner partner. *Venite, mi amici. Cenemus!*"

He took Theo's arm and pulled her away from the couch. She was grateful for his hand on her arm, for her knees had turned to water.

The other professors and guests moved to the couches, conversing in hushed tones. In the corner one of Paul's musician friends took up a kithara and started to play. The undergraduates sorted plates and serving utensils over by the covered dishes of food. A strained air of normality settled over the room.

"Here," Dr. Waterman said firmly, choosing a couch across the circle. She climbed onto it, and he settled himself behind her. She saw Di already stretched next to Julian, and Grant nodding to June Cadwallader as he took the place next to her.

"Disgraceful display," Dr. Waterman muttered under his breath. "Absolutely outrageous." He leaned forward and poured two cups of wine from the flagon on their table. "Here," he said, handing her one. "You probably need this. I know I do."

Theo drank gratefully then set down her cup. "What—" she started to say, but he shook his head.

"I think it best if we all just try to forget that little scene. Both of them should have known better. What was Grant thinking? I will have to speak to him. And Julian! He of all people should be setting an example. Completely irresponsible." He refilled her cup.

"Dr. Waterman," she tried again, "I'm sorry about—"

"It's not your fault at all. No, it's not," he insisted as she opened her mouth. "The two of them behaved like a pair of children. Now please, let's just forget it. My digestion is already upset enough, and I was looking forward to this."

He waved his cup toward the boy setting large silver plates at the tables, followed by a pair who carried a silver basin and ewer of warm water. She saw Grant hold his hands out to be rinsed under the scented water, and wished that they were back at their favorite Chinese restaurant and that she had never heard of the symposia.

"No you don't. You'll enjoy this. I promise," Dr. Waterman said. Theo sighed. It was getting unnerving, the way everyone around here read her mind all the time.

Dinner arrived soon after, to her relief. Dr. Waterman was a courteous partner, filling her plate for her from the highly seasoned dishes proffered by the servers, explaining what each one was, gently quizzing her by asking the names of the ingredients in Latin. Theo was glad she had spent time reading that copy of Apicius. She knew exactly what he was trying to do: distract her, keep her from paying too much attention to the brooding looks both Julian and Grant constantly sent in her direction. His kindness touched her, so she did her best to play along with him. In the end it worked and she *was* distracted, so that when the dinner had reached the sweets-nibbling stage and Dr. Herman started asking Latin riddles, she was able to drink her wine and laugh and groan with the rest.

Paul Harriman took out a flute and played a duet with his friend from the music department, a lively tune that sounded more Irish than Greek. Marlowe rose from his couch where he had dined with the girl in the disheveled costume and began to dance. Everyone clapped, and Paul increased the tempo of his playing. The girl leapt up to join him, and after a minute so did another; Theo saw that it was Dr. Herman's green-eyed friend.

Marlowe jigged and leapt with abandon while somehow still managing to take swigs from a bottle without spilling a drop. His partners were less adept, but matched him drink for drink. Then, unable to restrain themselves, first one, then three or four of the undergraduate servers jumped in as well. Marlowe roared his approval and waved a hand in invitation to all the diners to join them. His eye lighted on Theo.

"C'mon, Theo! You too!" He waggled his bottle at her. She laughed but shook her head.

"Well then! It's getting a little close in here, my friends!" Marlowe shouted above the crescendoing music. He leaned forward and formed a huddle with his partners, dancing in place as he exhorted them. Then, with a shout that sounded suspiciously like "Yippee hi-yi-yi-yi!" he ran for the door, followed by the dancing women. Theo heard the outside door of Hamilton Hall bang open, and wild cowboy yells rise into the chilly November evening.

Dr. Waterman chuckled. Theo glanced back at him in surprise.

"They'll not be a happy crew in the morning," he commented, refilling his cup.

Theo heard another *whoop!* from outside the building. "Won't they get in trouble? They're a little, uh, loud."

"No. Julian will smooth things over." At the mention of Julian's name his expression sobered. "The campus police are an understanding lot. They'll leave them to run it off."

"So long as nothing gets in Marlowe's path. Did you see what happened to those squirrels they came across last time?" called Di, dabbling her fingers in her wine and holding them up to the light so that wine dripped from them like blood. She had evidently been listening in.

Dr. Waterman frowned at her.

"Wish I could have gone with them," said Dr. Forge-Smythe wistfully. Everyone laughed, and Renee tweaked his wreath with a coquettish smirk.

By one-thirty Theo had had enough. It was getting harder and harder not to rest her head on the soft cushions and abandon herself to the warm languor that Julian's wine seemed to induce in her. Most of the faculty were still chatting and laughing with tireless vigor, but their student guests were drooping. Theo looked at Grant and saw that he was still watching her steadily.

"I'm falling asleep. Is it all right for me to leave?" she murmured to Dr. Waterman.

"What's that? Had enough? But it's early yet." He peered into her face. "Well, maybe not so early. Yes, you may certainly run along if you wish, but we'll be at this for a while longer."

"Next time, maybe. Thank you, Dr. Waterman. You were very kind."

He made a dismissive noise. "It was nothing. I hope you enjoyed yourself a little, anyway. See you on Monday."

Theo slid off the couch and walked up to Julian. From the corner of her eye she saw Grant rise as well.

Julian regarded her, leaning back on his cushions. His hair was tousled, which made him look boyish, and his eyes were their usual warm turquoise as they rested on her. "I'm sorry to see you leave so early, my dear. I hope you enjoyed your first symposium."

She resisted the impulse to reach out and smooth his hair. "Thank you very much, Julian. I did."

"Then you must come to them all. Good night, my Theodora."

Grant came to stand behind her. She tensed, but Julian nodded politely to him as well. "Good night, Proctor."

Theo felt him nod in return, felt him slip an arm around her and lead her to the door of the Great Room. At the doorway she paused and looked back. Julian still watched her, but it was impossible at this distance to read his expression.

In the entryway Grant knelt at her feet. Theo stared down at him. "What are you doing?"

"Helping you with your sandals." He slipped one then the other onto her feet, rose, and looked at her. Then, without a word, he folded her in his arms and fastened his mouth on hers.

It was a strange kiss. Even through her haze of wine and weariness she could feel that. There was passion, yes, in the way his lips took hers, rich and greedy, his tongue probing and coaxing so that she had to cling to him lest her knees give way as she concentrated on returning the kiss.

But there was something else in it too, something that had little to do with desire. With a shock of embarrassment and chagrin, she realized what it was. The door to the Great Room was still open. When she broke the kiss and looked up, she could see that Julian had had a plain view of them. *Are you watching, Julian?* that kiss had said. *No roll of the dice could give anyone this. Not even you.*

Theo jerked away from him. "Why did you do that?" she whispered fiercely, grabbing her coat from the rack.

Grant looked at her, his face expressionless. "Why do you think?"

"You knew that Julian could see us. I don't care what you think, Grant, but I'm not going to be a pawn in whatever game you've decided to play with him." Her hands shook as she tried to do up her buttons.

"You're not a pawn. You're the prize." Grant took his cloak from the rack and settled it over his shoulders.

"Damn it, that's a load of bull. Don't you *dare* ever kiss me again unless you do it out of love, not to score a point on someone."

He sighed. "You don't understand, do you?"

"No, it's you who doesn't understand. Good night, Grant. I'll see you on Monday. *Monday*," she emphasized, as his mouth opened in protest. "I don't want to see you tomorrow until you've had a chance to think about just what it is you want." She swept past him and into the starry night.

Eight

ON MONDAY MORNING THEO arrived to teach her Latin class a few minutes late, hoping to avoid Grant a little longer. It was no use. When she walked into her classroom she was greeted by whistles and catcalls from her students, and saw the reason why. An enormous bouquet of deep shell-pink roses, two dozen at least, stood on her desk, and Grant and half his class peered around the door that connected their rooms. The words *mea culpa* had been written in foot-high calligraphic script with colored chalk on her blackboard.

"That means 'my fault', right? C'mon, Ms. Fairchild. Whatever he did, you *have* to forgive him. Those are the most gorgeous roses I've ever seen," gushed one of her students.

"Thank you, Kelly, your translation is correct. How would you say, 'I'll think about it' in Latin?" she replied crisply, picking up an eraser and ignoring Grant. The entire room groaned.

After class Grant sidled back around the door. Theo shooed away her remaining students, mostly girls, who looked disappointed as she closed the door behind them.

"And?" said Grant.

She studied him for appropriate signs of contrition as she put her books away, and decided to let him stew a little longer. Glancing at her watch, she said, "I'm sorry, Grant. I've got Rhetoric in three minutes. We'll have to talk later."

"No we won't. I told Arthur you'd be late to his class this morning." He stepped forward and put his finger on her lips to stop her indignant sputter. "I apologize, Theo. You were right. I shouldn't have kissed you like that in front of everyone. It was rude and embarrassing to you. But I don't apologize for my feelings about Julian."

"But why? Why don't you like him?"

"Do *you* like him?"

Theo sighed and fingered one of the roses, stroking its velvety petals. "Yes, I do. I wasn't sure about him when I met him at the start of school. He gave me the creeps those first few days. But since then he's been very nice and not at all creepy. Some of it is just his manner, I guess, and I'm used to it now. Yes, I do like him."

"Do you trust him?" Grant persisted, taking her by the shoulders.

"What has he done to make me *not* trust him? Grant, what is it with you and him? He's never seemed hostile to you. At least not till the other night. I still don't understand what that was about, either." She shook her head.

"Can we make a bargain? I'll keep out of Julian's way if you'll promise to be careful around him." He looked earnestly into her face.

"Careful of what?"

"Just careful." He pulled her closer. "Please?"

"Grant—"

He bent his head and kissed her neck. She closed her eyes as her arms crept up of their own accord to hold him. "I missed you yesterday," he murmured in her ear. "All I could think about was how you'd looked in your toga that night. And what it would have been like to unwrap you and—"

There was a faint cheer from somewhere. Theo opened her eyes and saw a row of faces peering over the edges of the window ledge.

"We have an audience," she said, pulling away.

"Let's give 'em a good show, then." Grant pulled her back and kissed her on the lips. The cheers grew louder.

He pulled back and smiled with satisfaction. "You're blushing, you know."

Despite her rapprochement with Grant it was Tuesday before Theo felt comfortable resuming her usual study spot in the Great Room. She did not want to run into Julian, knowing what he must have seen the night of the symposium, embarrassed at the image she and Grant must have presented. But when he passed her in the hallway later on Monday morning he was his usual affable self. After a few more chance encounters with him she began to relax.

In fact, no one referred to the symposium. She had expected to hear some rumor of Marlowe and his band of merry women getting their wrists slapped for running roughshod over the campus, but not a whisper of it came to her. Theo concluded that what Dr. Waterman had said about the blind eye of the campus police must be true. It seemed odd, but not odd enough to waste time thinking about.

A few days after the symposium Theo blew into the grad student lounge for coffee with Grant. A northeast storm was beating the last of the campus's leaves into a pulp, making the brick walkways treacherously slimy. Theo had run all the way

MARISSA DOYLE

from her room, dodging the chilly rain and slippery patches, but warmed by her news.

"Umbrellas have been around for several thousand years, but I don't suppose you own one," Grant scolded, helping her remove her dripping jacket.

"I do, smartypants, but in this wind I wouldn't much longer. Oh, good. You ordered," she said as their coffee arrived. She held her cup in her hands to warm them and smiled out at the rain streaming over the window next to her.

He looked at her over the rim of his cup. "All right, what is it? You look fit to burst."

"Pooh. I'm happy, that's all. My mom just called. She wanted to know if you had any plans for Thanksgiving." She put down her cup and took his hand. "It's a bit of a drive, but if we left right after my last class Tuesday we could be in Philly by nine, barring traffic. We can think up some new Latin insults for my Dad on the way down, and if he's not feeling too shy we can get him to do Cicero's *In Catilinam* after he's had a little wine. It's his favorite oration."

Grant stared down at their joined hands. Theo cleared her throat. "That is, uh, if you didn't have any other plans for Thanksgiving break," she continued in a small voice.

He had never mentioned family. He must be going back to them, wherever they were. She should have thought about that. But when Mom had suggested she invite him for Thanksgiving it had seemed like such a wonderful idea. "Of course, I should have known you'd want to go home to your own—"

"No, that's not it. I'm sorry, Theo. I'd already arranged to go to New Hampshire over the holiday. Olivia needs me to take care of a few things, and there's some work for my project that I need to do up there." He looked embarrassed.

"Porcupines not learning their lines?" she said before she could stop herself. "Or is it the moose again? Or is Olivia—"

She made herself stop. He had told her, point blank, that Olivia was merely a friend and colleague. Why couldn't she just accept his word and stop torturing herself like this?

Grant leaned forward and took her hands again. "Or do I need to go keep my other girlfriend happy? No, Theo. You're the only woman who has any claim on my heart. Some day you'll meet Olivia, and then you'll understand. But I have responsibilities at Eleusinian that I can't shirk. I'd planned all along to go up there sometime this fall but I haven't been able to tear myself away. And now I have to pay for it by disappointing you." He glared down at his coffee and muttered, "Damn!"

Theo squeezed his hands. "Did you really want to come?"

"Yes!" he said, then continued in a quieter tone, "I would have loved to see your father declaiming, '*O tempora! O mores!*'"

"It *is* quite a sight." She sighed. "I guess I'll just have to concentrate on those papers over Thanksgiving instead."

"I'll make it up to you. I promise."

"No, it's all right. It's not your fault. I should have thought before I blurted it out like that. It's just that...that I'm going to miss you."

Grant looked back down at his cup. "I'll miss you too...my love."

The memory of that whispered 'my love' carried Theo through Thanksgiving and her parents' disappointment at not meeting Grant. She did manage to get one of her final papers written over the holiday, which was a relief; the end of the semester always seemed a lot closer on the Monday after Thanksgiving than it did the Wednesday before.

But when she arrived to teach her class that Monday morning, eager to see Grant after nearly a week apart, he wasn't there. Dr. Waterman took his Monday Latin class for him. Theo moped alone in the Great Room that afternoon until Julian stopped to chat with her and invited her to his office to try a new bottle of wine he had brought back from his cellar in Rhode Island. She went, feeling defiant; if Grant couldn't make it back from the Institute when he was supposed to, she didn't see why she couldn't have a friendly talk with Julian about her paper on Greek influences in Etruria.

The chat went on till nearly seven, so it only seemed sensible to accept Julian's invitation to dinner at a little Greek restaurant just off-campus, where the owner himself, evidently an old friend of Julian's, served them.

Once or twice Theo could hear Grant's voice plead "*be careful around him*" in her mind. But Julian couldn't have been nicer. He ordered their meal then explained each item, comparing their preparations to what was known of ancient cuisine while chatting intermittently to the owner in flawless modern Greek.

When intense dark coffee in tiny cups and ouzo were finally brought, Theo had forgotten everything unpleasant. Julian's turquoise eyes were warm and friendly as they rested on her, the ouzo and coffee danced sensuous tangos on her tongue, and though she couldn't forget about Grant's being late she had put aside her unhappy thoughts of him, at least for now.

Julian sipped his coffee. "I notice that Grant Proctor isn't back yet."

Damn. Why did he have to bring that up now? "I think he's due back tomorrow. At least, Dr. Waterman said he'd be here in time for his class Wednesday."

"It's a long drive from Eleusinian. Five or six hours, anyway. And I wouldn't be surprised if it were already snowing up there. Still, it's very beautiful, and quite comfortable for such a remote place."

"You've been there?" Theo couldn't help asking.

"Years ago, for a brief visit. When Olivia went up there. You've heard Grant mention Olivia Weaver, I'm sure."

"Once or twice," she said neutrally.

"Olivia taught here before she went there. Does Grant enjoy being at Eleusinian with her? I suppose he must, if he couldn't tear himself away. Ah, well. That's Olivia for you. She has that effect. Poor Paul was devastated when she left us."

Theo took a sip of coffee, hoping her hand didn't shake too badly. "Was he?"

"Oh, yes. Inconsolable. But Olivia seems to have gotten over him now that Grant's there. Quite well, from what one hears. Academia is a small world, you know. Rumors do circulate...here, Dmitri. Another ouzo for us both, please. Are you all right, my dear? You look a little pale. Another ouzo will fix that."

When she finally did see Grant, it was late on Wednesday. She had poked her head around his door Wednesday morning after class, but he was busy explaining reflexive pronouns once again to a very earnest and inarticulate math major and did not see her. He didn't meet her for their usual lunch together in the lounge or for coffee in the afternoon, and her mood plummeted; not even Marlowe delivering an invitation to the department's Saturnalia party at the end of the term could make her smile. It wasn't until nearly eight that night that he wandered into the Great Room, where Theo was working on a paper.

"Theo!" he said as he tossed his coat onto the table, which was covered with her books and laptop. "There you are! I've been looking for you all day." He pulled a chair next to her and pecked her on the cheek.

She reached over and retrieved one of her books from

under his coat. "Have you?"

"Well, of course. I missed you—"

"How's Olivia?" The steadiness of her voice amazed her.

"She's fine. I told her all about you, and she can't wait to meet you. How was your Dad? Did he do an oration? I kept thinking about what fun it would have been to meet him."

"No, he didn't. But he made some suggestions on my Rhetoric paper."

"You'll have to let me read it." He leaned toward her again, his eyes serious. "I mean it, Theo. I really missed you. I didn't know it would be so bad."

"Did you take care of everything up at Eleusinian?" she asked, not looking at him.

"Mostly, I think. I'll have to go back up at Christmas break to start on my project, but took care of everything else. Stop typing for a minute and look at me. What are you working on that's so absorbing?"

"My paper for Dr. Forge-Smythe's class. Julian gave me a few ideas for my topic over dinner the other night, and I've found lots of interesting references, thanks to him."

He was frowning. "You had dinner with Julian?"

"Yes, I did. Why not?" Her hands were frigid, poised over her keyboard, but she would not move them.

He took one and pulled her around in her seat. "Please look at me for a minute?" He took her chin in his hand and looked into her face. It was impossible to maintain her distance when he did things like that. She felt some of the ice in her midsection melt under his steady gaze.

"Okay," she sighed. "I missed you too. I was disappointed not to see you Monday, and a little hurt, I guess." Or a lot. Julian's comments about Olivia had raised up the insecurities she thought she'd mostly laid to rest. But he should know about her, shouldn't he?

"But I'm here now," he began, then stopped. "You look... different," he said with a frown, turning her face from side to side. "You didn't cut your hair or anything over Thanksgiving, did you?"

"I haven't done anything to myself, except perhaps catch up on sleep a little."

"Well, something's different about you." He sat back in his chair and looked at her, frowning. "Sometimes I'd almost swear..." He shook his head. "Anyway, it was so beautiful up there, the snow and ice and stillness. I kept wishing you were there to see it. And..." he hesitated, then said, almost in a rush, "I read another modern novel."

That was such a non sequitur that Theo was forced to smile. But something in his voice made her glance up at him again. He was looking at her with an odd intensity, almost as if he'd never seen her before. And with some-thing else, too—an uncertainty that made her put aside her pique and turn to him. "Which modern novel did you read?" she asked gently.

"*Pride and Prejudice*, by Jane Austen. You said you liked that one best next to *Persuasion*. So I read it." Again there was that strange note in his voice.

"Did you like it?"

"Yes, of course. But that wasn't important. It—*he*—helped me make the decision."

"He?"

"Mr. Darcy."

"Ah." Again Theo wanted to smile, but Grant's face wouldn't let her. "What decision did he help you make?"

He stared down at his hands, clasped loosely in his lap. "I can't tell you—not yet. I don't even know if it's possible, but I'm damned well going to try." He swallowed. "Darcy fell in love with Elizabeth. But he couldn't actually win her until he gave up Pemberley."

Theo blinked. "Darcy *didn't* give up Pemberley."

"No, not in the real sense. But he had to give up the old Darcy—everything that he'd always been, everything he'd always lived by—and become a different man before he could truly love her. That's what I mean by Pemberley. He gave that up, but gained so much." He looked up at her, and Theo drew in her breath. There was such longing in his eyes, and an enormous sadness...but also determination and hope. "I have to give up Pemberley too, I've decided. It's as scary as hell to even think about. I wish Austen had spent more time in Darcy's head, showing how he came through re-making himself, because I'm terrified. But I want my Elizabeth more than anything else I've ever wanted. *Anything.*" He reached up and touched her cheek, then slid off his chair to his knees and wrapped his arms around her.

Theo held him close, blinking back tears. Here she'd been nursing a silly, imaginary grudge, and he'd been— "Oh, Grant. I—I don't want you to have to give anything up for me," she whispered into his hair.

"But I do want to. It's the only way I'll truly win you." He drew back a little to look up into her face, and now he was smiling, the sadness replaced by joy. "Trust me, dearest, loveliest Theo." He kissed her, a lingering, tender kiss, then stood up. "You go back to your papers. I need to start figuring out how to get rid of Pemberley."

"You're getting frazzled, my dear. I've watched you reread that paragraph for the last five minutes. Come on up to my office for a moment. Dr. d'Amboise is prescribing some rest and medication."

Theo looked up from her book at Julian, who stood over

her in the Great Room. "But it's my last paper. I'm almost done with it," she croaked. She had to be. Exams started in three days and she had to start reviewing.

"Fine. Take a break now so you can edit it tomorrow with a fresh mind." He pulled her chair away from the table and took her hand. "But for now, come along, Miss Fairchild. My word is law here, you know."

Theo smiled. "As you command."

"That's much better."

In his office he handed her a glass of wine. "Just a small one. Enough to banish some of that tension."

"Thank you." Theo took a sip, closed her eyes, and sighed as it trickled down her throat. She *did* need a break. It was so easy to get drawn in to the words on the page and forget everything else.

"Which class is this paper for?" Julian set down his glass and came around behind her. "Hold still." He took her glass and set it down as well, then ran his hands lightly over her head before sliding his fingers through her hair.

At his first touch Theo jumped—there were rules about contact between students and faculty, after all—but a scalp massage just felt so *good* right now. "Roman Religion and Philosophy. I'm writing about the concept of divinity through Roman history. Oh jeez, that's wonderful," she managed to answer.

"Of course it feels good. A healer on Cyprus taught me this years ago. Tell me, what is your view of the divine? Does it coincide with the Romans'?"

The tension in her forehead and temples melted away. *I know what I think is divine right now,* she wanted to say but didn't. "For the Romans there were different levels of divinity, because their religion—mmm, yeah—was so full of borrowings from other people. I'm not sure there was an absolute. I have to admire their—their, uh, pragmatism, though. I think their chief embodiment of divinity was Rome itself."

"Turn your head a little—there. Isn't that better? They still call Rome the eternal city, so I suppose in a way they were right." Julian's hands worked their way down her neck and onto her shoulders. "The Greek concept of divinity was something else again. We talked about the gods once before, didn't we?"

Theo made herself focus on his words, not his hands. "The Romans borrowed a lot of their religious concepts from the Greeks. If it worked for them, they appropriated it and made it their own."

"I've often thought about that." He gave her shoulders a final squeeze and waved away her thanks as he moved back to his chair. "You look better already. Now, where was I? Ah, utility and the divine. Think about it, my dear. Picture the Roman Empire, expanding out of Italy and spreading across much of the known world, encompassing dozens of cultures and societies within its borders, taking in ideas as well as trade goods and taxes. Isis and Mithras and other gods imported from other lands became popular as time went by, and took their places by the old gods.

"But what happened to those old gods who were pushed aside when they were no longer wanted or needed? What happened to the millions of prayers and sacrifices that were made in their names? If one were fanciful, one could feel sorry for those old gods, called into being by human need and then cast aside by human inconstancy. A melancholy fate, don't you think?"

Theo smiled and sipped her wine. This was almost as much fun as their conversation about the heroes of mythology. "It must have been. Imagine how they must have felt when Emperor Constantine converted to Christianity. It was the beginning of their end. Their altars bare, no prayers and songs of praise to listen to, less and less worship to bask in. How sad for them."

"Ah, you follow me precisely. Your reputed ancestor, godly Emperor Constantine. He has a great deal to answer for, don't you think? Casting the poor Olympians from their homes in men's hearts? Dying peacefully in his bed was far too good a fate for him. So what does a god do when he is no longer a god? One must pity him, no?" Julian heaved a sigh, but his eyes still twinkled at her.

"Oh, I don't know," she said. "Would he stop being a god, even though no one worships him?"

"A very good point, my dear. A leopard cannot change its spots."

"Then it might be a rather nice existence for them, don't you think? All the advantages of being gods, with none of the tiresome having to answer prayers and perform miracles for ungrateful humans. And none of those dreadful burnt offerings." She smiled at him. "The smell must have been awful."

Julian laughed in delight. "You're wonderful, my dear Theodora. Absolutely perfect. I love to play with these ideas with you, because you always understand. I can't be the stern academic all the time. Now, you must forgive me my musings, and I must let you get back to your work." He bent and refilled her glass. "After you've finished your medicine, that is."

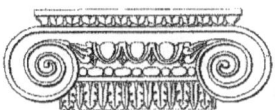

Nine

IT WAS THE FINAL day of the term. Theo had taken her last exam that morning. Now she was having lunch with Grant before she went back to her room to pack and go home for Christmas.

She stared out the window at the bedraggled courtyard below. The inch of snowfall the night before had done little to beautify the flowerbeds below, empty save for decaying dead leaves and litter blown in by the wind. She felt almost as empty, all the words in her brain poured into papers and exams. And as for her heart...that was feeling the emptiest of all.

In the three and a half weeks since that evening in the Great Room after Thanksgiving, she'd barely seen Grant. He'd been as absorbed in books as she, consulting obscure texts in the department library, firing off questions to other universities, and emailing Olivia. Theo had tried her best not to mind about that, but it had been one more thing to trouble her. She'd thought that their relationship had turned a corner; his talk of Darcy and Pemberley had sounded almost like...like a declaration. But maybe she'd been wrong; it was almost as if he'd forgotten she existed. He'd sounded almost surprised when she called him to make this lunch date. She was surprised that he'd even answered his phone. She closed her eyes and leaned her head on her hands.

"Are you awake enough to drive home tonight?" Grant asked her, a frown in his voice.

She dropped her hands and tried to smile. "I'll be fine. The car knows the way home." Then, because he was still frowning at her, she straightened in her seat. "And you? What will you be doing?"

"I'll head up to New Hampshire tomorrow for a little while. Then I'll be going to Italy. To...to visit some friends."

"Italy. How nice," she murmured, and turned back to the window. Which meant over a month without him. She had invited him to visit over New Years', hoping that this time he would say yes. But he hadn't mentioned Italy before. A visit wasn't looking very likely. The empty garden below looked downright cheerful, compared to how she felt.

"I'll call you. And write. I promise. I—I'll be working on my Pemberley project. I hope I can have it well underway by the time the semester starts."

"Will you? That's good," she replied tonelessly. She bent to pick up her handbag and fished around in it for a tissue. That darned heating duct was blowing right in her eyes, making them sting and water. Then her hand closed on something square. "Oh," she said, pulling out a little box. "I forgot."

"What's that?" asked Grant, craning his neck.

"A Christmas—sorry, Saturnalia present from Julian. He gave it to me last night at the department party, but I never got a chance to open it." She undid the wrapping of vivid turquoise silk, just the same color as his eyes. Grant scowled at it as it fluttered to the table.

Under the silk was a plain box. Was it plastic? No; it was warm to her touch, and less shiny—ivory, she suddenly realized. Wow. Wasn't it protected or something? Where had he found it? Inside was a tiny crystal bottle shaped like a Greek amphora. She held it up to the light and smiled with delight. "How pretty!"

"There's something in it," Grant said, still frowning.

Theo pulled out the stopper. The scent of lilies and hyacinths filled her head as she sniffed it, followed by a familiar tingly sensation.

Grant snatched the vial of perfume from her and sniffed it too, then leapt up out of his chair as if it had bitten him. "What does he think he's playing at?" he almost shouted. Heads turned to look at them.

"Stop it, Grant. Give me that before you break it." She rescued the beautiful little bottle from his grip and replaced its stopper.

Grant stood next to their table, breathing hard and staring at the bottle in Theo's hand. "Give it to me, Theo. You don't understand. It's dangerous. I thought I'd noticed it around you. What is he up to?"

"Dangerous? That's ridiculous. I think it's a lovely present." She wrapped the bottle in the square of silk and tucked it with the box back into her handbag.

"Did anyone else but you get one?"

"How should I know? And why should I care? Sit down, Grant. What's wrong with you?"

"You won't be seeing him over the holiday, will you?" He finally sat down but looked in danger of leaping up again at the slightest provocation.

"See Julian? Of course not. Why should I?" She smiled. "Do you know Dr. Waterman feeds his fish something that smells like that perfume? And the incense at the symposium was the same. Don't you like it?"

"I like it perfectly well. But—"

"But Julian gave it to me. If it makes you feel any better I didn't give him a present. And I certainly didn't expect to receive one from him. Which reminds me."

She had bought a Christmas present for Grant weeks ago, when their humanities classes had still been going well. Over the last week she'd waffled over whether or not to give it to him, but that seemed silly and childish. She bent to her book bag and pulled out a wrapped box. "Merry Christmas," she said, handing it to him.

He swallowed and took it from her. "For me?"

"Octavian doesn't have hands to open it, so I guess it's yours," she said, only slightly bitterly.

He looked at her and tore off the paper, and pulled out the charcoal gray scarf she'd chosen for him with such care, to bring up the gray of his eyes.

"It'll keep you warm up in New Hampshire—" she nearly choked, but steadied her voice. "It's cashmere. You can touch it sometimes, and try to remember what your senses are for. J-just a little memento of your hu-humanities classes this fall." She rubbed at her eyes with the back of her hand and tried to smile.

"That's one class I seem to have flunked," he said bleakly, stroking the wool.

She tried for a casual tone. "It's...not a big deal. Things change. I understand that."

"'Not a big deal?' Is that what you think?"

"I..." She looked away, still blinking.

"It's a damned big deal. More important to me than you know. I just haven't been very good at letting you know how much." He sighed and got up from the table, then came around and knelt by her, putting his arms around her.

The clock tower outside chimed twice. Theo glanced up,

startled, from Grant's serious face.

"I know. You need to get going. Just listen to me a moment longer. We'll start again in January. Maybe I'll be ready by then, if I try hard enough over break."

Theo opened her mouth to speak. He leaned forward and pressed his lips to hers.

"Please wait for me," he whispered into her mouth. "I don't have any right to ask that of you, but I will anyway. Theo, I love you, even though I've been terrible at showing it. Trust me." Then he kissed her as he hadn't since before Thanksgiving.

Dizzy, Theo pulled away and stood up. He rose too, and pulled her into his arms for a brief moment. "I'll call. And write. And...do me a favor?"

She looked at him.

"Don't use Julian's perfume. Please."

Theo was happy to be home with her family, even her three older brothers with their insufferable elder brother airs. And with Dido, who with a flick of her long tail ignored Theo when she stumbled yawning into the house at ten that night but was snuggled purring against her neck by morning.

She rested for a day then tackled correcting her Latin class's exams and term papers, and emailed her grades in to the university on Christmas Eve afternoon. All the while Grant's enigmatic words and behavior replayed in her mind, over and over, while she tried to decipher their meaning.

How should she read him? His brooding silences, his angry outbursts at Julian, his protestations of love—what did they all mean? *Did* he love her? Or did he just want to keep her from liking Julian any more than she already did...and if so, why? She remembered the expression on his face as they parted that last dreary afternoon—the look of sad longing in his eyes had nearly made her run back to him.

At seven on Christmas Eve, just as she was about to go out with her family for dinner, the doorbell rang. Her mother answered the door and came back with a box.

"It's something for you, dear. Our poor mailman—it's Christmas Eve! I asked him if he'd like some eggnog, but he said no." She handed the box, postmarked "North Errol, New Hampshire" to Theo.

"It's a good thing he didn't. One cup of Dad's eggnog and he'd be arrested for OUI." She took the scissors she had been using while wrapping presents and slit the tape sealing the box.

A cloud of scent rose from it as she lifted the flaps, similar to Julian's perfume but different: more spicy and musky, with hints of evergreen. Her mother looked startled and sniffed the air.

"What's that smell?" said her father, knotting his tie as he came down the stairs. "It reminds me of—" He stopped abruptly and looked at Theo.

The source of the evergreen scent became apparent at once: pine cones and pine needles had been used as protective packing around a small box made of thin sheets of a polished tan-brown material.

"How interesting. That's horn, isn't it?" said Dad curiously, peering over her shoulder. "Is your friend in New Hampshire implying a classical reference? There were two gates leading up out of Hypnos's house in the Underworld, through which dreams were sent to men. The false ones went through a gate of ivory, while the true ones went through a gate of horn."

"Open it already," said Mom. "I'm dying to see what it is."

Theo took out the delicate box and opened it. Inside was a pouch of white linen. She upended it onto her hand and a ring tumbled out. She picked it up, feeling numb, and examined it.

The setting was a rich reddish gold, shining with the soft patina of age. It held a small smoky gray oval intaglio. Theo remembered looking at the seals and carved gems with Julian in the Museum earlier in the fall, but could not recall seeing any that quite resembled this one. The carved image was simple but beautifully detailed. It depicted a flaming torch, held aloft by a fist. There was no note in the box. There didn't need to be.

After they got back from dinner Theo sat up late, staring into the tiny glittering lights on the Christmas tree in the living room and petting Dido on her lap. Every now and again her hand strayed to Grant's gift, which fit her ring finger perfectly.

What was she to think? "Guess he's trying to tell you he's carrying a torch for you," her brother Marcus had joked when he saw the ring. "I love you," Grant had said again as they parted that last afternoon. Theo turned the ring on her finger. Which was more real—his silences, or this? She scooped up Dido and buried her face in her soft fur. Cats were as transparent as glass, compared to some people.

"Theo?"

She turned. Her father stood in the doorway in his bathrobe and pajamas. "Mind if I come in?"

She patted the sofa cushion. He sat, and she saw his nostrils flare as he settled next to her. She had worn some of Julian's perfume for going out tonight, hadn't she? And felt guilty for wearing Grant's ring at the same time.

"Happy to be home for a minute?" Dad asked. He picked up her left hand and turned it this way and that in the pale light from the tree, looking at Grant's ring.

"Yes. Things were getting a little intense at the end. It's nice to be able to relax and not think for a little while."

"Intense academically, or personally?"

"A bit of both."

He nodded, and then said abruptly, "What is that scent I keeping getting whiffs of around you?"

"It was a holiday gift from the head of the department. Some perfume. He's become a good friend over the last few months—no, not like that. Just a friend. Why?"

"Oh." Her father gave a small cough of embarrassment. "It...er, brought back some memories, that's all. Do you happen to know what it's called?"

"No, I don't. The bottle wasn't marked. What sort of memories, Dad?" she asked, starting to grin. To her glee, she saw him redden as he cleared his throat again.

"Nothing important, really." He looked up then and met her eyes. "All right. Maybe that's not quite true. But it happened a long time ago, before your mother and I even met."

"*That* kind of memory?"

"Quiet, *insolens filia*," he said with mock sternness, and stared broodingly into the tree. Theo waited.

"It was when I went to Italy and Greece, the first time," he said at last. "I was still an undergraduate, had almost no money, and carried everything I owned in a backpack for two months of wandering around, mostly on foot. It's probably the most fun I've ever had in my life."

"I'll bet it was." Theo smiled at his wistful tone.

"I was in Thessaly for a few days after going to have a look at Mount Olympus, and was following a stream down to the next village. It was still a fairly unpopulated part of Greece, and I was enjoying the peace and nature for a few days before I hitchhiked down to tackle Athens. The afternoon was very hot, and I decided to nap for a bit in the shade of a tree. I took off my pack and my shirt, splashed some water from the stream over myself, lay down, and fell asleep almost at once. I woke up just a short while later, to judge by the sun's position, and found that I wasn't alone." He took off his glasses and polished them on his bathrobe.

"Yes?" she prompted. "Go on."

"I'd been joined by a very attractive girl who looked about my age. She was blond and blue-eyed, which wasn't all that uncommon a thing in that part of Greece, and was wearing a simple shift. At first." He coughed again.

Theo's grin returned.

"Stop that. I can *hear* you smiling, *muliercula*. Anyway, I don't think I need to go into further details. When I woke again she'd vanished. I rather feared for my pitiful belongings, but nothing was missing. And the only thing she'd left behind was the ghost of her scent. Exactly like what you are wearing. I almost thought myself back beside that stream when I came downstairs and smelled your perfume."

"Did you ever find out who she was?"

"I backtracked to the last village I'd been in, pretending to have lost something, to ask around after her. No one of her description lived there, so I ran like hell all the way to the next, only to hear the same story. Only one or two old men in the tavernas had any hints for me. 'You'll never see her again,' one cackled. 'She comes out when she's hungry, and leaves when she's sated.' 'Ask the river what her name is,' said another. 'He's her father, after all. Count yourself lucky she didn't decide to bring you home to meet her sisters or you might never have gotten away.'"

"Daddy," Theo said softly, wonderingly.

"I've never told anyone else that story. It's not something you tell anyone else, because no one would believe it. I guess there aren't enough lonely shepherd boys left in the hills of Greece to keep the nymphs happy any-more. I must have looked like manna from heaven, if you'll pardon the mixed metaphor." He sighed. "You're sure you don't know where he got that perfume?"

"No."

"Pity. Well, good night. Better get to bed before we scare Santa away." He got up and turned off the tree, but Theo sat in the dark for a while longer, stroking Dido and thinking.

Part Two

Epithalamium

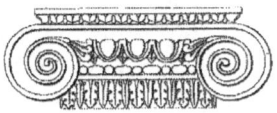

Ten

"THE FIFTH DECLENSION DOES not contain a great many nouns, but a lot of the ones it does include are both common and useful, such as *res*, meaning thing, and *dies*, or day," said Theo at the front of her First Year Latin class.

"Like *Dies irae* in the Mozart Requiem," said the music major in the second row. "Days of wrath."

"That's right, Aparna. Thank you. All right, the endings are here. Please copy them over, then we'll do a practice drill with them with the vocabulary list."

Theo dusted off her hands and wished once again that there were whiteboards, not blackboards, in these class-rooms. The feeling of chalk dust on her hands always gave her the shivers. She moved away from the board to give everyone a clear view of it and went to stand by the window.

Outdoors, the early March sun looked washed out and watery. Spring always seemed furthest away in March in New England. Back down at Sneed, the daffodils would be up and opening by now.

"Miss Fairchild? Is that *spes*, third one in the first column?"

"Is my writing that bad today? Yes. It means 'hope.'"

Hope. It was Theo's favorite word lately, because all she could do these days was hope for life to brighten. Maybe it was the miserable cold and frequent storms that had arrived with the start of the new semester and had stayed interminably since. But no one in the department had been very lively, either. Paul had lost all his flirtatiousness and treated her with such grave courtesy that she had been moved to ask Di Hunter if he were ill. Marlowe remained his merry self, but in a subdued way, and SpongeBob had not made an appearance since the Saturnalia party, not even for the department's Lupercalia party in February with its coy fertility references and general rowdiness.

Strangest of all, Renee Frothington-Forge-Smythe had taken a fancy to her. She hung around the department a day or two a week and invited Theo out for drinks or lunch, then fussed over her hair and wardrobe like a sophisticated elder sister trying to launch a gauche younger sibling in society. Lately she had started taking Theo shopping at her extensive number of favorite boutiques.

Where Theo felt in the most need of hope was with Grant. He had written to her several times over the month of Christmas break, postcards of bemused-looking moose from New Hampshire and of the Sibyl's Cave at Cumae in Italy, and three lengthy letters full of such longing and love that she was almost frantic for classes to start again so she could respond— for he had neglected to include a return address on any of them. Nor had he responded to emails or texts.

But when she'd come back, ready to fall into his arms, it was to find that he had reverted to absentminded preoccupation once more. Theo had spent a bad few days her first week back, trying to reconcile the beautiful love letters she had received with the coolness of their author.

But that wasn't all. Grant looked positively haggard, as if he hadn't slept in days, and pale as a ghost when he'd returned from Italy. Theo had been shocked at his appearance but he had waved aside her suggestions that he see a doctor.

"I must've picked something up on my trip," was his careless comment. "I'll be fine. Don't worry about me."

But he hadn't improved, and she was worried. There was no more talk of Pemberley, no more talk of—of almost anything.

Only Julian had been himself. He had greeted her with a warm embrace when she looked into his office on the first day of the new semester, and carried her off for a talk-filled dinner that very night. Since then, she'd had dinner with him almost every week, delighting in his conversation. And not telling Grant. That made her uneasy, for she had promised him that she would be careful with Julian. But she *was* being careful, whatever that meant. Julian didn't say or do anything that she would have been uncomfortable telling either her mother or the university's ethics committee about, and if it was good enough for Mom and the committee, it would have to be good enough for Grant.

Not that he ever asked where she was on those nights. She was always careful to shower away any traces of Julian's perfume, which she always wore when she went out with him. The expression of pleasure on Julian's face when she wore it was worth the risk of annoying Grant. If he'd even notice.

A restless rustle moved through the classroom. Theo turned from the window. "All set? All right, Matt, what would '*spes*' be in the ablative plural?"

"But if I tell him you were with me, it'll be all right," said Renee, her blue eyes wide.

"It's not that he'll care where I was. It's that I'll have missed his class," Theo tried to explain once more.

"To go shopping with his wife. Surely that's a good enough reason to skip Henry's class, don't you think? I've found the cutest little shop in Hingham—almost as good as something on Newbury Street. They've got lots of things that would look yummy on you, and Talbot's is only a little ways away. I just *love* classic clothes."

Theo sighed.

"Please? Pretty please?"

"Why are you doing this, Renee? I mean, it's very kind of you to be nice to your husband's students and all, but..."

She and Renee were having lunch in the lounge. Theo had actually come to like Renee. It was impossible not to, once you got to know her. She was so beautiful that even the most jealous woman was forced to give in and admire her eventually. Furthermore, she had the manner and personality of a Siamese kitten: imperious, playful, and utterly charming.

"It's my hobby. I love pretty things. And it's almost as much fun finding pretty things for other people as it is for myself. After all, Henry has his hobbies, like that nasty metal shop of his. So why can't I have mine?"

"Because the last time we went shopping, I would've maxed out two credit cards if I'd let you have your way. As it was I spent far too much."

"Yes, and you should've seen the eyes of all the men in this department bug out whenever you walked by wearing one of those new blouses."

Well, that was kind of true. Julian had paid her a quiet compliment when she'd worn the white linen one to dinner last week, but his eyes had spoken volumes more. If only Grant were the one to be doing the noticing—

As if her thought had called him into being, she saw Grant

walk into the lounge, head bowed, and sit down at a small table in the corner. While Renee chattered about the new spring colors and what necklines would be doing, Theo watched him slump in his chair. When a waiter arrived he pulled himself together enough to order something, then subsided back into a near stupor. This illness of his had persisted since January, well over a month and a half now. He claimed to have seen a doctor back in February after she'd finally called and made him an appointment, but if the visit had done him any good, she had yet to see it.

After a moment he stirred, reached down into his bag, and pulled something from it. A group of lunch-goers walked by just then, obscuring Theo's view. When they'd passed, she saw that he held a small silver flask, gazing at it with a strange expression of mixed revulsion and determination. As she watched, he seemed to steel himself. Raising the flask to his lips, he drank the contents down in a rush then sat back, grayer than ever and almost panting.

Before she could even think or say a word of excuse to Renee, Theo was across the room. She knelt at his side.

"Grant! What is it? What did you just drink?" she demanded, taking his hand.

He slowly turned his head and stared down at her as if his eyes wouldn't focus properly. "Theo?" he mumbled.

She reached over and picked up the flask, looked at it suspiciously, and raised it to her nose.

"No!" said Grant suddenly, lunging for it. She just caught a whiff of something awful, like decaying vegetation overlaid with sulfur and petroleum, before he snatched the bottle away from her, looking even more dreadful. "Don't touch that! Don't even go near it!" he gasped.

"It's horrible! What is it?" she asked again, fighting back nausea. He screwed the cover on it and shoved it into his bag.

"Nothing. Don't worry about it, Theo. It's all right. You'll see," he said, trying to smile reassuringly at her. It made him look like a death's head.

"No, it's not all right. Is that what's making you sick? What are you doing to yourself?"

He looked into her eyes, and she could see a shadow of the old Grant, her beloved wise fool, gaze back at her. "Recreating myself, Theo. It's my Pemberley. So I have something to give you when...when..." His eyes closed and he swallowed hard.

"What's wrong with him?" asked Renee from behind Theo. She had followed and was staring at Grant with horrified fascination, hugging her arms around herself.

"I don't know. He's been sick ever since the semester started. He just drank something that seemed to make him sicker, but he won't tell me what it was," she murmured back.

"You're right. I won't. H'lo, Renee. Nice to see you. Take care of Theo, won't you? Tell her I'll be okay in just a little while longer." Grant opened one eye and looked at them blearily.

"That's ridiculous and you know it," Theo said furiously.

Someone cleared his throat politely behind her. Theo turned and saw Grant's waiter holding a plate and a large glass of water. "Excuse me, please," he said, and set the plate down in front of Grant. "Anything else I can get you, sir?"

"No, thank you." Grant took a drink of water and sighed in relief. "Go with Renee, Theo. I'll see you tonight. I promise." He turned to his plate, which held a large and very rare hamburger.

Renee took Theo's arm and pulled her away without another word

"But he never eats hamburgers," said Theo, looking back over her shoulder. "He told me once that he was good friends with a cow a long time ago and hasn't been able to eat beef since then."

Renee pursed her lips. "Come on. Let's go. You heard him." She threw a couple of twenties down on their table and propelled Theo toward the door.

Even after an afternoon spent with Renee and her cheerfully inconsequential chatter, Theo could not get the picture of the gasping, whey-faced Grant from her mind. Nor could Renee's gift of a magnificent silk scarf, hand-painted in shades of turquoise, soothe her worries. She bolted an early dinner and was in the Great Room by six, waiting for Grant to keep his promise and prepared to brave the terrors of his neighborhood in Little Athens to knock down the door of his apartment if he didn't.

She didn't have to. He came into the Great Room shortly after seven-thirty, still pale and weak-looking but more in control of himself.

"I'm sorry, Theo," he began, flinging himself down in the armchair opposite her. Back around Halloween he would have sat down next to her on the sofa. She tried not to dwell on that fact. At least he'd showed up tonight.

"Would you care to explain to me what's going on? Are you sure you've been to see a doctor?" she asked, managing to keep her voice quiet.

"I know exactly what's going on. No, a doctor won't help. And no, I can't explain it. Not yet. Actually," he continued, holding up one hand to silence her, "I'm pleased with how it's going. I was worried I wouldn't be able to continue to teach."

"Well, your students have more sense than that," she replied severely. "Several of them have been to see me because they're concerned that you're going to drop dead in class some morning. I promised them I'd deal with your remains if they came and got me right away, but they didn't seem very reassured. What the heck do you mean 'you're pleased with how it's going'? Do you have any idea what you look like?"

"Good answer. Knew I could rely on you," he said, ignoring the second half of her speech.

"Grant—"

"Wait, Theo. I won't say anything else, so don't ask. But I think I can promise you that I'll be better by the end of spring break."

Theo got up and paced around the couch. "That's in another, oh, three and a half weeks. So you're telling me that if you're not dead by then, you'll be cured?"

"In a manner of speaking, yes. I'll be going up to Eleusinian for the break, and once I get back—"

So he would disappear back up to New Hampshire once again. "Grant," she said, interrupting him. "What do you think this looks like from my viewpoint? You tell me you love me in letters, but you avoid me like the plague when we're face to face. You look like you belong on life support but you're pleased with how well you're doing. And every time we might have a chance to spend some free time together over a vacation, you vanish up to New Hampshire. I'm—it's starting to hurt too much to love you." She sat back down and wrapped her arms around herself.

"Oh, Theo." Grant's knuckles whitened as he clutched the chair's arms. "I haven't handled this very well, have I?"

"I don't even know what it is you're trying to handle." She straightened and held a hand out to him. "Can't you tell me? Can't you let me help you?"

He stared at her for a long moment while she held her breath and willed him to stand up, to come to her, to come *back* to her and allow her to help him face whatever it was he was going through *"Please,"* she whispered.

He tensed as if he were about to rise—and then slumped back into the chair. "I'm not trying to hurt you—truly, I'm not." His gaze dropped. "It's just that...after spring break..."

She bit back her disappointment and took a deep breath.

"All right. After spring break. At that time we will sit down and decide what we should do. I love you, Grant. But I can't keep loving you if you keep pushing me away."

His eyes closed, and he swallowed convulsively. But his voice was steady when he finally spoke. "As long as you're willing to listen to what I have to say to you then. Most of it won't be very believable, but it's true nonetheless." He let his head fall back and stared up at the ceiling. They were both quiet after that.

It was a relief to have dinner with Julian a few days later. Theo didn't have to be on guard, to worry that he would collapse or do anything else inexplicable, to feel pushed away. It was restful to know that she would have a quiet evening of pleasant, non-emotionally harrowing conversation.

"Pretty scarf," he commented as he pushed in her seat at the Greek restaurant that he had taken her to before. As if by magic, two waiters appeared with a bottle of wine and a platter of olives and cheese.

"Thank you. Renee gave it to me because she liked the way it looked with my hair." She stroked it and looked up at him. "Actually, it matches your eyes."

"Does it? Well, then. My eyes are upon you, Theodora," he said, making a threatening face at her. "Literally."

She smiled. "You're far too nice to be able to look convincingly predatory."

"And you're far too clever to be caught by any common predator. Not that it wouldn't be tempting to try. But I'd rather be your friend." He held a glass out to her, then raised his own. "You're pensive tonight. Is everything all right?"

"Oh, it's...you know. Same old, same old." She shrugged

and tried to look more lively.

"Are things with Grant Proctor still troubling you?"

Hell. She didn't want to think about that right now. "Well…yes. I've been worried about his health. Have you seen how pale and tired he looks all the time? He's promised he'll be better after spring break, but I—I just don't know."

"I hope you can resolve things with him, one way or another. I don't like to see my friends unhappy." Julian's expression was concerned. "What are you doing for spring break, anyway? Going home?"

"No. Dr. Waterman asked if I would fish-sit for him and I said yes. I also thought I'd try to get work on course papers done that week so that I'm not so swamped at the end of the semester. Like I was last year." She popped a black olive, fragrant with rosemary and olive oil, into her mouth.

"You did very well last semester. But getting a head start is a good idea. I'll be busy with projects too. Finalizing the annual department trip, for one thing."

"Trip to where? That sounds exciting."

He raised an eyebrow. "To Greece, of course. We visit several site museums, do a little digging if I can arrange it, and have a wonderful time. You should consider coming."

Theo remembered her father's story of his first visit to Greece. His 'nymph' was probably now a wrinkled grandmother in a black dress and kerchief in some village somewhere. "It does sound wonderful. But I'll need to get a summer job and earn some tuition money."

"Are you sure I can't tempt you? It's not for the whole summer, after all." He chose an olive from the tray and ate it. "The olives there make these taste like cardboard. The afternoon sunshine would turn your hair to molten gold as we sat outside *tavernas* drinking retsina, and all the old women and young men would cluster around you to stroke it." Julian's voice was low and caressing. It insinuated itself into her middle and coiled seductively around until she felt hot and short of breath.

"Of course you can tempt me. How can I not be tempted when you say things like that? But I'll have to be good and resist." Julian was watching her with narrowed eyes, the way a hawk watches its prey before it dives for the capture. It made her breath come even shorter.

"What will I do if you successfully resist temptation? It would be a very lonely trip if you didn't come. I would be forced to request that you to return to school early in August and have dinner with me every night like this to atone." He pretended to look stern as he refilled her glass.

"I would have to do as you say, of course, *Magister,*" she said with mock submissiveness. "But it would be more pleasure than punishment."

"It would, would it? We'll see about this summer, *kalliste* Theodora." He smiled. "I can be very persuasive, you know."

To her surprise, later that week Grant came to her in the Great Room. Theo watched him over the top of her book as he prowled around, hands behind his back, stooped and pale but full of febrile energy. That had to be an improvement; the last few days she wasn't sure he would have the energy to teach his class, much less pace the room.

She sighed to herself and said aloud, "You're going to wear a path in the mosaics, which would be a shame. They're one of my favorite things here."

He didn't smile, but at least sat down on the couch next to her. She looked up hopefully, but he was frowning at the floor. "I've been thinking," he said suddenly.

"I'd think I'd noticed." She put a slip of paper in her book.

"What have you been thinking?"

"That it's time for you to come to Eleusinian. This summer. I want you to spend the summer with me in New Hampshire."

Theo felt her mouth fall open in surprise.

"There's a small guest cottage that you could stay in, if you liked, or you could stay in my—" He looked down at his hands. "We give summer classes in Latin and Greek for high school and college students. You could teach and earn some of what you'll need for the year. The faculty are wonderful. More amazing than anyone you've met, even here. And we could be together. It's beautiful in the mountains in summer, warm in the day and cool at night, and the stars are so close when we lie in the meadows on clear nights—"

"Not to mention the porcupines and moose," she murmured.

"And the porcupines and moose," he agreed, his mouth curving into the smile she hadn't seen since fall. "Maybe you'll be able to teach the moose to pronounce their *s's* and *t's*."

A feeling of unreality washed over her. Once she would have danced with happiness at this invitation. But now? A fleeting vision of impossibly blue water and white stucco walls beckoned in her mind, hot sun on her shoulders and chill pine-scented wine on her lips.

"Olivia's thrilled at the idea," Grant continued enthusiastically. "She can't wait to meet you. In fact, she said she'd come back here with me after spring break to—"

"What?" The seductive visions of Greece abruptly vanished. Olivia, coming here?

"Olivia called and told me today that she'd come for a visit. She used to teach here, remember? So she'll be able to see her old friends and have a chance to get to know you before the summer."

"Whoa. Wait one minute. I haven't said I'm going anywhere." Theo rose and began to retrace Grant's path around the couch, too agitated to sit still. Olivia? Here? No. This was her place, her turf. Things were strained enough between her and Grant without adding Olivia to the mix, no matter what assurances he'd given her. "We shouldn't be talking about what I want, when we still don't know what *you* want."

Grant stared at her. "But—Olivia—" he began weakly.

"This isn't about Olivia! If I went to Eleusinian it would be because of because of *you*, not her. And I don't have any idea whether or not I want to. I can't commit to go with you for the whole summer when I don't even know if we'll be speaking to each other come the end of the month."

Grant's face was white, whiter than she had ever seen it. "Not speaking? But—this is for you. Everything I've done is because I love you."

Theo felt as if he had punched her. "So you've been pushing me away because you love me? Is your definition of love to avoid me for days on end and keep secrets from me and refuse to let me help you? Because if it is, I—I'm not sure I want that kind of love."

They stared at each other for the space of a few seconds— or was it an infinity?—and it was as if the fire in her went out. She stared at him, her hands rising to her burning cheeks. Then she snatched up her bag and fled the Great Room.

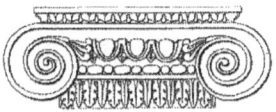

Eleven

OVER THE NEXT DAYS Theo slunk out of her room to attend classes and slunk back as soon as they were over, carefully avoiding even glancing into Grant's classroom on their teaching mornings. He seemed to avoid her as well; at least, she never caught even a glimpse of him, to her relief.

But eventually a little pride had spread, scab-like, over her pain. If this was how things were going to be, then so be it. She would have to get through the rest of the year co-existing with Grant in the department. But she was still careful not to pass by his door on her way to teach her Latin class, and after class went straight to Dr. Waterman's Rhetoric class without looking to the left or right.

And after another few days she decided it was time to reclaim all her former habits, so one evening she packed up her reading and grimly marched over to Hamilton Hall, to study on her accustomed couch in the Great Room.

To her relief, the room was empty. "Though it's nothing to me if he should choose to work here. It's time for me to get over it," she told herself sternly, fluffing the cushions on her couch before she made herself comfortable.

The room was quiet. It generally was, but tonight the silence seemed almost tangible. She glanced around her, then over at the other end of the couch. Right there was where he had sat that night, clutching his head like it was about to explode, his face a mask of misery—

Hadn't she been miserable too? Hadn't she cried her share of tears?

You were miserable, yes. But you weren't ill and confused and unsure how to handle things. There were a few things, though, that you were. Impatient, unfair, unkind. Too ready to see injury and insult where it probably wasn't intended. Too busy feeling your own sadness and hurt to be mindful of someone else's.

Dammit, he'd hurt her! Falling in love too fast and deep with a man who couldn't seem to return her love, watching her dreams of happiness with him turn to ash—or worse, fade to nothing, because they'd never been real in the first place. It—it just started to hurt too much.

So you lashed out in return.

"Stop it," she said aloud to the calm impartial voice of her conscience in her head. "I won't listen anymore." She slid down in her seat and curled up into a tight ball of pain, putting her hands over her ears as tears squeezed from the corners of her tightly shut eyes.

"Theodora?"

"No. No..." she said to the voice. She didn't want to hear it anymore, listen to it explain to her exactly how she'd messed up things with Grant—

Hands closed over her own, gently but inexorably pulling them away from her ears. She struggled, but the hands raised her to her feet. Even before she opened her eyes, even before the arms had gathered her against him she knew who it was, and let herself collapse against Julian's chest.

"Ssh. My poor Theodora, it's all right. It's all right," he murmured, holding her tightly as he stroked her hair. "That's right. Let it all out."

The song of his rich clear voice flowed over her, smoothing away her grief and pain until her very bones seemed to dissolve under the warmth of his hands, and only his arms kept her from falling to the floor. Her tears gradually ceased and she felt empty and peaceful, like a bubble floating above a stormy sea. She would be content to stand there all night, safe in the harbor of his arms, if staying there would keep the voice of her conscience at bay.

After a while—she was not sure how long—he drew back to look at her. "Better?" he asked softly.

She nodded and reached up to wipe away a lingering tear. As she did, she saw Julian's face change. He was staring at her hand with an unreadable expression on his face.

"Julian?"

He took her hand and examined it closely. "That's an unusual ring," he said at last. "Where did you get it?"

Grant's ring. She had forgotten about it. Or had she left it on in unconscious hope of...of what? "It's Grant's. He gave it to me. For Christmas. I—I'm not sure if I should still be wearing it, though."

"I see." He stared at it for a moment longer, his face still carefully blank, then let it go. "It's an interesting piece...but I'm more concerned about you. What made you so very sad?" He pushed her hair back from her face, then softly touched her cheek. His eyes were so close, closer than they had ever been. She could fall into them, like sliding into a warm tropical sea, let their blue depths hold her...

"It's Grant. I don't know what to do," she whispered. "He—I don't know if he loves me or not."

143

"Do you love him?" His voice was gentle, but demanded an answer.

"Yes." To her surprise, the word came out with no hesitation. "And I thought he loved me. But he's been so strange lately that I don't know what to believe."

"Perhaps it's time you two spent some time apart, to give you some perspective." He was rubbing her back gently, rhythmically, so that she wanted to purr like Dido.

"We sort of were. But then he asked me to come to the Eleusinian Institute with him this summer."

Julian's eyebrows rose. "Do you think that would be wise? Olivia—" He sighed. "I dislike speaking ill of colleagues—even former ones—but Olivia is not to be trusted. She—well, the word 'man-eater' comes to mind. I was actually relieved when she left here. She did not...reflect well on my department."

Theo winced. Was that it after all? He'd denied having any romantic feeling for her, but if he wasn't sure... "He insists that they're just friends."

"Hmmph. I'm not convinced. What did you say to him?"

"I didn't. I was too upset. I can't—won't—go with him, if he and Olivia—"

"Of course you can't, if that's the way things are. My poor sweet Theodora." Julian was silent for a moment. "You know, you really must think about coming to Greece with me this summer," he finally said. "I think it would do you a world of good."

"Oh, I—"

"There's time for you to think about it. I'll hold a place for you until the moment we step on the plane. I want you to do what will be best for you. Not that I don't think that coming with me isn't the best choice you could make." His voice smiled. "Come to my office tomorrow afternoon. We can talk about it more and I can show you the trip brochures that just arrived."

Yes. Tomorrow. Tonight she didn't want to have to think anymore. The pressure of his hands on her back increased and she gave into it, resting her head on his shoulder again. Her eyes felt incredibly heavy. "Yes, Julian," she whispered.

"Get some sleep. You're worn out with all this upset," he said, a few minutes—or was it hours?—later. "I'll see you tomorrow afternoon, yes? Will you let me take you out to Dmitri's for a quiet evening?"

"Thank you. I'd like that." She lifted her head and smiled at him as he released her.

"Then it shall happen. Good night, my dear." He lifted her hand and kissed it in a charmingly courtly gesture.

Theo slept well that night, better than she had for a while. She ran back to her room after her final class of the day with Dr. Forge-Smythe to dress for dinner with Julian, choosing the turquoise scarf to casually drape over her shoulders, then hurried back to Hamilton Hall.

On the second floor she tiptoed past June Cadwallader's office on her way to Julian's. Walking past June's office always gave her an uneasy feeling. This time was no exception. She could feel the woman's cold eyes on her as she passed, and would have sworn that the temperature immediately outside her door was lower than in the rest of the hallway. Unfortunately, the department mailboxes were in June's office. Theo usually waited until June was at lunch to check hers.

At the end of the hall she saw that Julian's door was half closed. Should she come back? Then she heard Renee's voice coming from behind it. She smiled and started forward.

"What do you mean 'why didn't I tell you before'? You never asked me," Renee was saying plaintively. Theo stopped.

Julian's voice answered, low and angry. "I distinctly remember commenting to you on several occasions that he seemed familiar. Why didn't you say something then?"

"I didn't think it mattered. I assumed you'd figure it out yourself. After all, *I* never forget a man, even if I've never touched him. Marlowe knows, and so does Arthur, I think. Why don't you yell at them? I didn't think it mattered anymore, anyway," she repeated. Theo could hear the pout in her voice.

"Of course it matters! The only one to defy me and get away with it—"

"He didn't exactly get away with it, did he?"

Julian ignored the interruption. "—was right there before my eyes, the one they gave him when he returned to Athens! I thought he was some minor nobody from somewhere else. Concealed himself well, though not well enough. The unmitigated gall of him, daring to come here and interfere in my business, just like before! He'll regret the day he set foot in my department—I'll see to that—"

Theo backed down the hallway. Who were they talking about?

Julian's door opened. Theo ducked hastily into one of the seminar rooms and peeked around the corner just in time to see Renee go striding down the hall, her cheeks an agitated cerise. She stayed in the seminar room to give Julian a few minutes to compose himself, and puzzled over what she had heard. *Who* had defied Julian, and concealed himself, and was interfering with him again? When she had counted ten minutes on her watch, she slipped out of the room and returned to Julian's door.

"My dear Theodora," he said as he rose from his desk with a smile, looking cool and unflustered. If she hadn't just overheard his conversation with Renee, she would have assumed he had spent a quiet afternoon alone in his office.

"Look at these. Don't they tempt you a little?" he said, spreading a sheaf of color brochures before her, the photographs white and blue and drenched in golden sunlight.

Theo picked one up. "Of course they do. I don't need these to be tempted to come. I just don't know that I can afford to go."

"And if that were not an issue? Would you come then?"

"I don't know. It's not a simple yes-or-no decision." She traced a finger over the arc of the Ionian Islands on the map on the brochure's reverse.

"I understand. Keep this and look it over. If you have any questions about the trip, you can ask me any time. Think about it over spring break next week. You'll be here?"

"I'll be fish-sitting for Dr. Waterman," she reminded him.

"Ah, yes. That's right." He sat back down in his chair, looking thoughtful. "So you will." He made a steeple of his hands and stared down at them for several long seconds.

"Julian?" she said softly.

"What? Oh, I'm sorry. Wool-gathering for a moment. Yes, think it over during the break. Perhaps something will happen to help you decide." He smiled. "Wine, Theodora?"

On the Friday morning before break, Theo found an envelope on her desk when she came into her Latin class. She set the students an impromptu translation exercise and opened the note.

> *Dear Theo,*
> *I know that you've been avoiding me these past several days. Truth be told, I've avoided you as well. Not because I didn't want to see you, but because I didn't know what to*

say. I've hurt you, and for that I am more sorry than words can express. Pain has been my companion for so long that I can tolerate it well, but I should not expect that of others. And I love you too much to ever want to see you hurt in any way. That is the first point of this letter: to tell you that I love you, despite my behavior over the last months that might say otherwise. And despite what you may think about my feelings for anyone else. I will say it again: I love you, you alone, forever.

Second: Some weeks ago you said that you would give me until the end of spring break to pull myself together, and that we would decide then if we had a future. I know I feel quite certain of what my decision is, but I understand that you might not be so sure. Will you hold to that promise, and let me prove to you that I am capable of loving you as you deserve to be loved? Meet me Sunday night at the end of break, and you will see then the new man I have become.

I leave for Eleusinian this evening. If you wish to reply to this note, leave one in my department mail-box. I'll check it after lunch and brave indigestion at June's hands.

Third: There is no third point. So I'll reiterate the first. I love you, Theo. And I live for Sunday, when I'll finally be able to prove it to you.

Grant

Theo reread the letter three times, feeling her throat tighten and ache with each reading. Did he love her as he said? Would he be able to prove anything to her by next Sunday? Would she be able to listen, to expose her still raw wounds to him once more and trust him not to etch them deeper?

No. She couldn't sort all that out right now, not with her Latin class sitting before her, shifting and sighing as they scribbled on their papers. There would be time enough for thinking it over next week. She pulled a leaf from the back of a notebook.

> *Dear Grant,*
> *Thank you for taking time to write me before you leave.*

She nibbled on the end of her pen. Might as well be honest.

> *You're right; I was hurt. I'm sorry for having struck out in my hurt, like an injured animal at bay, but that's precisely how I felt. I'm looking forward to a quiet week at Dr. Waterman's to lick my wounds and help me feel a little more human again.*

There. He'd know where she was, just in case. Maybe he would come back early…

> *I will do as we agreed and meet you on Sunday, and will listen to all that you wish to say to me. I'll see you at eight o'clock in the Great Room, if that's okay.*

Close on a gracious note. This would not be the place to express her hope that Olivia sat on a porcupine next week, or was mauled by a bear in drag.

> *Safe trip to Eleusinian.*

> *Theo*

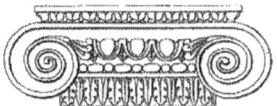

Twelve

"ONE TEASPOON, ONCE A day. Maybe a little extra in the tanks in my room and the kitchen; they tend to eat more—"

"—and don't forget to keep an eye on the heaters for the tanks on the three-season porch. It's all right, Dr. Waterman. I know the routine. I'll take very good care of your fish." Theo patted a tank.

"I know you will. I just worry about my little friends here. Can't help it." Dr. Waterman shrugged sheepishly and rumpled his hair.

"I understand. I hated leaving my cat with my parents when I came here. I miss her dreadfully, especially when I'm going to sleep at night and don't feel her lying on my feet so I can't turn over."

He laughed. "That's not a problem I have with my fish, thank goodness."

She followed him down the hallway back to the living room and went to stare out the sliding glass doors to the bay below. The water was a glorious but very cold-looking blue. "Where's this conference? Can I reach you on your cell phone if necessary?"

"Well, er...I'm not actually going to a conference." Dr. Waterman turned faintly pink above his beard. He looked away and picked some invisible lint from his coat sleeve.

"Oh." Theo was nonplussed. "A vacation. That's nice."

"No, not quite a vacation. I'm going to visit my wife," he said in a rush.

His *what?* "I didn't realize you were married."

He grimaced down at his sleeve. "We decided some years ago—career demands, that sort of thing—that we were better off living our lives this way. But we get together as frequently as possible. I don't like to talk about it—it works for us, but others don't always understand. I should have known you would."

Oh, gosh. The poor man! "It's no business of mine, Dr. Waterman. It must've been a hard decision to make, though, even if it's what works best for you."

"It was. I miss Trite a great deal. But we're both happier this way." He looked up at her and smiled. "You're a good girl, Theo. I'm glad you're my student."

She walked him out to his car and waved as he drove down the long driveway, then wandered around the corner of the house to the patio that overlooked the water. But it faced east and was too shady and chilly this time of the year. Instead she went back around and sat down on the front steps in the fickle March sunshine.

How sad for Dr. Waterman. Theo liked him very much, found his friendly paternal manner with her comforting. He should have had a house full of boisterous teenaged children and a charming, loving wife instead of tank after tank of rare fish and sea life. What was this mysterious wife like, whom he could neither live with nor without? Probably a female Grant Proctor, she thought with a smile. If she were to stay with Grant, would they end up like this? Unable to handle being together but unable to part?

"Mmmmreooow?"

Theo started and looked around. That had sounded just like...but it couldn't be. "Dido?" she called incredulously.

"Mmmmrrurrph."

A large cat ambled up the driveway, sleek and gray, with a magnificent fluffy tail. It stopped in the center of the circular drive, stared at Theo, then uttered a joyous 'prrrt?' and trotted up to her.

"Hello, handsome," said Theo, reaching down to let the cat sniff her before running her hand down its back. It felt too well-groomed and fed to be a stray. "You must belong to a neighbor. I thought you were my Dido for a minute. You sounded just like her."

The cat closed its eyes as she rubbed the side of its face and sat down next to her.

Theo chuckled. "I get the hint, buddy. All right, I don't have anything else to do just now." She smiled down at the furry face. The cat regarded her through eyes half-closed in ecstasy, and began to purr loudly.

"I'll bet Dr. Waterman doesn't like you hanging out here, just in case you take a fancy for a bit of fresh fish for dinner, huh? God, I miss having a cat around. Tell you what. I won't tell him you were here if you promise to behave yourself, okay?" She switched to rubbing the cat's other cheek, and the purr grew louder.

There was nothing like a purring cat to help put life into perspective. "Maybe you're what Grant needs," she mused aloud. "A cat might be able to teach him a thing or two about immediacy and proximity. Not to mention the joys of snuggling."

Right on cue, the cat reached up and put a tentative paw on her leg. Then it climbed onto her lap and gazed up at her worshipfully. She reached under its chin to scratch it there.

Grant. And Julian. She would have to think about both of them now. Two men were trying to convince her to spend the summer with them, Grant with words of love, Julian with...what? What would Grant have to say to her on Sunday that was so important—and so mysterious that she might not believe him?

"Murrrn," the cat said reproachfully as she stood up and dumped it to the ground.

"I'm sorry. I didn't mean to do that." She glanced up at the sun sinking behind the trees. "Anyway, it's starting to get dark. Time you went home. 'Bye, kitty." She bent down and rubbed its head for a minute, then turned to the door.

"Mreeeee?" said the cat, close on her heels.

"Hey, stop that! This isn't your house," she said, blocking the doorway with her foot. "I'll see you later." She slipped through the narrow opening and shut the door firmly behind her.

It was nice to just eat and sleep and stare at Dr. Waterman's hypnotic fish. She didn't open even one of her books for the next two days, and only exerted herself enough to drive into school to feed the fish there and stop at the store for necessities. In the afternoons she pulled a chaise longue from the terrace around to the western side of the house and sat in the sun, happy to be outside for a little while after the vile weather of the winter. Every afternoon the cat came back to visit her to be petted as she relaxed in the chaise and thought of nothing. It was positively idyllic.

But on Monday afternoon as she sat outside, the clouds began to thicken and the wind to blow.

"I knew it couldn't last," she said to the purring cat on her lap as she gazed up at the gathering clouds. "It just figures. I'll bet it snows tonight and is cold and gloomy for the rest of the week."

The cat blinked at her.

It didn't snow. It did, however, start raining as Theo made a chef's salad for dinner that evening. She stared out the dark kitchen window as the first tentative drops turned into a downpour, and went back to rinsing lettuce. Rising wind muttered and moaned in the eaves, making her shiver. It was eerie to listen to, though the attic vents in her own parents' house made a sound like a banshee when the wind blew hard enough in the right quarter. It was different when it wasn't your own house and you didn't know that that peculiar yowling sound you were hearing right now was perfectly normal, really—

The lights flickered for a second before resuming their steady glow. She froze, then laughed out loud. "What are you so jumpy about, Fairchild?" she murmured to herself. "You've been here before. There aren't any skeletons in the closets upstairs. Just a lot of fish. And they don't make any noise, remember?"

The yowl sounded again. This time she realized it came from outside, near the terrace. She took firm hold of herself, and wiping her wet hands on a towel went to the exterior light panel, turned on the outside floods, and peered out the sliders.

Rain blew in sheets through the arcs of light cast by the floodlights, pounding on the bluestone paving. As she opened one of the doors an inch, she could hear the surf crash on the rocks below, but nothing else. "Filthy night," she muttered, and had started to slide the door shut again when a flash of green caught her attention. She stared hard at where the light met the darkness, and realized that there was a pair of glowing eyes there, not far above the ground, staring back at her.

"Meeeet?" said a familiar voice.

"You'd better swear to me on the other eight of your lives that you're going to behave yourself, you," Theo crooned as she blotted the dripping cat with a bath towel.

It purred furiously and butted her arm.

"I'm not joking," she continued. "All right, I think I've gotten as much water out of you as I'm going to. Now listen to me. If you so much as glance at one of those fish with a funny expression on your face, you're out."

The cat ignored her, jumped on a kitchen chair, and started to wash itself. Theo watched it for a moment then went back to making her dinner, glancing at it now and again as she chopped tomatoes and ham and peppers. It was cozy to be in a large, comfortable house on a rainy night with a cat for company. She put some bits of ham and cheese onto a saucer, thought for a moment, and went into the garage. Dr. Waterman kept a bag of kitty litter out there to sprinkle on icy walkways in winter. She poured some onto a square of newspaper, scooped up the cat, and dug its paw into the litter. "Just so you know. I don't want to have to do any cleaning up later," she said to it.

The cat blinked at her, and she laughed. "You're too clever by half, puss. Okay, here's dinner." She set the saucer on the floor next to her seat at the kitchen table, and smiled down as the cat sniffed judiciously at it and began to eat.

"What do you know? I've got a dinner guest. This calls for a celebration." She set her salad on the table and turned back to the counter. Julian had given her a bottle of his wine on Friday as she left the department. A glass of sunshiny Riesling would be just the thing on a night like this.

After dinner the cat watched Theo wash their dishes, then

followed her around the living room as she turned out lights after checking on the fish. Before she turned off the last lamp she opened the slider. "Go home?" she said brightly.

The cat didn't move.

"Yeah, well, I know it's awful out, so I guess I don't blame you. You can stay here, I suppose. I hope your owners won't worry." She patted a chair in invitation. "Sleeps?"

This time the cat might have sneered.

"Well, it's as good a place as any," she said to it. They stared at each other for a moment. She had watched the cat all evening, but it hadn't so much as glanced at any of the fish tanks. She'd gone around the house to check on them just in case, but all were covered with mesh or with solid covers.

"Fine, then. Sleep where you want. I suppose I can trust you. I'm going to bed now, fuzzball." Theo picked up her wineglass, turned off the last light, and headed up the stairs to the guestroom. When she turned on the bedside lamp and looked around, the cat was sitting in the doorway. It watched her as she undressed and pulled on her pajamas and waited while she brushed her teeth in the bathroom. When she climbed into bed, it leapt up by her feet.

"Oh, you think so, do you?"

The cat blinked at her once more, then started to knead the quilt with its front paws, purring. Theo watched it, feeling half pleasure, half pain at the sight.

"I'd rather have my Dido, but I guess you'll do in a pinch," she whispered, and turning on her side, switched off the light.

She was too hot. The quilt was suffocating, pinning her down when she wanted to move and stretch. She kicked it off and rolled over, dimly aware of the rain and wind outside.

In sharp contrast with the weather the air in her room was warm and still, like a lazy Mediterranean afternoon. She rolled over and reached for the glass by her bed. A wineglass: that was right, she had brought it up with her, hadn't she? Well, it was wet and cool, and maybe Julian's wine would help her sleep again. She took a long drink, sighing as sweet languor trickled through her limbs, then yanked off her pajamas and stretched out naked on the sheets. The smooth cotton felt so good on her bare skin, cool and caressing—

She was thirsty again. There had been a little left in her glass when she drank before, hadn't there? She reached out and found it suddenly in her hand, and gratefully drained the cool brightness. Still so thirsty...but the cup was full. She drank twice more, then fell back into dreams.

Someone was in the bed with her. She couldn't see his face in the darkness; whenever she tried to see, it was as if her eyes would not work properly. He held a cup of wine to her parched lips and fed her grapes, juicy and sweet, that seemed to burst inside her like tiny roman candles, and then yet more wine. She tried to turn her face away, to ask who he was and why he was doing this to her, but she had lost all will, all ability to move. Eventually she couldn't even remember why she wanted to know those things. There were only the plump sweet grapes, and the cool liquid trickling down her throat—and then the hard, tireless body in hers, drowning her in pleasure, again and again.

A phone was ringing somewhere. Its harsh, insistent jangle hurt, and Theo pulled her pillow over her head until it stopped. When blessed silence returned she pulled the pillow off and tried to sleep again, but something bothered her. Her mouth was dry. She groped for the bedside table. Her fingers closed around something cold and oddly textured—a cup made up of angles and facets.

"Drink, Theodora," said a rich, familiar voice.

She nearly dropped the cup. But a warm hand was steadying hers. "Be careful, please, my dear. That's my favorite cup. But what better one to let you use?"

She knew that voice, the way it seemed to caress words even as it spoke them. It had spoken to her in her dreams—"*Julian?*" She gasped and nearly leapt from the bed, but a wave of dizziness made her fall back weakly onto the pillow. "What the—how did you get in here?" She reached nervously around her. "Where are you?"

He chuckled, capturing her flailing hand and kissing it. "Open your eyes, Theodora. You should be able to see me. You've had enough of my wine by now."

Theo blinked. "They are open," she whispered.

"No. *Open* them. Look at me, and see," he commanded, and touched her hand to his face.

She turned toward her hand and blinked. And there he was, his eyes heavy-lidded and amused and very blue, his sleek gray hair tousled, his muscular chest shaking slightly with repressed mirth at her expression of incredulity. *Bare* muscular chest. And bare torso, and bare— She sat up quickly again, and once more dizziness forced her back, dizziness so strong that she nearly fainted.

Julian. She'd been sleeping with Julian. But it had all been a dream, hadn't it? Those endless hours of intense sex—she had dreamed them, right? She had to have, because anything else was impossible. If only she could think straight—her thoughts felt as if they were dripping one at a time from a very slow faucet.

"It started out as a dream, my dear, because that was the easiest way to reach you. But not for long. Not for long." He held the cup out to her once more. It resembled what it had felt like, a piece of rock crystal but of a dazzling clarity and glow.

Julian followed her gaze. "A diamond," he said. "Pretty thing, isn't it? Henry made it for me a long time ago. Drink, darling."

She shook her head and began to inch away. "Julian, I—this is—"

He held it to her lips and looked at her, and she found herself obediently opening her mouth. The cool tingling wine slipped easily down her throat and seemed to smooth away her questions and worries even as she drank, leaving her languorous and relaxed. She drained the cup and fell back into the pillows, marveling at their softness. And when Julian took her in his arms and kissed her, she sighed with wordless pleasure.

"Very good, my darling," he murmured, his hands wandering over her body till the languor had turned to eagerness. "There's nothing for you to worry about. Everything is going beautifully. Oh, my Theodora." He kissed her deeply. "I knew it would be a beautiful thing. But I believe it will be even better than I'd hoped."

When Theo came to herself again it was daylight. She opened her eyes and saw Julian lying on his side, gazing down at her with a smile that could only be called smug.

"Good afternoon, darling," he said cheerfully.

"Julian!" Memory crashed down on her again like a cold wet wave. She was in bed with Julian—Julian!—and she'd been drunk—had he drugged her?—and they'd—they'd—

"Drink, Theodora," he said firmly. That strange heavy cup

brimming with the golden honey-and-champagne-tasting wine filled her mouth and she found herself gulping it down. He nodded with satisfaction. "We've been busy, you see. It's not an easy process, but you're coming through with flying colors. Almost done by now, in fact. I didn't expect it to go so well, but I should have known you'd excel." He bent and kissed her.

Theo felt the dreamy lethargy begin to steal over her again, but she fought it. "Almost done...with what? What do you keep giving me to drink? This is not—"

"Let's see. Which shall I answer first? The drink is a concoction of my own. Ambrosia dissolved in Riesling—*my* Riesling, of course—and flavored with a little bit of nectar and a few other special ingredients. My secret blend. I'm rather proud of it." He smiled modestly. "You've been thriving on it. And the fact that my wine grapes are ambrosia-fed makes it have twice the effect. If Arthur can feed it to his fish, why can't I give it to my grapes?"

Arthur...fish. A memory shimmered at the edge of her mind, but when she turned to it, it had vanished. Who was Arthur? Did it matter?

Ambrosia, though...*that* she thought she could remember from...from somewhere. "Ambrosia," she said carefully, through the tingling silver haze. Ambrosia. The food of the gods.

"But of course. I think my cocktail has worked well, though you also tolerated the straight ambrosia nicely." He waved a hand and pulled a small silvery pellet from the air, then popped it into her mouth. She remembered the grapes he had fed her in her dream, and felt the same strange sensations within her as it melted in her mouth and slid down her throat.

"But you've been drinking small quantities of my wine since November, which probably helped prevent unfortunate overreactions. Now, let's see how you're progressing. Put the cup on the bedside table for me, darling. No, no," he said gently. "No hands. That's for humans."

"But I am human," she whispered.

"Not human any more, my Theodora, not any more. You're mine now, and very emphatically *not* human. Weren't you listening? You've had enough ambrosia now to make the entire population of Boston sprout wings and glow in the dark. I wanted to be very, very sure that you were completely changed. Oh, do be careful, love. That's my favorite cup, remember, and Arthur wouldn't like his window broken." He smiled down at her triumphantly and waved the cup down from the ceiling where it had been bobbing erratically. "But that was very good for a start, my dear. Very good. Now, I do believe it's been nearly an hour since we've made love. We mustn't let that happen again."

It wasn't until much later that Theo realized how many days she had spent in a daze, in what felt like an endless, disorienting dream: drinking and eating what Julian gave her, feeling his body on hers, relentless in his passion. Sometimes it was difficult to remember her own name as she lay feeling herself melt away and turn into something else. But when she tried to think, to understand what was happening, all meaning would slip away.

At some point Julian finally let her rise from bed. "You've changed, remember," he cautioned, helping her stand. "Things will seem different. You've already seen how much stronger your sense of touch is."

Theo felt lightheaded as she swayed on her feet, the last cup of ambrosia wine she had drunk still effervescing inside her. The pressure of Julian's eyes on her was enough to make her overbalance. She cried out but didn't fall.

Julian reached up and pulled her back to the floor. "What

did I tell you?" he chided.

"I don't remember," she whispered.

"Hmm." He frowned. "Perhaps I've overdone things a bit. Come, my goddess. You need to learn this now. School starts again next week, and Sunday night is coming."

Sunday night? Yes, she was supposed to do something on Sunday night...in the Great Room. She had to talk to someone—or did she? "Sunday..." she murmured, and got lost in the feeling of the word in her mouth. Sunday... Sunday... What *was* a Sunday, anyway?

"I've called a symposium, just for the immortal faculty and staff. They need to meet you in your new capacity. I thought it would be the perfect way to do it." He pulled her into his arms and kissed her. "You'll be magnificent, *ediste* Theodora. I know you will."

After that, memory began to come back to her in scattered fragments. She saw a fish tank and remembered that she was supposed to be taking care of them for someone while he was gone. And something about a school. When she happened to see a book bag on the floor of the foyer, overflowing with note-books and texts, she began to remember that she was supposed to be doing something with them. She picked up a file folder labeled in her own handwriting and thumbed through it with growing unease, then carried it to Julian.

"This is mine, isn't it?" she asked him.

Julian barely looked at it. "It was, once."

"I was—am—I mean, I was studying, wasn't I? It's there somewhere in my head, but when I try to think about it, it slips away." She rubbed her forehead and frowned.

"My poor darling. You're still adjusting to it all." Julian took the folder from her and blew on it. It turned into a goblet, brimming with wine. He handed it to her with a smile. "Yes, you were a student," he continued. "But you aren't any more. Drink, my dear."

Theo took the goblet but did not bring it to her lips. "I was a teacher," she said slowly. "I wanted to get my doctorate, didn't I? It was very important to me. And then—"

"And then I found you." He guided the goblet to her mouth. "Now drink, and don't worry about your past."

And then she remembered other things. Julian was one the professors...and there were others, too. She remembered Dr. Waterman, and realized that it was his fish she was supposed to be taking care of. And that nice Dr. Forge-Smythe, with his pretty wife—she knew them, too. Only...only they weren't what they'd appeared to be, were they?

"You're gods," she said to Julian one night, after they'd made love for what felt like hours. "It—you're just pretending to be college professors."

He drew back and smiled down at her. "We aren't pretending—we *are* college professors. But yes, we are gods as well. *The* gods, I suppose you might say. But you are too, now, *eme philotate* Theodora—don't forget that."

Theo pushed that thought away. It was too much to deal with just now "But how—? What—"

"Do you remember—no, I suppose you don't, right now. We talked about it once, you and I, just before exams last semester. 'What do gods do when no one worships them anymore?' As I recall, you caught on right away. 'But how liberating for them, not to have to answer prayers anymore,' you said. You were right, of course. I got so tired of having to rustle the leaves in the oak groves at Dodona so those dreary old oracles could think they were interpreting my divine will."

"You—you're Ze—" She choked on the name.

"I've had so many names that it doesn't really matter. I am who I am, and right now I happen to be Dr. Julian d'Amboise, head of the Classics Department at John Winthrop University. Most suitable, don't you think? And the others—Paul and Diana. Henry and Renee. Freddy Herman. Marlowe, for crying out loud. I've always warned him that he's far too obvious, but fortunately most mortals are too blind to see the noses on their own faces. And Arthur, of course. He's almost as bad as Marlowe, with his fish and his endless laps in the university pool. And now, you. My new goddess." He bent to kiss her.

Theo thought hard, grasping for threads of memory. They had talked about the gods once—she could almost remember— "Dr. Bellow. And...and June."

He shifted uncomfortably. "Yes, them too."

"But why here? Why now?"

"Because we wanted to live. Some gods—the nameless, faceless ones worshipped by the men who made stone tools and lived in caves—did die, because they're forgotten. We did not want to share that fate. We refused to be forgotten, even when a new god ousted us from our rightful place."

"How could anyone forget you?" She reached up to touch his face.

He smiled and kissed her fingertips. "The new god was very eager for us to be forgotten. Ironically, though, it was his own followers who kept us alive. The monks preserved our memory when they copied the writings of the ancient Greeks and Romans, even though they had been directly responsible for our downfall. I've always been amused by that. It was the birth of the universities that set us free, which is why we're here. We lead pleasant and useful existences, keeping our own memories green by teaching the classics. Poetic justice, I always thought."

She was silent for a minute, struggling to make sense of it all. The gods—here. And now. And— "What about me? Why?"

"Ssshh." He put a finger to her lips. "The 'why' is easy. Because I wanted you. 'Beloved of the God' indeed. Who would have guessed your name would be so apt?"

She blinked up at him and asked, shyly, "Do you love me?"

"Why, my dearest! How can you ask such a question?" He held up a hand, and his diamond cup appeared in it. "And now you will drink, my dear. Don't let all this trouble you. All will be well." He chuckled. "All will be very well indeed. I don't know if I can wait."

The wine was making her sleepy again. "If you can wait for what?"

"Nothing that need worry you, dear Theodora." He waved his hand in the air and sent several small bolts of lightning shooting about. She flinched, and he laughed once more and kissed her.

"It can't hurt you. You're an immortal now, remember?" He raised one finger, and a small spark of blue-white lightning hovered above it. "Here. Take it."

She shrank from his hand. "Julian—"

"Take it, Theodora," he said kindly but firmly. "Don't you understand? You *can*. You are as immortal and divine as I am now. So take it."

She reached out a trembling hand to his. The little dancing bolt leapt and hovered in her hand, not at all hot or hurtful. It was like having a bright dragonfly capering on her fingertips, airy and curious, just gripping her lightly with tiny feet.

"It likes you," commented Julian, his eyes very turquoise in the shimmering, sparkling light. "Send it away, and call it back."

"But how—"

"Just tell it."

Go, she said in her mind to the brightness in her hand. The light vanished.

"Now call it to you," he urged.

That was harder. How was she supposed to do that? She settled for a picture, a mental image of an electric spark swaying and flickering on her fingers, and there it was again, a soft gold this time, less spiky and jagged, more flame-like, like a small torch.

A torch...

Another memory, as faint and fitful as the light that clung to her finger, teased at her and then was gone.

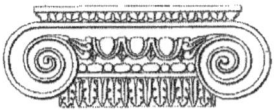

Thirteen

"IT'S BEAUTIFUL." THEO'S EYES shone as she stared at herself in the mirror in Julian's office.

She was wrapped in yards of whispering white silk, its edges embroidered with golden oak leaves. Gold oak leaf bracelets encircled her wrists, and as she watched, Julian reached over and set a deep saffron veil and a wreath of gold oak leaves on her head.

"*You're* beautiful, my Theodora." He regarded her in the mirror with deep satisfaction. "Quite perfect. All of it—perfect." He smiled.

Theo smiled back at him, though she wasn't quite as convinced. These last few days had been like a fairy story, at least on the surface. For long stretches she could live in that surface place, practicing her new divine powers and dreaming through cups of Julian's ambrosial wine. But not always. Though she could remember a little more now, it wasn't much: little flashes of her father, declaiming in Latin...books she had loved a long time ago, like Jane Austen... teaching at that school with the funny name...shopping with Renee... Memories appeared like pinpoints of light and were gone just as quickly, and the darkness they left behind seemed even darker afterward.

But Julian was always there, touching her, kissing her, feeding her ambrosia and wine until her senses were overwhelmed. It was so tempting to just live in the moment rather than to struggle to think, to remember, to reclaim who she'd once been.

Now he was handing her an oak wreath identical to the one he'd crowned her with and bowing his head. She let go of her uncomfortable thoughts and placed it on his sleek gray hair.

"Is this really happening?" she asked, looking into his smiling face. "Is this real? And this?" She waved a hand, and tiny butterflies made of rainbows began to flutter around them.

He responded by pulling her hard against him and kissing her, long and slow and deep. "*That's* real. And so is this." He took her left hand and slipped a ring onto it.

Theo lifted her hand and stared at it. The setting was of a tiny cluster of oak leaves, encircling a disc of lapis lazuli. Another memory slid into place: it was the seal they had looked for together in the museum, last fall.

"You see? I knew then that this was real, Theodora. It *is* happening, and I couldn't be happier." He ran his hands over her hips. "Happy as I am to be going to this symposium, though, I wish it were already over so that I could take you home and back to bed."

"Home?"

"To my house. It's all prepared for you, dearest. Surely you don't want to return to dreary Graves and sleep alone again, do you?" He laughed and kissed her. "Let us go. It's nearly time. Are you ready for our little presentation?"

But as they swept down the stairs toward the Great Room, Theo shivered. Despite her casual creation of the lovely little butterflies in Julian's office, her new powers still mystified and confused her and were not always so well-behaved: she counted herself lucky that she had summoned butterflies, not wasps. Only yesterday she had tried to summon a glass of water and instead created a bucket, which promptly poured itself over her head. And Friday she had shattered every light bulb in Dr. Waterman's living room, simply by pointing at the light-switch without thinking. Julian had assured her that her control over her power would improve, that she would soon be comfortable with her new senses and abilities. But now she had to emerge from the cocoon he had spun around them, and try out her still-wet wings. It was frightening to return to the real world when she herself no longer felt real, when memory of her past had faded into gray, consumed by the present.

Worst of all, now she had to deal with others, human and divine. What would the rest of the faculty say when she came in to this symposium with Julian?

"Do they already know?" she asked him nervously, holding his arm as they came to the doors of the Great Room.

"Let's say some may suspect. But they would presume nothing before I formally declared it. I am their master, after all."

Their master. He said the words with such careless assurance. She shivered again.

Julian opened the doors with a wave of his hand, then paused and looked down at her with an odd expression. To her surprise he took her in his arms and kissed her as he had just kissed her upstairs, deep and slow and long.

Through the kiss Theo heard the hum of conversation from the Great Room abruptly cease. Another memory teased at the back of her mind, something to do with being kissed here like this some other time...but then Julian took her arm once more and led her inside.

If anything, the Great Room was even more beautiful

tonight than any of her hazy memories of it: more candles glowed around the room, more incense wafted up from small bronze holders and filled the room with the scent of ambrosia. But this time the candelabra were not sensibly sitting on tables but drifted about the room, hovering wherever they thought they were needed by the laughing, chatting, white-clad guests. This time there were no costumed undergraduates serving wine and hors d'oeuvres. Instead five fauns, goat-legged below, human above, stepped daintily through the room on polished hooves, carrying pitchers of wine and trays of food.

"Oh," said Theo softly when one turned and smiled at her, sweeping a courtly bow. Though they were no more than four feet tall, she knew that they were not children. She nodded politely back, noticing with delight the creature's delicate pointed ears, topped with a wispy tuft of hair.

"Julian!" called a voice. It was Paul who bounded up to them, and yet it wasn't. His blond hair was almost metallic in its shine, and his forget-me-not blue eyes were preternaturally bright. Theo remembered that she was seeing him as he truly was, her perception undimmed by mortal eyes.

"And my lady," he added softly, bowing to Theo as well. With a twirl of his fingers he called into being a golden rose, spun from candlelight, and handed it to her.

She took it with a smile and thanked him, and heard a collective sigh from around the room. Looking up, she saw Julian nod his approval to Paul. Could she return the greeting? She stared hard at her hand and concentrated. *Music!* she thought, unable to articulate any further. A blob of light appeared which quickly formed itself into a tiny silver bird. It strutted back and forth on her hand, fixed her with its bright eyes, and sang a few liquid notes. She handed it to Paul with a relieved smile, grateful she hadn't conjured a frog instead, and said, "For when your own music must rest."

The sigh from around the room was even louder that time, and a scattering of applause sounded.

Paul laughed and held up the little bird. "A charming gift from a charming lady," he cried, and set it on his shoulder. "Welcome indeed," he said more quietly to her.

It was like a signal. All the assembled guests, the department faculty and some others Theo did not recognize, began to move toward her and Julian.

Marlowe reached them first. She was pleased that she could remember his name. "Show-off," he muttered to her. "As if it weren't obvious enough what's happened. How much did he give you?" He waved his silver cup under her nose, and an aroma of ambrosia wafted from it. "Nice to have you among us, though I was maybe expecting it to happen some other way. I always liked you."

"Thank you, Marlowe. I like you too. But what do you mean, some other w—"

Renee, clad in a pale pink *stola*, interrupted them. She threw her arms around Theo and hugged her. "That was spectacular, darling! You look lovely. It'll be so nice to have another— another *woman* around." She sniffed and looked pointedly at Di Hunter. "We'll have lots of fun together, you'll see. We have to go out for a drink soon, so we can talk."

"I tremble to think," murmured Marlowe to no one.

"Quiet, you." Renee sniffed. "You're one to talk."

"True. We must remember that our rooms are just a few doors apart in the proverbial glass house."

"Really, Marlowe. I'm a respectably married woman." Renee almost succeeded in looking scandalized.

"Like that's ever stopped you? Hmm. Maybe I ought to get married. It seems the fashion these days. Too bad you're already taken, Theo." There was a strange twist to his smile that bothered her.

"What's wrong?" she asked him.

"Don't you remember?"

"I'm trying to, but I don't know what it is I'm supposed to be remembering."

"Whom, you mean."

"Marlowe, what are you talking about?" She put a hand on his arm and looked at him imploringly. "Do you have any idea what this has been like for me? There are moments when I literally struggle to remember my own name, let alone all the other fragments of memory that keep flitting through—"

"Now, now, Marlowe, that's enough. Don't monopolize Theodora. That's my job." Julian appeared suddenly at her side.

Marlowe bowed and stepped away from them, but Theo heard him mutter under his breath as he did so, "—what he'll say when he gets here. He *is* my friend, after all."

"What did you say?" she called after him.

"Nothing, darling." Julian took her arm and walked her away from the frowning Marlowe. They came face to face with Dr. Waterman, arm-in-arm with a woman.

Theo couldn't help staring. Dr. Waterman's companion was almost as beautiful as Renee, with elegant upswept hair and delicate features, all a soft pale green. She wore darker green robes that complimented her skin, and a necklace of enormous pearls. She smiled sweetly at Theo.

"Julian." Dr. Waterman bowed his head shortly. "Theo." His face was expressionless.

"Arthur. And Amphitrite! How lovely to see you, my dear. So kind of you to come on such short notice. Theodora, my darling, this is my dear brother's wife, Amphitrite. Trite, may I present my beloved Theodora?"

"Welcome, Theodora." Her voice was soft and musical. "Arthur has often spoken of you and your kind care of his pets."

"Thank you." Theo took the woman's outstretched hands in hers. Her skin was warm and supple, but some-thing about it was not quite right. With a little start Theo realized that the backs of her hands, her arms, and indeed much of her that was visible was covered in the tiniest of scales.

"I have a present for you. A little gift from my home, to welcome you here." She reached into a fold of her robe and took out another strand of pearls, as magnificent as her own. She reached up and fastened them around Theo's neck. "There. I think they become you. Wear them often. They become sad if you do not."

"Thank you," breathed Theo, touching them in awe.

"Thank you, Trite. It is a lovely gift for my bride," said Julian warmly. Theo saw him look at Dr. Waterman as he spoke. Dr. Waterman did not meet his eyes.

"And how nice it is to see all three brothers here. I have not seen so many of our kin gathered together in many years," continued Amphitrite. Theo followed her gaze and saw Dr. Bellow standing in a corner, hovering possessively over a wo-man she recognized as the President of the university's assistant.

"Not everyone is here tonight," put in Dr. Waterman. He glanced at Julian as he spoke. "I didn't see June arrive."

Julian shrugged, but a faint line appeared between his brows. "I didn't expect her to. I believe that she had plans to visit the Bahamas this week, so it's not surprising that she isn't back yet. But now that you mention it, we do all seem to be here. Almost all, anyway."

Just then, the Great Room door banged open. The candelabra flew into the corners of the room, trying to shield each other from the gust of air that rushed in. From outside Theo heard the clock in the tower chime eight times.

"Ah," said Julian with satisfaction. "I think our company is now complete." He took Theo's hand and kissed it. "Shall we continue greeting our guests, my dear? Perhaps some refreshment first."

He held out a hand and a large crystal goblet appeared in it, brimming with gold liquid. He held it to her lips and she drank, feeling a fresh wave of blissful calm spread through her. It was too bad Dr. Waterman did not seem to approve of her new estate; his displeasure had been evident. But what did that matter? Everyone else had been delighted with her—Paul, Renee, Marlowe...her euphoria slipped a little. Maybe not Marlowe. But everyone else.

The candles emerged from their corner and redistributed themselves once more as Theo and Julian moved back to the center of the room. They illuminated the nervously conversing knots of guests that had gathered at a distance in a rough circle around one trio.

Theo saw that Marlowe was one of the three. His dark beard, usually so extravagantly full and curling, looked disheveled. As she watched him, she saw why: he kept reaching up to tug at it with an air of abstraction. She wanted to call out to him to leave it alone before he tugged it out by the roots, and had actually opened her mouth to do so. But Julian spoke first.

"Welcome, guests! I'm delighted you were able to come," he cried in his richest, fullest tone.

The three of them turned. For the first time Theo noticed that two of them wore not togas or *himations*, but normal twenty-first-century street clothes. That was surprising. Julian was a stickler for proper attire at symposia. But their lack of costume didn't seem to bother him. In fact, he looked positively elated at the sight of them: his eyes were shining with suppressed glee.

The tall woman wore a smartly cut gray worsted pants suit. Her hair was short and curling around a face that was handsome rather than beautiful. Her calm gray eyes surveyed them coolly.

"It's nice to be back, if only for a visit. You're looking well, father," she replied in a clear, silvery voice.

Father? What? Theo looked up at Julian and saw his mouth twist a little. If this woman was his daughter, that would mean she had to be...a little bubble of pleased excitement expanded in her chest. Athena had always been her favorite goddess, and now here she was...but why was her greeting so chilly and strained?

She turned back to the newcomers. Her euphoria fled as she met the wide, shocked eyes of the third person standing there, and memory—all of her memory—returned to her in a sickening, choking flood.

Grant.

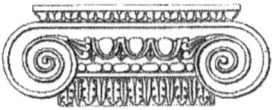

Fourteen

"HOW CLEVER OF YOU to arrive at this moment, my friends," continued Julian. "You're just in time to meet my beloved consort and hear our announcement. Theodora, this is one of our former professors, now of the famed Eleusinian Institute. May I present my daughter, Olivia Weaver?"

"Oh, cut the horse puckey, Julian," said Olivia. "What do you think you're up to?" She looked at Theo and her brows contracted.

"And I believe you already know Mr. Proctor." Julian took her hand and raised it to his lips as he stared at Grant.

Theo stared also, still drowning in a torrent of thoughts and words and memories that threatened to submerge her completely. Grant. She'd forgotten Grant. This was what she had been struggling to remember. This was not...this was not what she... Grant! Images flashed through her mind like lightning: Grant's dimples as he spun her stories of orating moose, his eyes wide and wondering after their first kiss, his austere beauty wrapped in a snowy white toga one November night, the agony in his face as he sat in the lounge drinking that foul-smelling liquid...

But that was nothing to the pain that she saw in him now. "Grant," she whispered. More memories flooded back. She was supposed to meet him here tonight, to discuss—to discuss something—

Olivia was still looking at her with that small frown. "I'm waiting, Pops. What are you up to now?" she asked, more sharply.

Through a haze, Theo heard Julian wince at the "Pops." "If you would all care to come closer, I'll be happy to tell you 'what's up' as Olivia so elegantly puts it," he said, voice raised to reach all the guests. He slipped his arm around Theo and held her tight against his side.

"No!" She twisted away from him. He'd done this all on purpose—had drugged her, kept her so befuddled that she could hardly remember her own name. And wiped Grant from her mind—the man she truly cared for—

"Theodora!" Julian's hand gripped her shoulder like a vise. He pulled her back against him and held her there; no amount of struggling could break his hold. She stood tensed and gasping as she stared at Grant and...Olivia? *This* was Grant's Olivia? Pallas Athena, chaste goddess of wisdom and war? This handsome but rather stern-looking woman was the Olivia she had mistrusted and disliked sight unseen?

"I would again like to thank you all for coming this evening," Julian began, intruding on her fevered thoughts. He smiled tenderly down at her. "Theodora and I are delighted that you could all be here with us tonight to acknowledge and celebrate our union."

Theo turned away, feeling physically ill. Grant's face contorted and he made a sudden movement. Olivia put a hand on his arm.

"It is not often that we meet a mortal worthy to enter our

ranks. And so it is with the greatest happiness that I present my Theodora to you. Of course, many of you already know her as student, colleague, friend. I have the unique privilege of knowing her as those things, plus more: lover, immortal, and now soon to be wife."

"No," she whispered.

"Indeed," Julian continued, "in the future, I hope and plan to present her to you in another role, one I think she is as ideally suited to as the others: mother of my children."

Theo stared up at Julian in shock.

"After the week Theodora and I have just spent together, I would not be surprised if this were to happen sooner rather than later," he confided with an arch smile. Someone tittered nervously.

On the edge of her field of vision Theo saw Grant's face turn gray. She tried once again to twist from Julian's grasp but he held her immobilized against him. He tilted her face to his and kissed her as he had outside the Great Room door, but with even greater relish. She whimpered.

"I knew as soon as I met this young woman that she was extraordinary." Julian gazed down at her, smiling. "As I came to know and then love her, a dream came to me, a dream that I knew only she would be able to help me accomplish. From our union will be born a new race of heroes, heroes who will help us introduce a new Olympian Age. Once again we will take our proper place and reign over a world set right. With my Theodora, I will give this to you."

Someone cheered then. And then someone else. In a few seconds all the gathered guests were clapping, with a few exceptions. Dr. Waterman was sadly shaking his head, his arm tight around Amphitrite. Marlowe was clapping, but his smile had a sardonic edge to it. Olivia actually looked amused as she looked at Julian. And Grant—

With a supreme effort, she wrenched away from Julian and ran to Grant, tearing off her veil and oak wreath as she did so. She caught him just as he seemed about to collapse. "Grant!" she cried fiercely. He sagged against her, and she remembered the feel of him in her arms, more ruggedly built than Julian, less elegant of form but so real, so *right*.

"Theodora?" Julian called over the fading shouts and cheers. He stalked over to them and tried to pull her away from Grant.

Theo clung to him. "No!" she declared into the now-silent room. "You tricked me, Julian. You seduced me into forgetting Grant. But Grant is the one I love." She held Grant's shaking form against her shoulder and stared defiantly at Julian.

"Deception?" Julian laughed softly. "Did you know he and I knew each other of old?"

"He said that he'd met you before," Theo said. Grant's body tensed.

"Had met me? Oh, that's rich!" Julian's laugh rolled over her. "He had more than 'met me.' He is my kinsman, my cousin. He once fought under my banner and rendered me an inestimable service. Once, indeed, I called him friend and mentor. *I*, Theodora. I called him these things, and looked on him as a wiser elder brother."

"Grant?" she said uncertainly, pulling back to look at him.

He did not meet her eyes. "It is true."

Julian's voice became low and venomous. "But it happened that one day we disagreed. My dearest friend, my wise elder brother had found something he cared for more, and gave it the one thing that would keep it from perishing of its own stupidity—stole it from me. Some say he had help," he glared briefly at Olivia, "though that has never been proven."

"Oh, get over it, Julian," Olivia sighed. "So he gave fire to man. You got more than your own back on him. Thirty thousand years chained to a rock while a vulture eats out your liver every day would seem to me more than adequate punishment for any crime."

Theo felt Grant jerk and nearly dropped him; only her new divine reflexes kept him upright, for her mind was wheeling. She stared at him, and read the truth in his eyes.

"Yes, Prometheus's punishment was sweet to me. And it was sweet to let my son Herakles be the one to release him: it made me look magnanimous. But even thirty thousand years of torture could not wipe out the insult. He had defied me. I let him come back to Olympus after Herakles set him free, let him resume his seat of honor. But he never resumed his place in my heart: as before I had loved him, so now I hated him. When our reign as the Gods ended, I didn't weep to see him leave. In time I assumed he had faded away, like so many other gods have."

Grant looked up at Julian and his back straightened. "I, fade away? I was probably the one Olympian least likely to do that."

"Why should I assume that? I thought you'd been dead for fifteen hundred years. I knew when you arrived here that you were an immortal. But the world is crawling with little gods who slink from life to life like beetles, trying to keep from being squashed. Only when it was clear you were interfering with Theodora did I take the trouble to learn which little insect of a godling you were."

"A little insect of a godling whose bite still stings, doesn't it?" Grant shot back. "And you didn't learn who I was till just recently. So much for being all-seeing."

Theo expected Julian to attack Grant; his nostrils flared and his eyes narrowed to slits as he glared at him. She drew herself up, prepared to shield Grant with her body if necessary. But then Julian's face relaxed; indeed, he smiled.

"Yes, you are right. I did just find out who you are. But I found out a few other interesting facts about you as well. Once you were among the mightiest of the Titans. But I hear that things have changed lately. Not feeling quite the thing anymore, are you? You should be more careful of your choice of beverages, my old friend. One doesn't really know where those fancy bottled waters come from, what nasty river flowing out of—"

"Julian! You said you wouldn't tell!" cried Renee suddenly, throwing herself at him. "You said you wouldn't tell them I told you. Now you've dragged *me* into the middle of this mess. You *promised*!" She burst into tears and started to beat on his chest with her fists.

"Go, quickly!" said a voice in Theo's ear. She looked up and saw that it was Olivia. She was staring at Renee. "Get Grant and go. I don't know what's going to happen next, but I think you two need to talk before anything else occurs. I'll try to keep the interruptions going after Renee calms down." She pushed at Theo's shoulder.

Theo did not need to be told a second time. She grabbed Grant's hand and began to sidle away from Julian and Renee.

My office is open, said a voice in her head. She looked up and saw Dr. Waterman staring at her. He nodded at her, and she nodded back.

"Come on," she murmured to Grant. "Upstairs." Halfway across the room she broke into a trot, still tugging Grant behind her. Passing the bust of Octavian on the stair landing, she resisted the impulse to give it a savage kick.

She pulled the unresisting Grant into Dr. Waterman's office, closed the door, and shoved him toward a chair.

But he did not sit down. He stood still, staring at the floor for several seconds. Then he slowly raised his eyes to her.

"You're wearing the *stola*," he said.

Theo stared at him. "What?" Then she remembered. Only married women wore the *stola*. Unmarried girls wore the toga. She flushed. "I hadn't noticed."

"No?" His voice was dry.

"No, I hadn't," she replied angrily. "I've barely noticed anything lately, because Julian's kept me so drunk on his ambrosia wine that I haven't been able to think two consecutive thoughts until just now."

"It's true, then. He's given you ambrosia. Marlowe said so." Why was he looking at her like that?

"He tricked me into it. He—" A sob filled her throat as she remembered. "He came to me in the sh-shape of a cat. On a rainy night, so I h-had to let it come inside and curl up on the foot of my bed—" She turned away from him, struggling to regain her breath.

"Oh, Theo." Grant's arms were suddenly around her. She turned and buried her face against his chest and let her tears flow. How could she have forgotten this? How could she forget his scent, his touch? The thought made her cry all the harder. He held her tightly, stroking her hair and murmuring under his breath until her sobs quieted.

After a few minutes he leaned back to look at her. "Well, you do make a beautiful goddess," he said with a ghost of a smile.

"Grant, don't—"

"Ssh. I'm sorry. I didn't mean to make you cry again." He gathered her to his chest.

After a few more minutes she was able to ask him, "Is it true? Are you really—who he said you were? Prometheus?"

"Yes, I am. Or I was. I haven't used that name in centuries." He sighed and continued stroking her hair.

"Prometheus," she said again, in wonderment. Man's first savior—until another savior came along to replace him. But he'd survived nonetheless, like the other gods—but for a better reason. "No one could ever forget how you defied Julian." She touched his face.

"Julian needed to be defied, or he would have been even

worse than he is. He was born a king, so it never occurred to him that he couldn't do as he pleased. So when he tried to turn on men and destroy them, I saved them. It was bad enough when I fooled him into accepting the lesser parts of animals for sacrifice. But when I gave man fire..."

Theo remembered the horrible twisting scar on his side and shuddered. "How did you stand it?"

"I...I'm not sure. Time and consciousness are different for the gods. It's part of why I'm still here, I think. That and the fact that men wouldn't let me die. And my own nature, the one they'd given me, betrayed me. I couldn't stop caring about them."

Theo gazed at him in wonder. Prometheus. She had fallen in love with Prometheus, had teased him and held him and kissed him, presumed to teach him how to love, dreamed of spending her life with him. And now—"Why didn't you tell me any of this?"

He smiled grimly, releasing her and taking a few nervous paces away, then back. "Would you have believed me? If I had taken you in my arms back at Christmas and said, 'Hello, darling, I'm Prometheus, and you've fallen into the middle of the 3025th reunion of Mount Olympus High School, watch out for that Julian character because he's got an eye for the ladies,' would you have listened to me?"

Theo bit her lip. "You've changed again. You were so sick before last week that you frightened me badly. Why are you better now?"

To her surprise he laughed. "Better now? Now? Oh Theo. I find myself in the grip of mortal illness, and you tell me I'm looking better!"

"Stop it Grant! What do you mean?"

"But I'm not better now. Oh, I may look better, and it'll take years to finally finish me off. But unless they find a cure for mortality, I'm sunk."

"For mortality—but you're a *god*."

"Not anymore." He looked down at the floor and smiled that mirthless smile again. "I am now as mortal as—as you used to be. This is what my Pemberley was all about. When I was ill after Christmas, it wasn't illness. I went to Italy then because the quickest path down to Hades is there, in Cumae. Don't you remember your *Aeneid*? I went there to collect water from the five rivers that flow out of Tartarus. Drinking the mixed water of those rivers was the only way Olivia and I could think of to kill the god in me and make me mortal. We weren't even sure it would work until just a few weeks ago."

"But why?" Theo cried in anguish.

"So that I could be with you. So that I could love you as a man, and live my life with you as a man, and die with you some day as a man." His words, quiet and steady, hit her like bullets. "Being a god has held little for me for centuries. I had nothing better to do, so I volunteered to come here for the year because we at Eleusinian like to keep an eye on Julian and his antics. And then I met you, and did something I'd never done before: I fell in love.

"You joked and kidded me about it, but I was in desperate need of those humanities classes you gave me. Even though you did your best, I failed. I couldn't love you back enough, or in the right way, or anything. I thought I was about to lose you, so I talked to Olivia over Thanksgiving about this idea I'd gotten from reading *Pride and Prejudice*. I wanted to become a man so that I could love you, and then one day I would die. The two things I had never done in all the millennia of my existence, the two things that my beloved mankind could do but I couldn't— and I would do them now with you and be glad of it. I drank that horrible water, and was grateful for every burning, twisting pain it sent through me as it destroyed my godhood, because every drop of it brought me closer to you."

"Grant..." A similar pain twisted her own vitals.

"Isn't it ironic? I probably finished becoming mortal just about the same time you finished becoming immortal. I'd planned on proposing to you tonight—telling you all these things, and asking if we could spend the rest of our lives together. Because I finally understood what the worst thing I could suffer would be: it would be to watch you grow old, and die, and know you were lost to me forever." A tear trickled unchecked down his face. "I failed, though. I was so wrapped up in recreating myself for you that I neglected you, and let Julian walk in and waltz out with you without a murmur."

"No! He doesn't have me. He tricked me!"

"Doesn't he?" Grant shook his head. "After thirty thousand years I thought I knew all about pain. But no one ever told me about the agony of seeing the woman you love taken by another. Yes, you were tricked—and I made it possible for him to trick you. You were distraught and bewildered about me—I was aware enough of that—and he played on those emotions. And now he gets a beautiful consort to bear him children and is able to humiliate me publicly in the process." Grant's voice was calm though more tears now slid down his cheeks.

"But I don't want him! I want you!" Theo said desperately.

Grant crossed the space between them to pickup her hand and looked at the ring Julian had placed there just an hour ago. "I'm not sure you have any choice in the matter. Maybe if I'd come home with you and put my ring on your finger myself back in December, none of this would have happened."

His ring! She looked at her right hand. "It's gone," she whispered. She tugged at Julian's ring, trying to pull it off. It would have been easier to pull off one of her fingers.

"Don't bother. He won't let you remove his ring. It marks you as his. Do you think he'd have left mine on your hand while he was trying to wipe your mind of me?" The hurt in Grant's eyes deepened as he looked at her hand. "Was it—was he good? Did you enjoy it?" he continued harshly.

Theo felt like she had been slapped. "Grant!"

They stared at each other. "Oh, Theo," he said at last, and looked down at his feet. "I've succeeded in ruining this beyond repair, haven't I?"

She reached out and took him by his shoulders. "No, it's not over! I'm not going to give you up just like that—"

"My darling Theodora," said Julian's voice suddenly, from nowhere. She jumped back involuntarily. "If you're done with your little talk with Mr. Proctor, we would appreciate it if you two could sneak back down here. We have some unfinished business to attend to."

"When I'm good and ready," she shouted back.

"Splendid! I'll see you in a moment, then." His voice was mocking.

And then Grant vanished.

"No!" Theo lunged across the short distance that had separated them, but he was gone. How had Julian been able to do that to him?

Grant's no longer a god, Sherlock. Julian can do what he wants with him.

"Not if I can help it," she said out loud, and stalked out of the room.

Fifteen

Down in the Great Room the guests still milled about, though now the fauns were huddled by the door, looking fearful. Theo gave them a reassuring smile as she passed, but they only looked more frightened. She probably had a face like a Gorgon right now; no wonder they were terrified.

Julian still stood in the center of the room, his gold wreath still straight on his sleek head, his tunic and *himation* unmussed. Renee was being comforted by Dr. Forge-Smythe and Amphitrite, and Theo had the irrelevant thought that Renee's pink robes would look quite nice on her pale green companion. Then her attention was drawn back to Julian.

Next to him Grant sat bound and gagged in a chair. There was a crown of willow twigs set awry on his brow. Theo frowned and moved toward him, hand outstretched to pluck it off, but Julian shook his head.

"No, my dear. I must ask you not to touch him."

"Must you humiliate him by tying him up and gagging him like a common criminal?"

"Alas, yes. I'm afraid I must." Julian looked sorrowful, but there was a glint in his eyes that belied his words and tone.

"Fine," she snapped. "What did you want me for?"

"What do you think I want you for? To join me so that we can complete our celebration here and start our life together."

"I don't think you were listening before, Julian. I said no. I don't want to be your wife or bear your children. You tricked me into being your lover before, but I don't want you. I love Grant."

"But darling, you agreed to be my wife. Remember?" He cocked an ear toward the ceiling with an exaggerated gesture, and Theo was horrified to hear the sound of kissing and her own voice saying 'Yes, Julian. I am yours,' at a level that reverberated and echoed in the room.

Grant winced and shut his eyes.

"That was in singularly poor taste, in my opinion," said Olivia. Theo had forgotten about her. She came to stand a few feet from Theo, her face grim.

"Taste is not the issue right now, my dear. Winning is." Julian glided over to Theo and put his arm around her. She tried to pull away and when he would not let her, held her-self as stiff and still as a statue.

"No, Julian, the verdict's not quite in." Olivia stared at him, hands behind her back, looking thoughtful. "Do you deny that you came to Theo in the form of a cat?" she shot at him. Theo jumped; Olivia had evidently been listening in to her conversation with Grant.

He frowned at her. "No, I don't deny it."

"Because you knew how confused she was over her relationship with Grant, and how comforting a friendly, purring cat would be."

"Perhaps."

"And do you deny plying her with enhanced ambrosial wine

in extraordinary quantities?"

"Really, Olivia, I don't see that's any of your busi—"

"Do you, in short, deny manipulating Theo emotionally and physically with drugs into bed with you, and keeping her under your will for a week by those same methods?"

Julian turned a dull red as he stared down at the floor, pacing a restless circle around Grant.

"Under those circumstances, I don't think that Theo's pledge to you is binding," Olivia finished triumphantly. "You cannot hold her to a covenant you achieved by trickery."

Julian glared at her for several seconds. Then suddenly he smiled. Theo felt her heart sink into the ground at the sight of it.

"Very well," he said, and raised a hand. And once again, Grant vanished. The ropes that had bound him slipped limply to the floor. The square of cloth that had stopped his mouth fluttered onto the seat; Theo could see where his saliva had dampened it. The willow crown tumbled down beside it.

"Grant!" She lunged toward the chair. But it was too late. "What have you done with him?" she snarled at Julian. "Bring him back here now!"

Julian turned to her. "Olivia may have won a hand for you, but I still hold the rest of the cards. My dear Theodora, I give you a challenge. If you want Grant Proctor, you can have him. Provided you can find him. I'll be generous, and give you until, oh, noon on Commencement Day. If you can find him before then, then you and he are free to go. If not—"

"No! You mustn't harm him!" she cried.

"Who said I was going to?" he said with another horrible smile. "I don't have to. If you can't find him by noon on Commencement Day, he goes free anyway. But you'll remain here as my consort and yield to my will in all things. And then we'll watch while life destroys Grant for me. Too bad it's considerably less than thirty thousand years this time. But the joy of watching him die of old age and illness, and in the knowledge that you are mine—well, I guess I would call that fair."

Theo stared at him, too angry and shaken for tears. Oh, Grant—

"Blast it, Julian," said Dr. Waterman, pushing forward. "This is going too far. We swore not to do anything to call mortal attention to ourselves, but you just made a department instructor disappear. Furthermore, I don't care for this game of yours. I'm going to help Theo find—"

Julian raised one hand, and Dr. Waterman was struck dumb. "Are you, Arthur?" he said gently. "I don't think so. You're my brother and cannot go against me. That goes for all of you here," he continued in a stronger voice. "You are my guests tonight and are beholden to me. If Theodora's going to try to defy me, she must do it without your help."

"Not entirely, Julian." Olivia's voice was loud and confident. "I'm not your invited guest. I choose to help find my colleague, and you can't stop me."

Theo turned, feeling hopeful for the first time. "You will?"

"Of course." She nodded calmly. "Grant is my friend."

"Is this your idea of filial piety, daughter? You sadden me." Julian sighed. "Well, this seems to have brought my lovely party to a halt. Such a pity. Would you all excuse us?" He turned to Theo and held out his hand to her. "Come, my dear."

She stared at him. "I don't think so."

"Would you do me the courtesy of speaking with me in my office for a few moments? Or do you fear me?"

Yes, as a matter of fact, she did. But it didn't seem politic to admit it in front of the gathered guests. She glanced at Olivia, who gave her a just-perceptible nod.

"Very well," she said with as much dignity as she could muster despite her fury and anguish, and started to walk toward the door ahead of him. In an instant she found him at her side, her hand in his.

"Manners, manners. Just because we are temporarily at odds doesn't mean we should treat each other badly."

She snatched her hand away. "Temporarily?"

"Of course. I *will* win, you know. In time you'll be glad of it. In the meanwhile, I should hate to see our friendship affected by this momentary discord."

They were on the stairs. Theo stopped. "If you were so concerned about preserving our 'friendship,' as you call it, then maybe you should have thought about that before you sneaked into my bed disguised as a cat."

"Please, my dear." He propelled her up the stairs and down the hall to his office, shutting the door behind them. He held out a chair for her. "I would offer you wine, if you would—"

Theo almost choked. "You *dare* to offer me your—"

He sighed again. "Very well, then. I thought it would be kind if I gave you the chance to yield now and save yourself several weeks of worry and upset that will only end in your failure. I assure you that Grant will be able to leave here unharmed, which is not something I can guarantee if you insist on searching for him."

"What's that supposed to mean?"

"Exactly what it sounds like, my dear Theodora. There are dangers in your attempting to rescue him, dangers that are unlikely to harm you as an immortal. But Grant is no longer a god, but is now prone to the frailty and weaknesses of mortal men. Furthermore, I only think it fair to warn you that the longer it takes for you to find him, if you ever do, the less able I am to guarantee that he will leave his captivity unscathed and unchanged."

"What do you mean 'unscathed and unchanged?'" Theo's throat suddenly felt tight and dry, so that she almost wished she'd said yes to wine. Almost. "You're not being very clear."

"Why should I be? I have no wish to help you in this. I merely thought you should be acquainted with all the facts before you made a final decision."

"You are *too* kind."

With a sudden movement he came around behind her and put his hands on her shoulders. "Stop being angry with me and listen for a moment. You're a goddess now, beloved by the Lord of the Sky, the King of the Gods. Think about that for a moment. As my consort you can do anything. *Anything.* See the world. Live a life of opulence beyond your wildest imagination." He bent to murmur in her ear. "Or even go back to Sneed and show them all what they lost through their own blindness and ignorance. Revenge can be sweet, even to gods. I should know."

Could it? A part of Theo's mind examined the thought of what returning to Sneed could be like for her now.

"Oh my dearest Theodora, the world can be ours," Julian whispered. His breath caressed her ear. "Even now it is lying before us. Let us take it together."

With a faint sense of surprise, she realized that she hadn't thought about Sneed in a long time. It didn't matter anymore. But Grant did. She didn't want the world at her feet, but Grant's hand in hers.

"Is there anything else you wished to say to me?" she said, trying to hold herself stiffly as he stroked her neck and arms.

"Can you deny that you were happy last week with me, Theodora? Can you say that you didn't take more pleasure from me than you had dreamed possible with anyone?" He tilted her head back and kissed her hard, then released her before she could even protest.

"I'll let you go now. Believe me, I don't take your and Olivia's combined powers lightly. But I will win, and I will welcome you back into my arms come May." He turned away and went to stand by his window, looking out at the night.

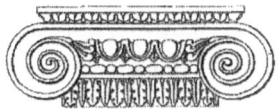

Sixteen

THE NEXT MORNING THEO was heavy-eyed as she trudged down the hall toward her classroom. She hadn't seen any department faculty yet, which was just as well, for she had no idea what she would say to any of them. As she passed Grant's classroom she glanced inside, expecting to see Dr. Waterman standing at the front of the room.

Instead, she saw Grant.

With a wildly pounding heart, she almost ran into the classroom. "You're okay!" she gasped.

"Oh. Hello, Theo. Nice vacation?" he asked, turning from the board where he had been writing.

"G-Grant?" she breathed, still staring.

He looked at her. And suddenly she saw that someone else looked through his eyes. Then she saw his features rearrange themselves subtly, until she could see Olivia's face shining through Grant's features.

"Did you want to see me?" he—she asked.

"Uh..." Theo floundered. "It'll wait. I—I'll catch up with you after class."

Olivia gave Grant's casual wave. "Lunch?" she said.

Theo nodded mutely and stumbled into her classroom. Fortunately her own students were almost as shell-shocked as she after a week of excess in Florida and other points south, and were subdued and undemanding that day.

At noon Olivia met her for lunch. Theo felt awkward as she watched her approach in Grant's shape. What was she going to say to her? Would Olivia think she was stupid, a harlot, or, worst of all, a cold-blooded Judas? By the time Olivia sat down opposite her with a friendly smile, she was nearly shaking with nerves.

"Hello, Theo," Olivia said quietly, holding out her hand. Grant's hand. "I'm very happy to meet you at last. Last night doesn't count. '

Theo took her hand in a daze. "You are?"

"Of course I am. Grant's told me so much about you that I feel like I already know you." Her eyes were warm and friendly.

To her horrified embarrassment, Theo started to cry. "But—I betrayed Grant. How can you possibly like me?"

"No. You were tricked into forgetting Grant. Julian's responsible for his disappearance, not you. You're as much a victim as Grant is. He loves you, and I respect him more than anyone else, human or immortal. I'm bound to help you both for that reason, but also because I like what he told me of you, and would like to see you both safe back at Eleusinian. Don't cry. We'll solve this together. Julian doesn't scare me."

"He scares me." Theo took a shuddering breath and summoned a box of Kleenex. She wound up with a stack of Christmas-patterned tissue paper. Olivia smiled and summoned a handkerchief for her.

"Julian has his weaknesses, just like the rest of us." She handed it to Theo. "Now tell me everything."

"Everything?" Theo buried her nose in the hanky. How was

she supposed to tell this goddess, famed for her staunch virginity, about what she and Julian—

"I can handle it, Theo. Just because I don't choose to participate doesn't mean I hate sex, or abhor others for it. But I'm mostly interested in what he said to you last night in his office."

Theo told her about her conversation with Julian. Olivia nodded. "He was playing games with you. Testing you. Trying to see where the chinks in your armor were, and trying to psych you out. Classical warfare technique, only now it's used in boardrooms. He's a master at it," she said as she energetically pursued tortellini in Alfredo sauce around her bowl with a fork.

Theo glumly watched her over her untouched Reuben sandwich. With her new senses it was too easy to tell that the corned beef in it was a week past its use-by date. And it was even more uncomfortable to sit here staring at a Grant who wasn't Grant, hearing his voice, watching the sunlight gleam on his soft dark hair and shadow his deep-set eyes.

Olivia looked up at her. "Hey. Don't worry. I told you before. We'll find him."

"If he even wants me to find him. If he doesn't hate me for letting Julian..." she trailed off, pressing her lips together.

"Theo, listen to me. All fall and winter I heard Grant talk about you non-stop whenever he came back to Eleusinian— how wonderful you are, how kind and patient with his fumbling attempts at loving you, how terrified he was that he would blow it all and lose you to someone who would love you better."

"But why couldn't he just love me? What made it so difficult? Julian's a god too, but he—" she halted, blushing.

"It depends on what kind of god you were. Julian and the others—even me, I suppose—were made in man's image. We were prayed to, spoken to, taken inside men's heads. So we learned to be human. But Grant—he was different."

"Different how?"

"He was one of the Titans who came before us, remember. He must have been a god once to men long ago, one of those nameless gods who are now lost. But he didn't get lost. He got made into something else by the Greeks and was revered by men. But not worshipped and prayed to the way we were. So he never got into peoples' heads the way we did, to see what it was like to be human. In a way he's more god-like than any of us, because he is so remote."

Theo stared down at her plate. "So that's why he had such a hard time responding? Because he just didn't know how? And I thought his humanities lessons were just a joke."

"Oh, no. Not to him. He took them very seriously. But until he could experience life as a man, he couldn't love you the way he wanted to. And he wanted to very badly—enough to become human."

"And I went and let his worst enemy take me without a fight," Theo muttered bitterly.

"Theo, I know Julian. He's my father. You never had a chance. I know how persuasive—and devious—he can be. You know you're not the first one he's done this to. Don't blame yourself for falling for his tricks."

Theo shook her head. Why didn't Olivia understand? "But how could Grant not hate me now? I could tell when we talked that he—"

Olivia put down her fork. "I can disagree with you till I'm blue in the face, but you won't believe me until we rescue him and he can tell you himself. Of course he was hurt and angry and upset. But blame you? He knows Julian too well for that. But this isn't helping us find Grant. We need to make a plan. Where should we start?"

"Do you think it's worth talking to anyone here?" asked Theo, wiping her eyes again with Olivia's hanky.

"No. Julian was quite plain about that. No one who had

accepted his hospitality last night can help us. We'll have to do it ourselves. We'll have to turn around and out-Julian Julian. Look for the chinks in *his* armor."

"Does he have any?"

"Well, not many." Olivia sighed. "But that doesn't mean he isn't capable of making mistakes. That's what we have to look out for."

Theo pushed her plate away. "He may be a god, but you—er, *we*—are too. Why can't we just...oh, I don't know...why can't we just use our powers and just *sense* where Grant is?"

Olivia smiled gently at her. "If only it were that easy. Don't forget who Julian is. There's a reason he's the king of the gods —he's the most powerful of us all. If he wants to hide Grant from us, he can, and no power of ours will reveal it. We have to actually search for him. Not that our powers won't help, but we're in for a long, hard task. In the meanwhile—" she hesitated, then looked seriously at Theo. "In the meanwhile, be careful. You know now how devious Julian is. Don't let him catch you again."

To Theo's surprise Renee was waiting outside her Republican Rome class that afternoon. She assumed Renee was there to meet Dr. Forge-Smythe, and nodded politely as she walked past her.

"Theo, wait! I want to talk to you," Renee called, falling in step next to her. She wore a luscious pink cashmere sweater that Theo coveted but knew would clash horribly with her hair. She sighed and tried not to mind.

"Here?"

"No. Let's go have a drink. I know I could use a glass of wine right now—oh." She saw the expression on Theo's face, then shook her head irritably. "Well, *I* could. You can have something else." She took Theo's arm and steered her down the hall. They passed June Cadwallader's office, and Theo involuntarily glanced inside. June was at her desk, as usual. She looked up at Theo with an unreadable expression. But before Theo could analyze it, Renee had propelled her to the stairs.

Renee brought her to a small fashionable bar frequented by young investment brokers who reminded her uncomfortably of the male teachers at Sneed. Renee, however, was smiling as she seated herself at a table and looked around her.

"I love it here. All these red-blooded young men who've sublimated their warrior instincts in the stock market." She shivered happily. "You watch—in five minutes four of them will have had drinks sent to our table."

"To you, not me. And besides, you're married."

"I know I'm married. But that doesn't mean I can't look. It's part of my job, after all. And you'll be getting your share of drinks too, girl. Looked in a mirror lately? You're immortal now, remember? They may not know it, but they can sense it. Especially since I took over your wardrobe." Renee patted her hair and smiled at the waiter who came to take their orders. "Two mojitos please," she said briskly. As soon as he had left, she turned back to Theo and opened her mouth to speak.

But Theo beat her to it. "Are you doing this on Julian's orders?" she asked, staring at Renee through narrowed eyes.

"Of course not!"

"No?" Theo raised an eyebrow.

"Well, not *really*," she amended. "He did ask me to keep an eye on you and make sure you were all right. But I would have done this anyway tonight, Julian or no Julian. Remember I said we needed to go out for a drink soon?"

A pair of young men in gray Brooks Brothers suits strolled by their table, smiling broadly at them. Renee smiled back.

"See? I told you. You could have your pick of this place if you wanted to," she whispered after they had passed.

"I don't want the pick of any place. I want Grant," Theo replied through clenched teeth.

Renee waited while their waiter served their drinks. "Well, you're not going to get him," she said bluntly. "I know Julian. He'll win."

"Look, if that's all you brought me here to say—" Theo started to rise, but Renee reached over and pulled her back down.

"It's not what I brought you here to say. But I do want you to listen to me. Drink."

"Why?" Suddenly suspicious, Theo sniffed at her glass.

"Oh for heaven's sake, there's nothing in it," said Renee, rolling her blue eyes.

"I can't help being gun-shy, can I?"

"I want you to drink because you're so uptight you squeak. Now relax and listen. I'll be honest with you. Who would you be better off with? The king of the gods who adores you to distraction, or a former god who barely understood love enough to hold your hand?"

"That's none of your business," Theo said stiffly.

"But it is. I want you to stay here. I *like* you. June and Di are insufferable and Persephone never was my type. It's lonely for me here. I was so glad when I heard about you, because I thought I would finally have a friend." She looked away.

Theo found that she was unexpectedly touched, but kept her voice brisk. "Renee, you're the goddess of love. How can you be lonely?

"I'm lonely because I'm bored. No one is interested in romantic love these days, outside of novels. I do love a good romance novel." She sighed. "Look around you. Who writes love poetry anymore? It's just awful. All anyone does is watch television and movies about sex and power and think they're love stories."

"Then you should be able to appreciate my position," said Theo. "Grant and I love each other. Why won't you help us?"

"Because Julian loves you too."

Theo snorted. "He would seem to be the exemplar of sex and power masquerading as love. Forget it, Renee."

"All right. You say you love Grant. So aren't his health and well-being the most important things to you?" Renee leaned forward and looked hard at her.

"Go on."

"Wouldn't it be nobler to give him up and yield to Julian, so that Grant can be released? What a poem that would make, renouncing your love to set your lover free! And you'd still have yummy Julian to sleep with in return for your sacrifice—"

To her own surprise, Theo laughed. "But I don't want to be part of an epic love poem and have my name inscribed in the stars. I just want to find Grant and live a normal boring life with him for the next fifty or so years. It's called 'happily ever after' in those romance novels you claim to like so much. You'll have to look somewhere else for inspiration for new poetry." She stood up. "I'm glad to be your friend, Renee. But not if you're going to give me silly lectures like this again. I'll see you later." She walked away from the table, dodging the waiter who was carrying two more mojitos to their table. From the corner of her eye she saw the investment bankers watch her leave with disappointment writ large on their faces.

"But he could be anywhere. Antarctica, for all we know." Theo lay on her couch in the Great Room late that Tuesday evening, staring miserably at the molded plaster ceiling.

Olivia slouched in a chair nearby. She had relaxed her Grant-form, and kept wavering back into her own shape as she sat. It was disconcerting to watch, to say the least. "No. Nothing like that," she said, rubbing her forehead.

"Why not? Julian says he's playing to win. So wouldn't the most inaccessible place on earth be the most logical place to put him?"

"Yes and no. You need to understand Julian. He *does* want to win. He's used to winning. But it won't be as much of a victory for him unless you have a chance at winning too, but fail. That's just the way he is. So he won't make it completely impossible to find Grant. If anything he'll leave a few clues around, mixed with a lot of red herrings. We just have to find them and figure out which are clues and which aren't."

Theo groaned. "All right then. Maybe he changed him into a moose and sent him back to Eleusinian." She squint-ed at her book bag lying on the floor beside her and tried to turn it into a porcupine. Instead it became a large red tomato pincushion, complete with pins and strawberry-shaped emery bag. She sighed and waved it back into its proper form.

She had expected Olivia to laugh, but she didn't. Instead she looked thoughtful and scribbled a line on the notepad in her lap. "I'll have someone look into it right away," she replied.

"You're joking, right?"

"No. Were you?"

"Uh, yeah," Theo said sheepishly.

"It's not all that far-fetched. Except that I don't think his power would be as effective there. But that's the general idea. Whatever it is, it won't be straightforward."

"So he could be right here, disguised as this sofa?"

"Conceivably." Olivia squinted at it, and Theo clutched at a cushion. *Oh, sorry, darling. I didn't mean to sit on you*, she thought absurdly. But then Olivia shook her head.

"No. He's not. Anyway, it was too uncomplicated a hiding place."

"What if Julian keeps moving him around?"

"That's another possibility," Olivia replied bleakly. "He never said Grant would always be in one place." She sighed, then gave herself a little shake. "Tell me again what Julian said to you the other night."

Theo closed her eyes and thought. Being an immortal would make graduate school easier: it gave her extraordinary powers of enhanced recall. She recited, "He said that though I would be able to search for him safely, Grant had lost the protection of being a god and...and the longer it took to find him, the less likely it was that he would be unchanged and unscathed." She opened her eyes.

"'Unchanged and unscathed,'" murmured Olivia. "That would imply that he has been somehow changed, and would likely suffer damage as a result."

"Changed how? Damaged how?" Dear god, no...

"I don't know."

The door to the Great Room opened then. Olivia sat up quickly and turned back into Grant, and Theo lifted her arm off her face and looked at the door.

Julian stood there, watching them.

Theo froze, for the expression on Julian's face as he stared at her recumbent form startled her. It was an expression of sheer naked hunger.

"Good evening, father," said Olivia calmly, taking back her own shape again.

Julian nodded briefly, not taking his eyes off Theo. The turquoise was dark and turbulent today. Then he turned on his heel and left.

"What was that all about?" she asked Olivia shakily.

"Who knows? Nothing, quite possibly. But you never know

with him." Olivia lapsed back into her slouch, and Theo went back to staring at the ceiling.

Had Julian walked in on them on purpose? It was the first time she had seen him since Sunday night, for she had avoided going anywhere near his office since then. On Sunday he had been his usual confident self. Tonight all traces of that had vanished. He had looked like a starving man as he stared at her from the doorway.

Could it be true? Could he be so intent on winning not just because it was what he was used to, but because he truly wanted her? As dispassionately as she could, Theo thought back over her week with him. Was the glow in his eyes, the warmth in his voice, the tenderness of his touch, love? Or was it just a passing fancy, the way it had been for him with dozens of other women, both mortal and immortal? What would have happened if Grant had never returned from spring break? Would she have been content with Julian?

Taking a deep breath, she thought again about their time together. No. Julian was not love. Grant was.

"Good morning, Theo. Or should I say Theodora?"

Theo looked up from her scalding cup of coffee. She had been staring into the steam curling up from it, hoping it would form a picture of where Grant was if she concentrated on it hard enough. All she kept getting were vaguely bovine figures, striding about before her in the wisps of steam. Moose, perhaps. She must make sure Olivia had the grounds of the Eleusinian Institute checked.

Marlowe stood over her, holding a cup of coffee and a muffin. He wasn't smiling.

"Hi, Marlowe. Call me whatever you want. My wishes don't

seem to enter into anything anymore." She waved the latest moose-like form into the air and nodded at the empty seat opposite her.

He sat down, still regarding her. "You don't look so good."

"Thank you." She took a sip of her coffee. It didn't burn her tongue, to her momentary surprise. Oh yes, wasn't it *swell* being a goddess? She was immune to such little annoyances as pain and injury now, wasn't she?

"I'm sorry. But you don't. Are you sleeping much?"

"When I can. I didn't think I'd need much anymore." Sleep had become a luxury these days: whenever she lay down, she was kept awake by obsessively imagining all the places where Grant might be. Worse, when she managed to doze off, was the danger that she might dream of making love with Julian, as she had both Tuesday night and last night. She had a sneaking suspicion that he'd arranged to have those dreams sent to her; Olivia had agreed it was a possibility. It didn't make the prospect of going to sleep very welcoming. Easier just to skip the whole thing.

"Everyone needs to dream. Even gods." He broke a piece off his muffin "That's what wine was supposed to be for. To let men dream awake. I thought that it would bring about a new world."

"You and Timothy Leary."

He finally smiled. "Better living through chemistry. Yes, well. I'm distressed at how my beloved wine gets abused and misused. As you are aware."

Theo felt a stab of anger. "I didn't do the abusing and misusing, if you'll recall."

"No, I guess you didn't. I'm sorry. Grant is my friend."

"Oh, and he isn't my friend? What is this? 'There's that stupid little tramp who trifled with my buddy's affections then went and slept with someone else?' I don't need this, Marlowe.

I'm trying to solve this thing. Getting scolded by you doesn't help. I can scourge myself quite well, thank you." She started to get up. Her coffee cup rose obediently after her, and Theo snatched it angrily out of the air before anyone noticed.

Marlowe looked up at her, and the frost that had edged his manner and voice melted a little. "Sit down, Theo. All right, I really am sorry. I can't blame you for falling for Julian's powers of persuasion. Especially since he had the help of my wine to do his dirty work." He sighed. "I wish I could help you. But I can't. And even if I could, I really don't have any idea of where Grant is."

"Yeah, thanks." Theo rubbed at her forehead again. The headache was back.

"Truce?" He held out a hand with a glint of his old smile.

She took it. "All right."

He picked up his coffee cup and touched it to hers. Instantly the steam stopped floating up from their surfaces, and the brown liquid inside the cups turned red. She smiled a genuine smile for the first time since Sunday, and picked up her cup filled with deep red fragrant wine.

"To Grant," said Marlowe, lifting his to her in salute. "Will you two have me back up at Eleusinian some day? I might stay longer next time."

We two. Tears burned the back of her throat. "If—no, *when* I find him, we would be delighted."

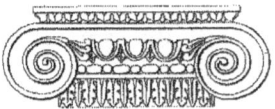

Seventeen

HER LIQUID BREAKFAST WITH Marlowe that morning made Theo feel better than she had all week. At least *someone* in the department was talking to her.

Dr. Waterman had, that first morning, asked her to stay after class. When the rest of the students had left and she stood by his seat, he'd looked at her with such a sorrowful expression that she wanted to cry.

"I tried to protect you from all this. Back at the start of the year," he said. "I saw that first afternoon that there would be trouble with Julian. I'm sorry I failed you, Theo."

"It's not your fault, Dr. Waterman." He looked as though he were about to cry, too. "It's..." She turned away.

He rose and folded her in a hug. "From Trite," he'd said after letting go. "She sends her love. I wish—" But when she opened her mouth to speak, he shook his head again and left.

Di and Paul and Freddy Herman had been almost painfully reserved all week, treating her with exaggerated politeness. Dr. Forge-Smythe too was sad-eyed, and kept encouraging her to have dinner with Renee "some night *soon*." And every time she walked by June's office, she would feel the woman's eyes on her like an ice-cold auger.

"I'm a wreck," she said to Olivia on Friday night in the Great Room. "Thank goodness it's Friday, but not for the usual reasons. At least I don't have to deal with anyone for a couple of days."

She was grading Olivia's class's homework while Olivia read over Monday's assignment in the textbook. Olivia had, somewhat shamefacedly, admitted that she was far more comfortable in Greek than in Latin.

"It's what I grew up speaking," she'd said, after asking Theo's help.

"What about Grant? He did too, I assume."

"No, not really. I don't know what the Titans spoke, if they even spoke. But he's at home in either language, far more than I am. He could have taught Greek just as well."

Theo felt a little glow of pride. Of course he could. He was perfect. Then she laughed to herself, mockingly. Too bad she hadn't thought that a few weeks ago.

"You're doing it again," observed Olivia.

"What?"

"Chastising yourself. I can tell by that look of misery in your eyes. Beating up on yourself won't help Grant."

"No, I suppose not." The sentences on the page in front of her were pulsating, large then small. She blinked at them and frowned, and they began to spiral. She clutched at the edge of the table.

"Theo! Are you okay?" said Olivia, looking up from her book.

"I don't kn—I'm—I was dizzy, for a moment. Damn." Theo rubbed the bridge of her nose and winced.

"Headache again?"

"All day. I took an ibuprofen but it didn't even touch it."

"It wouldn't. Not anymore. Oh dear, we need a training manual for new deities." Olivia looked sympathetic.

"Well, since you don't get new deities very often, I don't suppose there would be a big market for one. So, no more drugs for headaches and head colds and allergies?"

"You won't need them, because you won't get those any more."

"This headache feels pretty real to me right now," Theo muttered.

"You don't need drugs. You need some ambrosia. All the gods need ambrosia every few days. Not having it won't make you any less divine. But if you don't get it, you'll miss it—the headaches, and so on."

"No," said Theo flatly. "No ambrosia. I don't want it or need it."

"Theo, even I have it a few times a week. It's like—oh, I don't know. Like vitamins. You won't die without them but you won't feel very healthy, either. Where you're so new to immortality, you might need it more frequently than the rest of us do."

"Oh, fine. And end up the way I did with Julian, so drugged and euphoric that I forget I'm looking for Grant? No thanks. I'll do without."

Olivia looked worried and rumpled her soft Grant hair. Theo watched her and winced again, but not from her headache. She looked away and added, "Maybe if Julian would stop looking at me like a wounded stag, I'd feel better."

"Has he spoken to you at all?"

"No." She'd been avoiding him, though whenever they passed one another in the hall she could feel his mind reach out to her, and see his hands rise slightly, as if in supplication, then clench into impotent fists.

"I hate to say this, but I think you'll have to soon. None of the places where we thought Grant could be have panned out.

You'll have to talk to him, if only to try to prise some clues out of him."

"I was afraid you'd say that. All right. Next week, if I must." But she wasn't looking forward to it.

That weekend Theo and Olivia combed every building on campus, though Theo was not quite sure what they were looking for as they peered at commemorative statues and into disused broom closets. Theo kept the editor-in-chief of the campus newspaper, *The Torch*, busy by pretending to be interested in writing a graduate student column, while Olivia examined its office minutely in the shape of a small gray mouse in case Julian had been in a punning mood when he banished Grant.

"We're looking for a sense of Grant—a feeling of him. If he were in that tree over there"—Olivia pointed at an ancient hemlock tucked behind the Library—"we'd be able to feel it."

"So right now all we can know is where he isn't."

"Well, yes. But that narrows things down, doesn't it?" said Olivia brightly.

Theo tackled the department museum next. She and Olivia brought their classes up for a treasure hunt, giving them lists of items, words and images to find. Under cover of their bustle and chatter, she would try to examine as much of the collection as possible.

"What if he got turned into an intaglio and is put away in one of the locked drawers? How can I look there without a key?" she worried to Olivia while waiting for their classes to gather.

"You don't need things like keys anymore, remember?" Olivia murmured patiently. "Just don't be obvious about it when you search the locked places, that's all."

"Act casual. Act casual," Theo muttered to herself as her students scattered in the museum. She followed them from room to room, trying to look as unobtrusive as possible as she moved from case to case and statue to statue.

"Why, Miss Fairchild. This is an unexpected pleasure," said a gloomy voice behind her. Dr. Bellow had glided into the room on silent feet and stood next to her, stoop-shouldered and grim.

"Good morning," Theo replied as cheerfully as she could, and willed herself not to edge away from him. "I know it was short notice, but we cleared bringing our first year Latin classes up here with June. I hope we're not disturbing you. So...no Kirby today?"

Dr. Bellow's eyes were a flat black. With a little thrill of horror she realized that she could not discern pupils in them; they were like black holes, leading into nowhere.

"No, no. Not disturbing us at all. A treasure hunt? How clever. It's nice to have so much life up here for a change. My poor Kirby's down in my other office. We have a few students in the department who are allergic to dogs and object to his presence, so he's staying there." He smiled, and she shivered involuntarily. Allergies, heck. They were just tired of being sized up as potential dog food. Between him and his master—brrrrr.

"Was there something in particular you were looking for?" he continued, looking down at the open drawer before her. She had started on one of the locked cases.

"Oh, no. I never seem to have much chance to get up here and look around, so I'm taking advantage of being here now. I just love looking at these." Her voice was getting higher and more sincere with every word. In a minute she'd sound like Minnie Mouse if she weren't careful.

"Then you must come more often. I always enjoy visitors to my museum."

"Thank you. I should really go see how they're doing..." She inclined her head at the doorway, which the last of her students had just vanished through.

"Wouldn't you prefer to be alone and undistracted to examine these beautiful pieces? But of course you must go with your class. Happy hunting." His eyes gleamed with a faint hint of mockery.

"What?"

"Your class. Good luck on their treasure hunt."

"Oh. Right. Thank you." She scuttled away before he could say another word.

"He knew," she said to Olivia hurriedly in the hallway after they had returned downstairs and class was over. "He knew why I was up there."

"That's not too surprising, is it? Did he try to keep you from examining anything in particular?" Olivia looked alert.

"No. But he's impossible to read. How have you stood him all these years?"

"Everyone has a relative they love to hate. We're used to him. But I think we'll need to go check the museum out more thoroughly soon."

Julian passed then, amid a group of his second year Greek students. He said nothing but met Theo's eyes with his electric turquoise stare. She felt a jolt pass through her as their eyes locked, felt her mouth go dry and her heart thud slow and hard. A flashback to one late afternoon during their week together filled her mind. Julian had made love to her in a square of deep golden sunlight on the living room floor of Dr. Waterman's house. She remembered the faintly musty scent of wool rug, its roughness on her back and shoulders as she writhed beneath him to pull him closer, deeper...her surprised laughter as he rolled them over so that she was on top, straddling him, and his eyes, glowing in the sunlight like the Mediterranean itself as she moved once, twice, and then lost herself in a blazing glory of sensation...

"Theo?"

Theo realized that she was clutching Olivia's shoulder. Unblinking, Julian passed by, silent among the chattering students.

"I'm sorry. I...got dizzy for a minute." She shook her head and let her hand drop. Would this sort of thing happen every time she and Julian looked at each other?

Olivia frowned at Julian's retreating back.

On Tuesday Renee convinced her to go out for dinner. Theo in turn tried to convince her to invite Olivia to tag along, but Renee refused.

"She never liked me much. Always thought I was silly. Of course she's tremendously wise and skilled and powerful. But it always irked her that there was a power I wielded that she never could. She pooh-poohed it, but I knew it bothered her just the same. Especially after Paris."

"Paris? What does France—" Theo frowned, then swallowed. "Oh. *That* Paris."

"That Paris," agreed Renee. "Handsome boy, but not much sense. He was almost too easy to convince. Let's go."

Instead of one of her favorite trendy spots featuring Ozark-Szechuan fusion cuisine or the other latest craze, Renee brought her to Dmitri's. Theo froze when she saw the sign.

"No. Not there," she said, stopping dead in the middle of the sidewalk.

"Why not? We all like it. You've been there lots." Renee's eyes were wide and innocent.

"If you're planning on having Julian join us for dinner by accident—" Theo began angrily.

"Oh, puh-*leese*. Give me more credit for subtlety than that. And Julian knows better, too." She took Theo's arm and steered her inside. "*Bonjour*, Dmitri!" she trilled as he led them to a back table.

"He's Greek," Theo muttered at her.

"I know. He thinks I'm French."

Once they were seated, Renee turned serious. "I won't deny that Julian wanted me to come here with you tonight."

Theo felt her cheeks flush. "So I was right."

"No, you weren't. He's not coming. But he wanted me to talk to you. He's worried about you."

"I'll bet he is," snapped Theo. Good. If he was worried, maybe she and Olivia were getting close. But Renee's next words dashed her hopes.

"You look exhausted, Theo. You've got to stop running yourself so ragged looking for Grant and take care of yourself. You're not used to your new condition yet. I know it might seem like you don't need rest or to have ambrosia, but you do."

"If I'm immortal now, why do I need rest? If I can't kill myself with overwork, then I don't need rest."

"You do, you stubborn girl. Julian is almost frantic when he sees you looking so worn out. Oh, Theo, is it worth it? Listen to me. Julian had some of his wine sent here for you. Do us all a favor and have some? I'll drink it too, if it will make you feel better."

Theo sat back in her seat and shook her head. "What part of 'no' are you not understanding? I won't touch another drop of Julian's wine. I don't need any more ambrosia. I don't care if Julian is frantic. How does he think *I* feel?"

"I don't know. How do you feel?" Renee's eyes were overeager as she looked back at Theo.

A light clicked on in Theo's head. "How do I feel? Julian's heard I've been feeling faint and dizzy now and then, has he?

And now he's wondering if it's just a little ambrosial deficiency, or something else."

Renee had the grace to look uncomfortable, but she said frankly, "Can you blame him? If it were to happen that you were pregnant with his—"

"Being a goddess hasn't stopped me from the usual monthly annoyances, more's the pity. Maybe Julian isn't as all-knowing as he likes to think. You can inform him that I am not pregnant, and that if he's truly concerned for my health and well-being, he can tell me where I can find Grant," Theo shot back, staring furiously at Renee. At the two Renees—no, just one, but now she was wavering like a badly tuned television—

"Theo!" she heard Renee say in an exasperated tone. "Now do you see what I mean?"

"I'll be fine," she muttered, rubbing her forehead.

"When pigs fly, girlfriend. Julian is *not* going to be happy with you."

"Ooh. How terrible. I'm trembling."

Renee shook her head. Beyond her, Theo saw Dmitri stare at her with intent eyes, holding a wine bottle. She stared back, then stuck out her tongue at him. He scowled, and Theo saw his dark hair fade to silver just before he vanished.

Next Theo and Olivia moved their search into the city. They examined both Grant and Proctor Streets, the Greek and Roman art in the Museum of Fine Arts and the Gardner Museum, every tree on Boston Common, and all the animals at the Franklin Park Zoo. When none of those venues turned up any hint of Grant's presence, Olivia summoned a flock of barn owls to search farther afield in the wilder places around town.

"I'm drawing the line at Chestnut Hill and the Somerville

border. Any farther out than that is futile," she said to Theo a few evenings after the dinner with Renee.

"I'm beginning to think any point within it is futile, too," said Theo, rubbing her aching temples. The past few mornings Julian had been stationed near the front entrance of Hamilton Hall when she came in, giving her a sharp and anxious once-over. In fact wherever she turned these days he seemed to be there, watching her with brooding eyes. No wonder she was frazzled.

Olivia looked up at the bleakness in her voice. "You're losing hope, aren't you?"

"Can you blame me?" Theo replied. Her voice shook. "We've been searching everywhere, and haven't caught a single hint of Grant."

"One of the first things Grant told me about you was the conversation you had with him on the subject of hope. Do you remember what I'm talking about?" She unfolded herself from her chair and came over to sit next to Theo.

Theo closed her eyes and thought about lying on the grass in the October sun, gazing up into Grant's serious gray eyes. "I remember," she said quietly.

"It was what made him realize just how important you were becoming to him, and what he needed to learn in order to love you. You can't lose hope now, Theo. If you lose hope, you'll lose Grant."

"It was—it was the first time we kissed," she said, still gazing back in her mind's eye at the two figures on the grassy hillside.

"Well, he glossed over that part of things. I think he was still too shaken by it. I'm afraid I didn't much care for what I'd heard about you, until that conversation." Olivia smiled and let her disguise slip, so that she looked at Theo with her own face.

"You didn't like me?"

"No, not at first. I just couldn't picture him falling in love with a twenty-first century woman. I should have trusted his judgment better—he is far older than I, after all—but I was worried he'd be hurt."

"He *was* hurt," said Theo, lapsing back into gloom.

"That's the risk you take in love. He was also happier than he'd been in thousands of years. Your love gave him the courage to live, and to want to die."

"Don't say that, please, Olivia." Theo buried her face in her hands. Olivia put an arm over her shoulders.

"We'll find him," she said again.

"Do—do you still hate me?" Theo asked from behind her hands.

"Of course not. I liked you before I met you, once Grant had told me more. And I like you even more now. It will be fun when all this is over and we can go back home to Eleusinian together."

Memories—uncomfortable, some of them—swirled and roiled through her tired mind. She hesitated, then spoke. "I hated you too, you know."

"I'd guessed," said Olivia, unperturbed.

"Well, how was I to know? Grant kept talking about his great friend back in New Hampshire. And Julian..." Theo swallowed.

"Julian let fall some misleading comments about me, no doubt," she said dryly. "He was very angry when I went to Eleusinian. Oh, it was wonderful here at first. Our own little enclave at John Winthrop, for years and years. When any of us got to retirement age, we'd just pretend to move away to some old-age home in Arizona and take on a new shape to be rehired. Quite clever. But I got tired of it, and tired of them all. They've grown petty, a lot of them. Only Julian chafes under his comfortable yoke. I did too, but I had the option of running away. So I did. I don't think Julian will ever forgive me. So I'm sure he took great delight in dropping poison about me into your ears."

"I worried that *you* were what was keeping Grant from being able to love me," said Theo, lowering her hands from her tearstained face.

"And instead I was the one who encouraged him to go to Cumae over Christmas, so he could become human and love you."

Theo smiled, but her smile held no mirth. "'Lord, what fools these mortals be.'"

Theo peeked out the seminar room door. She had stayed behind after Dr. Forge-Smythe's Republican Rome class to scribble down some ideas for her class paper, and now the room, and, it seemed, the floor were deserted. Well, it was Friday afternoon. People tended to leave a little early. At least Julian didn't seem to be anywhere in sight.

She picked up her book bag and stepped quickly down the hall to check her mailbox in June's office. June had taken to locking her office at lunchtime, which meant Theo couldn't get her mail while June was at lunch. She had to endure June's fulminating stare every day now, which didn't help her emotional state.

A fresh wave of dizziness overcame her as she walked. It was getting progressively worse, and was starting to interfere with her class work. Theo paused by Dr. Waterman's closed door to catch her breath and contemplated summoning a cane to help steady herself. But the way her magic use had been going lately, she would probably just fill the corridor with a thicket of sugar cane. With a weak smile at the thought she resumed her walk, now creeping doorknob to doorknob. If she were lucky, June Cadwallader had left early and she could get her mail without feeling those dark eyes boring into her back. She already felt ill and tired enough without *that*.

She glanced down the hall. Hell. Julian's door was half open. No such luck that he'd gone already. Another rush of dizziness made her stagger slightly.

June hadn't left yet either. Double hell. Theo slipped in with a polite nod to her and went to look in her mailbox, taking out the ball of twine that had been wedged into it. That was the fifth time she'd found one there. Evidently June found it a convenient place to store it, or else she was just being annoying. Probably that.

Under the twine there was a department newsletter, put out by Di and decorated with obnoxiously cute computer clip-art. Theo rolled her eyes, which was a bad idea as it made her feel even dizzier. She steadied herself as unobtrusively as possible on the table below the mailboxes. It made a small scraping sound on the floor, and she could practically *feel* June watching her. She wanted to turn around and tell her that she wanted nothing to do with Julian and that June was welcome to him, but facing her basilisk stare was more than she could handle right now.

Along with the newsletter was a photocopy of an article about the excavation of the theater at Herculaneum that Dr. Waterman had promised her. She glanced at it but could barely read the title. Her awareness of June's eyes on her was growing until it felt almost physical, as if two holes were burning between her shoulder blades. She wanted desperately to reach back and see if her shirt were on fire.

There was one more thing in her box—a small envelope addressed only to "Miss Fairchild." She clutched her mail in one hand and almost stumbled out into the corridor. A funny smoky smell burned her nose, making her eyes water until she couldn't see. She gasped. was there really a fire here in Hamilton Hall? Smoke was everywhere, in her eyes and ears and throat, in her head—

"Theodora!" she vaguely heard as the choking darkness closed over her.

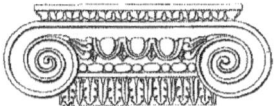

Eighteen

A FEELING OF COOLNESS, of sweet wetness, greeted her as she swam back up to consciousness. She tried to pinpoint where it was, but it felt like it was everywhere: on her skin, inside her, a sweet cool tingling that banished the dizzy burning smoke and soothed the pain in her head.

Then she realized that it was from the cup at her lips. She gulped eagerly, and blessed relief filled her. Another cup, yes. And another. After the fourth she let her head fall back with a sigh of contentment. She smiled and stretched, and opened her eyes.

Julian was gazing down at her.

"Ju...?" She struggled to sit up. What had happened? What—

"Hush. You fainted outside June's office. Fortunately I happened to walk by just then, my beautiful stubborn Theodora. Drink some more." He shifted the arm that encircled her shoulders to help her up a little.

More memory flooded back then. This was *Julian* holding her in his arms, holding the cup that she was drinking from so obediently...drinking cool, sweet, honey-and-champagne-tasting— "No!" she cried feebly, and turned her head away to hide it against his chest. Another bad move; the scent of his skin woke memories better left for-gotten.

"Yes. Enough foolishness, Theodora. You've refused any ambrosia for nearly two weeks now and it's made you ill. You're going to have as much as I say you need. I won't stand by and watch you suffer from your own stubbornness." He turned her head and put the cup to her lips again. "Drink."

There was no gainsaying the command in that voice. She drank another cup, felt the last of the dizziness and the ache in her head vanish. A familiar dreamy contentment stole over her.

No! said a part of her brain. *Wake up, idiot. Just because your head feels better doesn't mean you can let down your guard. This is Julian and Julian's wine, remember! Don't—*

"Look at me, Theodora," Julian whispered. He set down the cup and tilted her head toward him, and Theo realized that she lay on something hard, something smooth and polished, and that he was stretched out next to her, stroking her face as he gazed down at her. The hand caressing her cheek began to wander south.

Theo screwed her eyes tightly shut to block out his hypnotic eyes and shoved as hard as she could against his chest, then rolled away from him...and found herself falling. She landed ungracefully on hands and knees amid a litter of papers and files and realized they'd been lying on his desk and that her jeans were unzipped.

"Theodora!" Julian looked over the edge of the desk at her.

"Oh no you don't, Julian. You're not going to do that to me again." Theo climbed unsteadily to her feet, waiting for dizziness to strike once again, but instead found she felt better than she had in days. She scowled at him.

He met her scowl with his charming smile. "Why not? You

enjoyed it greatly the first time."

"Because you'd drugged me senseless with ambrosia. Just like you were trying to do now. But if I went to the campus police and accused you of using drugs as an accessory to attempted rape, they wouldn't believe me, would they? Just like they didn't seem to notice Marlowe and his erstwhile maenads that night at the symposium."

He ignored her. "I gave you ambrosia because you were so ill from lack of it that you were hallucinating in the corridor. What might have happened once you were restored to your right mind..." He shrugged, then vaulted lightly from the desk and landed beside her. She tried to back away but he caught her in his arms and began to kiss her neck.

"By the Styx, I've missed you," he murmured. "It's like having my heart torn out when you run away from me, or look at me with anger and disdain."

"No!" She tried to jerk away from him. Damnation! She'd forgotten his strength. He ignored her struggles and held her pinioned, kissing his way up her jaw.

"Tell me. Tell me you didn't remember this, and long for my touch again," he whispered into her mouth.

"Grant," she managed to gasp out.

"No! Not Grant. Grant wasn't there when we made love for endless, glorious hours. It wasn't his name you cried out as you came, but mine."

"Grant wouldn't have had to trick me into taking ambrosia to make me say his name when I came," she retorted. With another shove against his chest she broke free from his embrace and ran to the door. "I'll find him," she said, hand on the doorknob. "You aren't going to win."

"I always win, my dear." All traces of ardor had vanished from his face and posture. "You—and Grant—should remember that." A smile touched the corners of his mouth.

"Are you sure he still wants you?" he continued conversationally. "He's an intelligent being. Knowing you've betrayed him with me...well, it just might be kinder if you failed to find him. Then he could slip away at commencement, and you wouldn't have to put him through the unpleasant task of rejecting you to your face. If he were to see you now, with your blouse unbuttoned and your hair all tousled, what conclusion could he draw but that you prefer me?"

Theo looked down, swore mentally, and began to do up her buttons. "How would he know I've been here?" she demanded. "Unless you tell him—which would mean he's somewhere nearby..."

Julian shrugged and pointed at another scattered pile of papers. They lifted obediently into the air and settled on his desk, shuffling themselves into an orderly stack. "Maybe he is. But he might be incapable of understanding anything in his current state." He pretended to sigh sadly. "I can't imagine you wanting to embrace the physical Grant just now."

"In his current state—*what have you done to him?*"

"Nothing that shouldn't be reversible, assuming he has the strength of heart and mind for it. Stubbornness was always one of Grant's fortes, though others called it persistence and courage. I'm rather proud of myself for thinking of his hiding place. Not a bad job for short notice." He smiled at her, a teasing, faintly malicious smile. "No, I'll have to think about whether or not I tell him. Maybe I'll save it for a few days, as a treat. I imagine he's gotten a little bored by now."

"Behold the noble king of gods and men, who tortures his prisoners with lies," she said scornfully, to cover the fear that had gripped her.

"It's no lie that you slept with me, beautiful Theodora."

"After being tricked into it. I'm glad you've had your fun, Julian. Don't you dare try it again." She finished buttoning her blouse and opened the door.

"At least I hope you've learned your lesson about taking adequate ambrosia, my dear. You're welcome any evening to join me in a glass of wine, you know."

"Don't hold your breath."

Julian smiled and pointed at his desk blotter on the floor. It came into his hand. "I can afford to hold my breath, really. You have less than one month left to find where in the world I've put your dear Grant." He tapped the calendar on the blotter. "One month. I can hardly wait."

Outside Julian's office Theo leaned against the wall and closed her eyes. Her breathing was still uneven, and she desperately longed for a shower to get the feeling of him off her. But there were more important things to be done first.

She willed her breathing into calmness, then held it. Breathing, as Julian pointed out, was optional now. In the stillness, she listened. Apart from Julian humming cheerfully to himself in his office (which made her teeth grind), the building was empty. Good. She slipped down the stairs and into the Great Room.

It was full dark now, so Theo darted around the room turning on lights—she didn't dare trust her powers just now—and looked around. "Not a bad job for short notice" Julian had said when he taunted her about Grant. That must mean that whatever Julian had done with him the evening of the symposium, it was something he'd thought up on the spot. Which might mean that there was something in the Great Room that had given him the idea for it.

Not the furniture. Most of it had been piled away, with only the dining couches set up on the other side of the room. With a tentative wave, she sent a couch scuttling back on its short legs to rest against the wall. Then more confidently she moved the rest, apart from one chair.

Now, Grant had been tied in his chair, about here—a momentary sadness, mingled with anger, flooded through her, and she sternly pushed it back. That wouldn't help her find Grant. Julian had been next to him. Yes: when she'd stormed down the stairs and into the room, she had stopped...

Theo looked down at the mosaic floor. There had been a wreath at her feet, one of the pretty fillers the mosaic's designer had put in between the scenes from mythology. That would be right here. And so Grant's chair had been there—she waved it impatiently into place. Which would have meant Julian was...she stepped the six or seven paces forward and to the left...here.

She looked down.

At first, she was disappointed. At her feet was another of the floral patterns. But just to her left...she moved over a few more paces.

There was a beach scene before her: curling blue waves washed up on a sandy tan shore. Two figures stood on the sand, surrounded by seals that gazed raptly at them. One was a man, tall and strongly built, grappling with the other—but what was the other? A lion, from the savage jaws and wild tawny mane...but below, where paws and legs should be, was a thick, brownish-gray column, like a tree trunk. What was half lion, half tree?

"Proteus," said a voice next to her.

Theo jumped and looked up. Olivia stood there in her own form, regarding her with her somber eyes. "Are you all right?" she continued. "I was worried when you didn't show up for dinner."

"I—I didn't hear you come in. I thought the building was empty," Theo said, blushing and floundering.

"It is now. Julian just left. He looked very pleased with himself." She looked questioningly at Theo, who threw herself into the chair and stared miserably at the floor.

"I'm not surprised. He should be. He—" She bit her lip. "He almost got me again. I fainted when I was getting my mail and he took me into his office and gave me his ambrosia wine and—" She shuddered. "It was a close thing."

"I see," said Olivia after a minute.

"Do you see now why I was avoiding ambrosia?" Theo demanded. "If taking it will make me forget everything and fall into Julian's arms, then I'll have to learn to do without it."

"But there's no reason why it should do that," said Olivia with a frown. "I don't suddenly fall into a stupor and forget everything when I have it. Nor does anyone else I know. There must be something about his wine that does it to you."

"He did say it was double-strength, from grapes fed with ambrosia."

"That shouldn't give it this power over you." She sighed. "Oh, Theo. I told you to be careful of him."

"Well, I was unconscious when he started pouring it down my throat. I didn't have much choice."

"Then next time, have some of my ambrosia before you get to that state. I don't think it will have the same effect as his." She tapped her lips with one finger, staring at her shoes and thinking. "I suspect it's time I did a little research. Speaking of which, what were you doing, just now?"

"He—he talked about Grant. He threatened to tell him that I had betrayed him again. And that Grant might not want me to rescue him because of it—"

"Utter rot. Don't believe it for a minute. Go on."

Olivia's straightforward rebuttal was comforting. Theo continued, "And he said that he wasn't sure Grant would be able to understand him in his current form, and that his concealment of him hadn't been a bad idea for short notice. So I thought that maybe something in here had given Julian the idea for what to do with Grant. I think I've figured out where we all were standing when Grant...disappeared that night."

"You think Julian was standing here?" Olivia closed her eyes. "Yes," she said slowly. "It was about here. And that he saw Proteus?"

"I have to assume he did. I remember him staring at the floor. But what about Proteus could have given him any ideas?" Proteus, the old man of the sea, a prophet, and... "A shapeshifter?"

"That's Menelaus and Proteus," said Olivia, pointing. "When Menelaus was returning from the Trojan War, he was shipwrecked on Proteus's island. When he tried to capture the old man to ask for his help, Proteus turned into all sorts of dreadful things—a lion, a snake, a tree, a burning torch—" She looked at Theo, her eyes wide.

"A burning torch," Theo repeated. Prometheus's— Grant's—device, carved into his ring. "Does that mean Julian turned him into something?"

"It might."

Theo got up. "But we've already examined anything that might make any sense," she said, pacing and staring at the floor. Abruptly, she stopped. "Olivia?"

The other woman hurried over to her and looked where Theo pointed. Equidistant from where Theo had estimated Julian had stood but on its other side was another scene. This one was simpler: a man and a woman, standing in a doorway. The woman gazed adoringly up at the man as she pressed something into his hands, something round...an apple? No. Larger and rounder, like a ball.

"Theseus," she said softly to Olivia. "It's Theseus and Ariadne. She gave him a ball of string before he went—"

"Into the labyrinth," finished Olivia. They stared at each other.

Theo's dreams were not pleasant that night. Once she finally got to sleep, that is. She and Olivia had sat in the Great Room till late, discussing the pictures.

"But we don't even know if that's what Julian was looking at when he decided what to do with Grant. He could have been looking at Amphitrite, and changed Grant into a fish," Theo had argued.

"Do you really believe that?"

"No. I don't know what I believe."

"Then this is all we have to work with," Olivia said patiently. "So is it Proteus, or the labyrinth?"

But where was there a labyrinth anywhere? And what could Proteus have to do with any of it?

When Theo got up to teach her Monday morning class, she was tired and heavy-eyed. Though she usually tried to get breakfast first, there hadn't been time. Reluctantly, she went upstairs to get some coffee from the machine in June's office.

As always, June was there. Theo tried not to look at her as she sidled toward the coffee-maker with a mumbled "Good morning."

"You left your mail here on Friday," June barked, startling her into nearly dropping her cup.

"Oh. Er, yes, I did. Sorry. Thank you." So kind of the old harpy to remind her. But would June know what had happened after she'd passed out? Theo stole a glance at her face as she pulled the papers and envelopes from her box. Oh, yeah, she knew. She stuffed her mail in her bag and beat a hasty retreat.

Olivia was late for lunch that afternoon, so Theo pulled out her mail to read. Among it was a plain white envelope with no address. It was the note she'd seen on Friday, right before she'd fainted. Theo opened it and pulled out a small square of paper.

"It is painfully obvious that you are in need of a good dose of ambrosia. Do not, however, accept any from Julian's hand, especially in his wine. Some of his ambrosial wine contains varying amounts of water from the river Lethe. I will let you draw your own conclusions.

A Friend"

"Is that piece of paper a snake? You look as if it just bit you," said Olivia. She sat down across from Theo. "I'm sorry I'm late."

Without saying a word, Theo handed her the note. Her face felt stiff.

Olivia whistled as she read it. "Well, that would explain things. Lethe! No wonder you forgot everything but Julian when you drank his wine."

"He d-did drug me," Theo stammered angrily. "He swore he hadn't—"

"So he lied. Is that so surprising? What *I* want to know is who this 'Friend' is."

Theo struggled to bring her breathing under control. "So do I."

Lethe, the River of Forgetfulness! So that was what had made her forget everything—not only Grant, but herself, her life, her wants and dreams. It was almost worse than what he'd done to her physically. He'd stolen so much from her. But she'd found herself again...and now she would find Grant if it killed her.

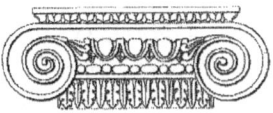

Nineteen

"IT HAS TO BE either Arthur, Marlowe, or Renee. The rest are too much in Julian's pocket, or wouldn't dare defy him," said Olivia, a few afternoons later in the Great Room.

The question of the identity of the "friend" who had sent the note to Theo was occupying almost as much time as searching was. At least it seemed that way to Theo.

"Well, it's not Renee," she said, irritably rubbing her eyes.

"Why not? She likes you."

"Yes, I know. So she wants me here with Julian so we can go shopping together for the rest of eternity. Do you know, she scolded me yesterday for refusing to look Julian in the eye and smile when we meet in the halls? 'Since he's probably going to win, don't you think you ought to be a little nicer to him?'" she mimicked bitterly.

Olivia winced. "Okay, so not Renee. Then Arthur or Marlowe. Which do you think?"

"Honestly, Olivia, I don't really care. I want to get out and look for Grant, not sit here and speculate about the author of anonymous notes." Theo rose and started pacing up and down the width of the room.

"We've done as much looking as is practical without further clues. If we can find out who this friend is and talk to him or her, we might get farther faster," Olivia explained patiently for the sixth time. "I think you need to get them each alone and question them.'

"Question whom?" said a cheerful voice. Marlowe had strolled into the Great Room. "Hello, Theo. Oh, uh," he dropped his voice, "Hi, Olivia." He looked around the room then asked, "How's it going?"

Theo looked at Olivia. "Well, er—"

"Now's your chance," said Olivia under her breath. "But not in here. Go sit outside or something."

Marlowe willingly followed Theo out into the April sunshine. Students milled about on the greens, and windows in all the buildings were opened to admit the warm spring air. Theo led Marlowe over to a cedar bench set in the ornamental plantings around the foundation of Hamilton Hall. Azaleas covered with swelling buds and tiny purple scilla and crocuses clustered around their feet.

"Spring at last," Marlowe said happily. "I always go a little crazy in the springtime. It's what comes of being agriculturally connected, I suppose. All those shoots and tendrils straining toward the sun wreak havoc with my attention span. But I can't say I regret it.'

A little crazy? "Crazy how?" asked Theo.

"Oh, I don't know. Restless. Impatient."

"Rebellious?" she suggested.

"What do you mean?"

"Restless and impatient enough to leave anonymous notes in my mailbox warning me about Julian's wine?" Theo watched him carefully

Marlowe's face became very still. "What about Julian's wine?"

"Someone left a note signed "A Friend" in my mailbox a few days ago, warning me that Julian was lacing his wine with water from the river Lethe and giving it to me so that I would forget things. Like Grant."

She was unprepared for his response. "What?" he nearly shouted, and leapt up.

"So it wasn't you, I guess." She slumped on the bench.

"Julian's doing *what* to wine? Dammit, this is what I was talking about before. Messing with my creation. How dare he?" He glared at her for a moment, then sighed and threw himself back down beside her on the bench. "So that's how he made you forget Grant, huh? I wish I'd known, so I *could* have warned you."

"It's okay, Marlowe." She reached over and patted his hand. "We'd just like to know who is trying to help me, so we could talk to them."

"So would I, my dear, so would I."

Theo gasped and turned. Julian stood behind them, arms folded.

"You should really be more careful where you choose to hold confidential conversations, my dear Theodora. You never know whose windows might be open on such a lovely afternoon." He gestured negligently behind him toward the brick façade of Hamilton. Looking up, she realized that their bench was precisely below his open office windows.

"So you wish that you could have warned Theodora, do you? Are you quite sure that you didn't, my dear son? You always have been an incorrigible boy. I'm not sure that I don't believe you did." He slowly moved around to face them.

Beyond him, Theo could see students sunning on the grass, leaping through the soft air to catch a ball—being normal and human and mundane. Couldn't they sense the towering angry shadow standing by the bench?

She stole a glance at Marlowe and saw that he was all too aware of it: fear had made the face behind the luxuriant dark beard go pale.

"Of course," Julian continued smoothly, stepping closer to her, "My Theodora should know better than to believe everything she reads in anonymous notes. Would you happen to have it with you so that I could see it?"

"No," she said, eyes narrowed. "And as it was a private communication, I don't think you have any right to ask for it anyway."

He smiled a humorless smile. "You forget one thing, my dear, one thing that it would be good for you to learn now. I *do* have the right. I have the right to do more or less anything I choose to do. Like this." He pointed at Marlowe and muttered "*Ampelos!*"

Theo jumped up, crying out and reaching for him, but it was too late. In Marlowe's place a sturdy vine was shooting out of the earth, twining around the bench as she watched it, leafing out as it grew. In a moment it had occupied the space Marlowe had, grown over the bench in an eerily man-like shape.

"No!" She turned to Julian. "You—you—"

"Bastard? Is that what you were going to say? No, not technically, I'm afraid." He looked down at the vine next to Theo, still writhing and sprouting leaves. "My, my. We are a little unkempt, aren't we? I shall have to send the gardeners around to give him a trim."

"Julian!"

"Oh, don't worry. Marlowe only has to stay this way until Commencement. This is just to keep him from interfering until then." He took her arm and turned her to face him. "I told you before, my dear. I *will* win. I won't permit anything that might jeopardize that. Of course, I'd be happy to restore Marlowe to himself immediately if you would only yield now."

Theo tried to twist out of his grasp. "No."

"But poor Marlowe. And poor Grant, too. I don't think he's terribly comfortable in his present state. At least he didn't seem that way at my last visit to him. Don't you want to spare him the agony?"

"Agony?" Theo jerked away that time, but Julian's hands shot out and pulled her back. She squirmed in his embrace. "This can't look good," she panted as she fought him. "Faculty members forcing themselves on students."

"Oh, no one can see us. I already made sure of that." He tightened his arms slightly, and Theo found that she couldn't move.

"I'm getting impatient, my dear. But it's been so long since I've had anything to be impatient about that I'm rather enjoying the sensation. Fight me, if you must. It will make my victory all the sweeter." He bent his head and kissed her slowly, still holding her immobilized against him.

"Why is Grant in agony?" she demanded when he finally ended the kiss and released her. "What have you done to him?" Involuntarily she wiped her mouth on her sleeve and was gratified to see him wince.

"Single-minded, aren't we? I don't choose to tell you, however."

"If you've damaged him—"

"Did I say I had? There are more kinds of pain than just physical, remember. Often they're even more effective." Laughing, he neatly caught her balled fists and kissed each one. "I shouldn't tease you this way, my poor darling. Oh, Theodora. Why can't we go back to the way things were that golden week together?"

"Because," she said icily, "they were never real to begin

with." She wrenched away from him, and with a sorrowful glance at the vine on the bench, went to find Olivia.

The following morning Theo stood in front of her class, dully assigning the day's homework. Teaching had turned from joy to chore without Grant to compete with. Though her students still carried on the rivalry with his class, unaware of course of what had happened, all the fun had gone from it as far as Theo was concerned.

"Please complete the exercises at the end of the chapter on page 256, and read, er, Chapter Twenty in the *Gesta Romanorum* reader and be ready to discuss it on Friday. *Valete*." She started to pack up her books as the class filed out, and wished she could go back to her room and sleep instead of go on to her Rhetoric class with Dr. Waterman.

"Excuse me, Miss Fairchild?"

Theo looked up. It was one of her students, the perky one who always sat in the front row. "Yes, Kelly? Can I help you?"

She shook her head. "It's not that. It's just that I was the first one in class this morning, and I found something on the floor. It belongs to you, I guess, but I didn't have a chance to give it to you before class started." She held out a small white envelope.

Theo could see her name written on it in a familiar hand, and Kelly, the classroom, and worry about her next class vanished as she held her hand out for it. She heard herself thank the young woman, watched herself scoop up her things and rush into the next classroom, saw Olivia look up in surprise as she shoved it under her nose.

"I think it's from A Friend. Read it. I can't," she said, and collapsed into a seat to watch Olivia open it and concentrated on not levitating as she was prone to do these days in moments of excitement.

Olivia scanned the note, written on a small square of paper identical to the last note. "Ah," she said with a smile. "Very interesting. All right, Theo. Go to class and meet me— hmm— meet me for lunch as usual in the Lounge."

"But—" Theo let go of her seat and started to rise. She hooked a foot under the desk and yanked herself back down. "But what does it say?"

"I think it best if I take care of this. You'll know after lunch. It couldn't be this easy, but we might find something useful."

"*What*?" Olivia was being perfectly maddening.

"You'll be late if you don't go now. Trust me. I'd rather you didn't get caught burgling the museum." She handed Theo the note and swept out the door with a fiendish glint in her eye. Theo read:

> *You might find something of interest in the locked gem cabinets in the museum, third bank over, second from the bottom drawer.*
>
> *A Friend*

"And I'm supposed to sit in class for two hours while you sneak up there and rescue Grant?" she panted, catching up to Olivia in the hallway.

"Grant won't be up there. And yes, you'll go to class and be patient for two hours. You live in a different time scale now, Theo. To an immortal, two hours is less than nothing. Go. I'll see you at lunch."

Rhetoric and Composition had never taken so long despite its being her favorite class. Dr. Waterman seemed to sense her mood and went out of his way to engage her, which made her feel worse, somehow. She knew that if Dr. Waterman could help her, he would. If only he could...but then an image of Marlowe's horrified face as his feet took root came to mind. She had poured a bottle of water on him that morning with a whispered apology and was going to ask Olivia for some ambrosia to sprinkle on him as well, as extra protection against root rot and aphids. She wasn't sure she could handle it if anything similar were to happen to Dr. Waterman.

Olivia was late, of course. Theo poked at her salad with a fork and stared hard at the door until she breezed through it with a broad grin on her face. Or rather, on Grant's face. The dimples made Theo's throat ache.

"Well, that was fun!" Olivia fell into a chair, still grinning.

"What was fun? Did you find whatever it was? Did anyone see you?" Theo pushed her salad aside and leaned forward expectantly.

"No, no one saw me. At least, not *me*. I'm afraid I did rather startle a couple of students in the library when I landed on the window sill—'

"'Landed on the window sill,'" repeated Theo faintly.

Olivia held her arms out and flapped them. "Yes, landed on the window sill. I should have peeked in first but I didn't think anyone would be there this time of day. But I took care of that and did my mouse trick next—it's very strange going from owl to mouse, you know. Does funny things to your sense of perspective, going from predator to prey—"

"Olivia!"

She laughed. "Anyway, the museum was deserted. Lights hadn't even been turned on yet. A few students have supposedly been complaining about Kirby's being up in the museum, so Dr. Bellow's been spending more time downstairs. Getting to the gem drawers was no problem. And," she held up a clenched fist and reached it over to Theo, "here we are." She dropped something from it into Theo's outstretched hand.

Theo looked into her hand and felt the blood rush into her face.

Grant's ring. The smoky gray quartz intaglio gleamed in its red-gold setting, the carved torch still sharp and detailed. "He isn't...?" she asked, with a hopeful look up at Olivia.

"No, he's not inside it. I checked that first thing. I thought that would be too transparent for Julian. But there must be some reason he hid it, and some reason A Friend thought it would be good for you to have it."

Theo slipped it on her right ring finger. "I don't care why. I'm just glad to have something—something of his."

"Yes..." said Olivia slowly, her brow furrowed. "What day is it?" she asked abruptly.

"Wednesday," Theo replied. "Why?"

"Wednesday. That means Julian will be in seminar till four. Hmm. Do you mind skipping class this afternoon? I'd like to try an experiment, and it would be best to try it when we know Julian will be busy. Eat, and let's go over to the Great Room."

Olivia had Theo put up a repelling circle around their usual seat in the Great Room. "It's good practice for you, and will keep anyone from bothering us," she explained. "It's also not so obvious a bit of magic that anyone's attention will be drawn to it right away. Everyone uses them all the time here, I've noticed, when they don't want to be bothered by students outside of office hours."

Theo stretched out on her favorite couch as Olivia directed, still fingering Grant's ring and trying to ignore Julian's on her other hand.

"Comfortable?" Olivia pulled up a chair and sat near her.

"Yes. What am I doing here?"

"You're going to try to find Grant. You're wearing his ring. It establishes a link between you. If you think about him hard enough and luck is with us, you might be able to catch a glimpse of him or where he is—enough to give us some further leads."

A shiver of excitement ran through Theo. "I might see him?"

"Maybe. Or see through his eyes. Maybe it won't work at all, or will only work sometimes. But we haven't gotten any other leads."

"What do I do?"

"I don't know. Whatever works for you. Close your eyes, maybe. Think about Grant. Reach out to him with your mind. Or maybe not thinking about him at all will do the trick. Try them both." She sat back and looked at Theo expectantly.

"Right now?" Theo felt uncomfortable with Olivia staring at her.

"That's the general idea."

"Could—could you move over a little? I don't think I can do this when you're—"

Olivia slid her chair back a few feet. "Better?"

Theo sighed and closed her eyes. "A little." She tried to relax into the cushions, comforted by their familiar, slightly nubby texture, and turned Grant's ring on her finger. The ward she had set around them dulled sounds from outside, so all she could hear was her own breathing, quiet and steady. She listened to its slow rhythm for a while, and thought about Grant. An evening from late last October came to mind, when they'd been here in the Great Room. He'd been sitting on the couch and she had leaned over his shoulder to look at a diagram in the article he'd been reading aloud to her. But instead she'd become engrossed in the feeling of his hair tickling her cheek, and his warm scent teasing her nose, and the sight of his hands holding the journal, strong and capable. She'd reached down and run her finger down the back of his hand, and he'd turned his head and smiled, she could *hear* the sound of his smile as he breathed...

Was her breath coming faster? No, she could still feel her chest rise and fall slowly. But the breathing she heard was ragged and uneven, and the air she felt in her lungs—it was chilly, yet still and musty at the same time, like a disused cellar. She opened her eyes and saw not sunlight in the Great Room windows but dimness as she walked. There were walls beside her, rough and damp, and the floor under her bare feet was cold. One foot was sore as she stepped on it, and she realized she was limping, trying to keep from pressing the sole into the dirty stone. She shivered and sank to the floor, leaning against the wall to catch her breath, and closed her eyes for a moment, feeling weary despair creep over her.

It was dark when Theo opened her eyes again, not merely dim but completely dark. Nor could she feel anything physical now—neither cold nor damp nor pain in her foot—only a tangible sense of sadness that covered her like a pall. She reached with her mind and pushed against it. It wouldn't give.

"Grant?" she called in the dark silence around her. *"Grant, it's me, Theo."*

The silence continued. But gradually she could sense something in it, a quality of groggy watchfulness that mimicked the silence.

"Grant," she said again, and reached out to it. Her thought-fingertips just brushed something that jerked away from her, and a low moan tore at her heart.

"Please, Grant. Come to me. It's Theo. I'm here," she whispered.

Something rushed past her in the dark, something large and angry and fearful. It shoved her away then withdrew, and she could hear it muttering softly to itself. "No. It's not Theo. Leave me alone, please. Please..."

"Grant, it is *me."* She reached out and began to feel around

her with her mind. Again she brushed against something that gasped and jerked, but this time it did not flee. *"Oh, Grant,"* she murmured, and gathered him to her.

He was shaking, only partly conscious and so lost in despair that she wasn't sure he understood she was there. Quietly she began to murmur in a low voice, words of comfort and tenderness, and gradually felt his shaking subside.

"Th-Theo—" he whispered.

"I'm here, Grant. You must be sleeping, so I was able to come to you because I found your ring. We're looking for you as hard as we can, and we'll find you soon. Can you tell me anything? Do you know where you are? Has Julian hurt you?"

At the mention of Julian's name the Grant-figure jerked. "Not Julian. Not—don't show me—Theo—no..."

Theo cursed herself. *"No, Grant. It's just me. I love you and am trying to save you."*

But a wave of disbelief came from the shrinking form. "Theo loves Julian. I saw..."

"What you saw was a lie. I love you, Grant. When I find you we'll go back to New Hampshire together, and I'll teach the moose and porcupines Latin so they can do Plautus for a change. We can be together and love each other without anyone keeping us apart—" She knew she was babbling, but she was afraid that if she was silent, Grant would run away and hide again. *"I love you,"* she whispered once more.

He sighed and relaxed, drawing warmth from her thought-body, and after a minute she realized that he had slipped out of this dream they shared and into deeper sleep—

Olivia was shaking her. "Theo!" she called anxiously. "What was it?" She reached down and touched Theo's cheek. "You were crying," she finished.

She blinked up at Olivia. By the sunset's glow in the windows she guessed she'd been—asleep? In a trance?—for a good two hours.

"I don't know. I was there, with him. It's dark," she whispered and clutched at Olivia's hand. "It's cold and dark, and he's hurt his foot—he limps when he walks, but he can't be still for long because when he's moving he doesn't have to think, because that's when the memories hurt the worst—" A fresh wave of horror overcame her. "He's in bad shape. He—he doesn't feel like himself, somehow. It's like he's imprisoned somewhere inside something else, and all he can do is hurt. He doesn't understand where he is or what's happened."

"Where?" Olivia demanded. "Where is he?"

"I don't know. It was dim. I could sense the walls on either side of me, like a hallway. But it was rough, like stone..." she swallowed and said, "Water?"

Olivia summoned a cup and handed it to her. "What else? Did you talk to him?"

"I tried to. He's so exhausted—"

Because Julian had been coming into his dreams. It was obvious from his words, disjointed as they had been. Had Julian been using the ring to reach Grant's mind? Could he just slip in and show Grant his memories of making love with her, like some poisonous home movie?

"I don't think we'll be able to get much from him anyway," she said. "All he knows is that he fears Julian and was terrified that I might be Julian, come to show him—show him images of me and him. He remembers me, but couldn't seem to understand that it was me there trying to help him."

Olivia looked pale but determined. "Then you've got to try again."

Twenty

THEO TRIED AGAIN THE next night and couldn't find him, but was successful the following night and again the night after. Grant didn't seem to remember her previous visits, except for one thing: on the subsequent nights he did not flee, but was easily coaxed to come to her. He quickly fell asleep as she spoke softly to him, as if he could only rest if she were there to guard him. She was happy to be able to give him peace, if only for a little while, but it made questioning him impossible.

Olivia was encouraging when Theo told her what happened the following afternoon. "You *are* helping him, Theo. Every night you go to him in his dreams, it means Julian can't. I don't know if Julian needs the ring to do it—probably he does, or else you might have—"

"Might have bumped into him in Grant's head? How nice." Theo shivered. "Well, it's not gotten us far, but I can be happy that I'm protecting him from that."

"Until Julian notices the ring is missing," said Olivia.

"Oh, please don't say things like that." Theo leaned back on the couch. "My head hurts again."

"Then I suggest you have some ambrosia." Olivia stared hard at the table next to her, and two large mugs appeared. She motioned one over to Theo, who caught it in midair and peered into it.

"Cocoa?"

"Well, it's—ahem—it's my favorite drink. Even Marlowe admits that really good chocolate is almost as good as wine. He drank his share of it at Eleusinian."

Theo drank. "I think you've got something here." The tingling of the ambrosia combined with the rich darkness of chocolate was wonderful.

"Don't search for Grant tonight," said Olivia suddenly, watching as she finished her cup.

"Huh? Why?"

"It's taking a toll on you. You looked peaked before you drank that, and you don't look much better now. It can take a lot out of you to journey into someone else's mind if you're not used to doing it. Rest for a night or two, and then try again."

"But I don't want to miss any chances—"

"You won't be of much use if you're too tired to be alert for clues. Go back to your room and get a good night's sleep."

A night of uninterrupted sleep would feel good. But she drew as much comfort from being near Grant, despite his state, as he seemed to from her. For always, in the back of her mind, was the chilling thought that these might be her last moments with him.

Despite Olivia's pep-talks, she was losing hope. They had searched the campus for anything like a labyrinth, but nothing had come of their search. Not that using the ring to talk to Grant had yielded any more of use. Would it be better after all to just give in to Julian now? At least Grant would be released from his bondage...though hers would just be beginning. Maybe

Julian would be kind and let her drug herself on his Lethe wine until the pain began to ease.

Like it ever would.

Theo went back to her room and slipped into an uneasy sleep.

A sound like a hesitant knock on her door woke her, so quiet that Theo wasn't sure whether she'd heard it or dreamt it. She listened for a moment; when it wasn't repeated, she closed her eyes and—

"Please," a hoarse voice whispered, out in the hallway.

Theo sat bolt upright, then nearly fell out of bed in her effort to reach the door. That voice—it couldn't be—she unlocked the door and yanked it open.

Grant stood there.

He shivered with cold though the night was warm. His nude body was smeared with dust and dirt; his hair was shaggy and unkempt, his eyes were red and tired, and he looked like the most wonderful thing on earth. She stared at him as her knees threatened to buckle, then pulled him into her arms. "Grant!"

He collapsed against her, still shivering. "Is it really you? Am I here? Theo—" His voice was weak and rough, as if he hadn't used it for a long time, and his tall frame shook as she held him.

"Oh, Grant," Theo murmured, her chest swelling with happiness. "How did you escape?" She pulled away to look at him again, and realized that he was naked. Tears welled in her eyes. She shut the door and led him to sit on her bed, tugging her quilt up over his shoulders. "My poor darling." She snapped her fingers and summoned a mug of hot tea, tossed aside the handful of smoking golf tees that appeared instead, and tried again. This time it worked. She held it to his mouth, and he gulped at it gratefully.

"I don't know," he whispered. "It was so dark, all the time—"

"I know. I tried to come to you and help you—someone told me where to find your ring—"

"Someone helped you? But who?" he asked, dazed.

"I don't know yet. It doesn't matter, now that you're here. I've been so worried about you!" Theo felt as if the weight of the world had been removed from her shoulders.

He leaned against her. "Kiss me, Theo. I've been so cold and afraid—"

She pulled him closer and began to laugh from sheer relief. She brushed his hair out of his eyes. It felt wonderful under her fingers. "I can't believe you're here. How did you escape?"

He shivered again. "I don't quite know. I was asleep, I think, because I woke up and there was light. It hurt my eyes—"

Theo stroked his face. He reached up and captured her hand to bring it to his lips. "I kept staring at it until I could stand it, and then I crawled over to it—"

She made a small sound, and held him closer.

"—and it was a door, left partly open, in the Administration Building—"

"We looked there, but it wasn't easy to check all of it as well as we should have. Olivia wanted to try again—Olivia! We should call her right away. You'll have to leave with her first thing in the morning, before Julian realizes you escaped." A tear slipped down her cheek. "Who could have let you go?"

"I don't know. I don't care. I'm here now." He closed his eyes and leaned against her. "Call Olivia later. I just want to feel you next to me right now." He shivered again.

"Come on." Theo tugged him further up the bed. Then she lay down next to him and pulled the covers over them both.

"You're still freezing. Let me warm you." She held him against her and wrapped her legs around his. He nuzzled his face into her neck.

"You smell just like you," he murmured.

"Who should I smell like?" she teased. Oh god, it was so good to have him back in her arms...closer than she'd ever had him before.

"I don't know. It's just—" He raised his face and looked at her for a moment, his gray eyes serious. Then, slowly and deliberately, he kissed her.

"Grant," she whispered, a few minutes later. "Do you—I can feel you—"

"Do *you* want to?" He kissed her neck, and she closed her eyes and made a soft sound of pleasure in her throat.

"Yes, I do. But if you're too tired—it can wait—"

"No. Now. What do you think has kept me going all this time? Knowing that someday I'd be able to hold you, and touch you, and make love with you. My dearest Theodora." He pulled up her t-shirt and cupped one of her breasts. "So soft," he whispered, and bent his mouth to it.

Theo closed her eyes. She had waited so long for this to happen, dreamed of it all those anxious weeks in the fall and winter and the even more anxious ones this spring, wondered what it would be like when they came together at last. Now Grant was safe, and they would be together for always. A memory returned to her, then, of something he had once said. "Are you sure, Grant? You don't want to wait until—"

"Wait until what?" He moved to the other breast, and she shivered.

"I thought you wanted to wait until we were in New Hampshire before we made love."

He was quiet for a minute. Or too busy. Theo didn't care which, so long as he didn't stop what he was doing right now.

"Maybe I did, once," he finally said, taking her hand and kissing the palm and each finger. "But I want you here and now. I can't wait anymore."

"Oh, darling." She kissed him back and slid her hands across his chest and down his torso.

"I've missed you so much," he murmured, kissing her hair. "All these weeks, longing for you and not able to touch you."

Theo froze "No," she breathed quietly. Then more loudly, "No." She sat up and stared at him, then ran a finger down his side. His smooth, unblemished side. "Your scar."

"What?"

"Your scar's not there," she said, scuttling back toward the foot of her bed. No, it couldn't be—please, no, it just couldn't—

"Damn," he muttered.

"No!" she cried, half-leaping, half-falling backward off the bed. He sat up and lurched forward to catch her wrists and pull her back toward him, and she caught a glimpse of turquoise eyes and tousled silver hair. "You called me Theodora. I sh-should have known th-then," she stammered furiously.

Julian tried to take her in his arms but she jerked away from him. "My dearest Theodora," he soothed. "I wasn't lying. I *have* been nearly sick with longing for you."

"So you pulled the cheapest, meanest trick you could possibly think of—oh, god, and I thought—I thought it was my G-Gr—" Nausea gripped her stomach.

"Just as someone cheated me?" He held a hand up and waved it. Theo looked up and lunged for it, but he yanked the hand holding Grant's ring out of her reach and laughed. "No, no, little tigress. It's mine now. No more midnight trips to visit Mr. Proctor's dreams and look for his hiding place. I'm getting most annoyed with this 'Friend' who keeps telling you things he shouldn't. Now I'll have to hide this little trinket someplace else.

But won't I have some interesting new memories to share with our captive friend?"

She lunged at him again but he caught her wrists and forced her hands down. "It's too late, Theodora. Give up now. You're not going to win. How can you, against me? It's less than three weeks until Commencement, and you're no closer to finding Mr. Proctor than you were in March."

"All right then. Assuming I don't find Grant, what's to stop me from just leaving on May 14th? What if I just get in my car and—" Theo stopped. Julian's ring on her left hand was starting to glow. Before she could do more than register the fact, thin silver cords sprouted from it like predatory vines, binding her hands together. She stared at them in horror.

"I wouldn't recommend it, for obvious reasons. That particular enchantment doesn't need me to be present to work. As soon as you made any attempt to leave me, something similarly unpleasant would happen. And if you do somehow depart before commencement and break your agreement, I will also break mine and Mr. Proctor's eventual mortality might not be so eventual. Do I make myself clear?" He gestured, and the cords vanished with a little puff of silvery smoke. Theo rubbed her wrists, feeling sick.

"Oh, while I have you here," he continued in a conversational tone. "I wanted to make sure your passport is up to date."

"My passport?" She stared at him. "What does it have to do with any of this?"

"Our trip to Greece this summer, of course. It'll be so much easier if we're not worrying about such mortal nonsense as passports at the last minute. Our minds will be on other things. At least mine will." He blew her a kiss and vanished.

Theo rose and showered. Then, unable to face returning to her bed where the rumpled bedclothes mocked her, she walked the campus until dawn.

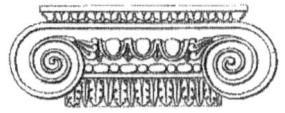

Twenty-one

SOMEHOW—LATER SHE WAS never quite sure how—Theo stumbled through the next weeks of papers, exams, and teaching duties in her First Year class. Olivia helped by grading her class papers and figuring out rough grades based on homework and tests, and Dr. Waterman didn't require a paper or exam from her for his Rhetoric class. He called her into his office the day after her horrible encounter with Julian.

"Your first year class's success is more than sufficient proof that you are a master of the language. Not to mention your performance in my seminar. Besides," his voice dropped, and he turned to peer shyly at one of the fish tanks in his office, "it's the only thing I can do to help. I wish there were more. Have you had any luck?"

Theo shook her head. "I don't want to say anything, Dr. Waterman. I don't want to get you into trouble the way I did Marlowe. Amphitrite would never forgive me."

"She would, and more. She and I both hope you'll come to visit us this summer no matter—no matter what happens."

Still, there were papers and exams for her other classes to worry about, not to mention Julian's continued psychological warfare. A week before commencement, Theo was horrified to find an invitation in her mailbox to a final department symposium, issued in her and Julian's names in celebration of their union, to be held on the day after commencement. Paperclipped to it was a note in Julian's hand, offering to help her pack up her things and move them to his house 'to save time'. She glared so hard at the note that it burst into flames, and June tutted and frowned and made a great show of turning on the fan in her office to disperse the smoke and smell.

Theo went outside to sit on the garden bench next to Marlowe's vine. She had set a ward around it to keep the university groundskeepers from cutting it back, and had conscientiously fed it ambrosia each week and watered it daily, and it had grown lush and leafy. She wondered with a sad little smile if Marlowe would be a foot taller and have a beard to his knees when he took his proper form again in a few days.

Olivia walked past her into Hamilton Hall, head bowed in thought, but Theo did not call out to her. They'd had an uncomfortable discussion the night before when Theo, nearly in tears, had asked Olivia if she thought Julian would let her say good-bye to Grant on commencement day.

Olivia had rounded on her angrily. "I'd thought you'd be saying good-bye to Julian, not Grant. Are you giving up?"

"No! But—" Theo looked imploringly at her, and saw her own sadness and weariness reflected in Olivia's eyes. She had taken over the bulk of searching these last days while Theo had slogged through her schoolwork. If Olivia was relying on *her* to keep their hopes up, then she must be despairing as well.

Theo sat for a few more moments by Marlowe, smiling sadly again as his leaves rustled softly at her on this windless late afternoon. "Thank you," she whispered. "I know what you're trying to say." She patted his trunk and went back to her room to sleep. Only in sleep could she escape the sense of impending doom that hung over her, closer with each passing hour.

On the day before commencement, Theo sat alone in the Faculty Lounge, not eating a salad. Well, there was one thing. She'd had so little appetite lately that she'd lost five of those extra fifteen pounds she'd been wanting to lose. But further reflection that Julian would be the only one to appreciate this fact dampened the little cheer she took from the thought. Besides, Julian admired her figure. "Modern women are far too skinny. Nothing to hold on to," he had commented once, sliding his hands appreciatively over her. "You, however, my lovely Theodora..." She resolved grimly to lose another twenty, just out of spite.

It was lonely sitting by herself. The indefatigable Olivia was out searching the Biological Sciences Building again, now that the labs were mostly closed with the end of classes. Marlowe of course was not there; she had not seen Renee for days—even Paul Harriman might have been nice to have around just now, if only for distraction's sake. She slumped in her chair and closed her eyes.

"Is this seat taken?" said a chilly voice.

Theo opened her eyes and nearly fell off her chair. June Cadwallader stood there, carrying a diet soda and surveying her with a disapproving stare. She took a quick glance around the room: it was nearly two, and most of the tables were empty.

"Er, no it's not," she replied uncertainly, and sat up as June seated herself and opened her soda. She took a drink and stared meditatively at Theo for a few minutes.

"You've given up," she announced.

Theo stared back. "What did you say?"

"You heard me. You've given up. You're going to let him win. I'd expected better from you. It was hardly worth the effort I went to, then." She shook her head contemptuously.

"The effort you—?" What interest could June have taken in her search? Unless— "You sent the notes from A Friend," she said slowly.

"Of course I did, stupid girl. Who else would have? I thought you might have gotten further than you did, with Olivia helping you. I suppose Proctor's diminished mortal state made it hard for him to help you find him." She shook her head once more and tsked.

Theo swallowed hard. "But why help me? I thought you hated me?"

"I do," June replied calmly. "I loathe you. But I loathe the thought of Julian's winning at anything even more. If I can't have him, I don't see why he should be able to have anyone else. That's why I'm going to help you again, though you don't deserve it."

Olivia said Julian had divorced June centuries ago. Evidently she bore one heck of a grudge. Theo opened her mouth to speak but June forestalled her. "Eat that lunch. You're going to need your strength. You've let yourself get into such a state that I doubt you have the fortitude to rescue a pencil stub."

Theo took a bite of her salad, her mind racing. How could she eat now, when there was hope of finding Grant? And June—how did she know where Grant was? Had she misjudged the woman all these months? She started to float above her seat, just an inch or two, and yanked herself back down, holding onto her chair with one hand.

June watched her with a grim expression. "Don't get any false impressions. I'm not doing this because I like you, or because I feel sorry for you. I just want you out of my hair."

Theo put down her fork. "All right, if we're being so honest—why do you want to get rid of me so badly? You and Julian have been apart for fifteen hundred years, according to what I've heard."

June's face remained impassive, but one of her hands clenched slightly. "I want you gone because I don't want things to change. Life has been very comfortable here for a good hundred and fifty years. If you and Julian go off and drop your litter of so-called heroes, our nice quiet existence here is finished."

Theo looked at her. "And?"

"And?" June imitated her rudely. Then she looked down at her soda. "And I don't want to see you as the new queen of the Gods at his side. So long as things stay as they are, I'll be the one who's remembered as the queen of Olympus. Not some upstart once-human wench who can barely control her own powers." She looked pointedly at Theo's left hand, which was still tethering her to her seat.

"Thank you," murmured Theo, savagely spearing a piece of cucumber. She was not sure whether or not to believe June. This could be her—or even Julian's—idea of a joke. She looked up and met June's cold brown eyes.

"Tell me something. How is it that you can help me, when Marlowe got turned into a grapevine just for talking to me, and when everyone else has been avoiding me like I'm infectious?"

For the first time, June smiled. It was not a pleasant expression. "Because I wasn't at Julian's awful little party, was I? I'm not bound by the rules he set that night. Olivia was right about that: even the king of gods and men can sometimes make mistakes." She smiled again, and Theo felt a surge of something that she had never again thought she would feel: not just hopefulness, but real hope.

She pushed back her seat and stood up, clutching the table to keep from levitating again. "All right. I'm willing to believe you. Will you help me, please?" she said, making a clumsy bow.

June looked at her. There was a reluctant hint of approval in her cold eyes. "At least your manners are good. All right, come back to my office with me. There's something there I need to give you." She rose, waited while Theo paid for her lunch, and stalked out of the room, not looking behind her.

At the top of the stairwell in Hamilton Hall leading to the faculty offices, June motioned her behind while she peered through the door. "All clear. Come on." She moved swiftly and silently to her office, and closed the door behind them.

"Try not to be seen by anyone. You know that Julian will be on his guard so close to tomorrow," she said, fumbling in a desk drawer.

"I'd guessed that," Theo said quietly, but her heart was starting to pound and her palms to sweat. Was Olivia back yet? Surely she must be done in the Biology Labs by now. She closed her eyes and prepared to send out a call to her.

"Stop that." hissed June, looking up with a ferocious scowl. "Do you want everyone in the building to hear you?"

"But—"

"But nothing, idiotic girl. If Olivia doesn't get back here on her own, you'll have to go alone. Here." She finished digging in her drawer and handed Theo something round and brown. It was a ball of twine.

Theo had seen her and Andrew Barnes using miles of it to pack up items from the museum being lent to other institutions. She had also found it wedged into her mailbox at least a dozen times. But why twine? What significance did a ball of twine... then it hit her She took a deep breath. "It *is* a labyrinth, then."

June looked faintly surprised. "You knew that?"

"I'd guessed. This just clinches it."

"Then why haven't you gone to find him yet?"

"Because I don't know where it is. I guessed it might be one when I looked at where Julian stood in the Great Room before he made Grant disappear—I saw a picture of Theseus and Ariadne in the mosaics."

"Not bad," said June grudgingly. "But I'd go back down and have another look, if I were you."

Theo paused and frowned. "I thought you said that you weren't there that night? How do you know where he stood and what he might have seen?"

June sniffed and patted the knot of hair at the back of her head. "I *wasn't* there. Not in person, anyway. Do you take me for a complete fool? Who do you think hires—and pays—the fauns to serve at symposia? Go and look again. But be careful."

Theo slipped down the stairs to the Great Room, her feet barely touching the ground. The miserable old cow could just have told her, couldn't she, and saved her some time? At least she wasn't going down without a fight. She chucked the bust of Octavian under the chin as she passed it on the landing.

The Great Room was empty, save for the usual beautiful golden afternoon light. She hurried around, staring intently at the floor. Where were Proteus and Theseus again? Julian had been—hmm, there, was it? Damn, that was right—she'd have to move the furniture again. An impatient wave of her hand sent the chairs and sofas scurrying into a corner, where they huddled nervously. The tables quickly followed but the lamps, tethered to the walls by their cords, flung themselves upward and out of her way, hanging in the air like oddly shaped birthday balloons.

There. Not far from the fireplace Theo found Proteus, and then the wreath pattern where she guessed Julian had stood. Yes, to her right were Theseus and Ariadne. So where else should she look? There was nothing ahead of her...She stood for a moment in a square of sunshine from one of the windows, and thought. What about the wreath itself? She backed slowly away from it, still staring. No, it was just nondescript leaves in a stylized pattern. What, then? What had she missed? She frowned down at the floor, and then she saw it. *Stupid girl*, she could hear June's voice say, and she nearly agreed with her.

There below her feet and directly behind where Julian had stood, forming a triangle with the pictures of Proteus and Theseus, was a third: a man playing a lyre, followed by a pale, beautiful woman.

"Orpheus and Eurydice," she whispered. "Walking back up from—"

The outside door into the building banged, and she heard the murmur of voices approach the Great Room door.

"You must come see the Great Room mosaics, Mr. and Mrs. Barnes," said one rich, clear voice. "Surely Andrew has told you about them?"

Theo froze. No—not Julian—please not now, when she was so close! She gestured sharply, and the chairs and couches leapt back into their places. She dove behind one just as the door opened. It spitefully backed up another few inches, bumping her shoulder. "Sorry," she whispered.

"They're quite well-known. We're most fortu—" Julian's voice filled the room as the door opened, then stopped abruptly. There was a pause, and then Theo heard a series of soft thuds around her. She looked up just in time to see all the lamps float back down into place. Oh lord—she had forgotten to set them back down! Julian had walked in and had to set them back down before he brought in the visitors, which would mean that he knew someone immortal had been in here rearranging the furniture... someone, for example, like her, having another look at the mosaics.

"—most fortunate to have them here all the time to appreciate." His voice was louder, and she could hear polite murmurs and quiet footsteps follow behind him. She peered around the edge of the couch and saw him gesture to Andrew

Barnes and a middle-aged couple that must be Andrew's parents. What were they doing here? Of course; Andrew was graduating tomorrow.

She looked back at Julian, who was still chatting animatedly. But while his smile was wide and warm, his eyes roamed the room, and there was a small frown in the cast of his brows. Theo withdrew and tried to make herself smaller. Why hadn't she practiced teleporting yet?

"Come over here, Dad. There's an incredible picture of the Cyclops," said Andrew eagerly, pulling them to the other side of the room. Theo let herself breathe. She had to get out of here before they made their way back over to this side of the room. But where should she go?

Look at the mosaics again, June had said. Theo touched the cool floor with a shaking hand. Julian probably knew this floor better than anyone. A memory of a fall afternoon full of golden light, like this one, came back to Theo: she and Julian, gazing down at the pictures, and Julian telling her how he, too, often came to contemplate them. Close on its heels was another: Julian circling Grant's chair, hands behind his back and head down as he paced, listening to Olivia. Then he had seen Orpheus as well.

Orpheus and Eurydice. Eurydice had been bitten by a snake and died, and Orpheus had gone down to Hades to bring his beloved wife back to earth. How did that tie in to the labyrinth? Unless—a small half-sob, half-giggle escaped her, and she clapped a hand over her mouth.

Unless Hades was where the labyrinth was.

Was there an entrance to the Underworld on the campus of John Winthrop University? Probably not. Surely Olivia would have known about it if there were. Well, if not Hades the place, then maybe Hades the god?

She peered out from behind the couch again and saw Julian

usher Andrew and his parents toward the stairs. She started to breathe a sigh of relief.

"I know you're in here, my dear. And that there must be a reason for your not wanting to be seen. I ask that you wait here for me while I give these good people their tour, and then perhaps you'd be willing to tell me why you left all the lamps in mid-air. Very careless of you, you know." Julian's voice, low-pitched but clear, reached her from across the room. There was the sound of the stairwell door closing.

Theo waited a moment then tottered over to it, still shaking, and slipped down the stairs to the basement. How could she have been so stupid as to forget the lamps? Maybe June wasn't so far wrong. Now Julian knew she was skulking around Hamilton Hall. Oh, why hadn't Olivia gotten back yet?

She carefully opened the door into the basement. If there was any justice in the world, Dr. Bellow would be in the museum at this time of day and she could search his office again for the entrance to the labyrinth. It was time *something* went right.

There was no justice. As she tiptoed down the dim corridor, Theo saw a rectangle of light spilling from an open doorway. Drawing closer, she could hear the squeaks and sighs of an ancient wooden office chair and the rustle of pages turning. Dr. Bellow was in his office, dammit. Olivia had said something about his spending a lot more time down here lately. Of course he would be ..if he were guarding the entrance to where Grant was being kept.

How could she get him out of there? She tiptoed back up to the second floor and looked cautiously around the door, listening for voices. The corridor was blessedly silent. She dashed down it to June's office.

"I went down to Dr. Bellow's office. That's where I need to go, isn't it?" she whispered fiercely at June without preamble.

June motioned her into the office. "Yes," she hissed back. "So what are you doing here?"

"Dr. Bellow's in there. And Julian caught me in the Great Room. How can I get past them?"

June frowned and drummed her fingers on the edge of her keyboard. Then she smiled. "Julian's on his way upstairs to show Andrew's parents the Museum. He'll find that it's locked, and that I don't happen to have the key handy."

"So?" Theo shook her head. "He doesn't need a key."

"*Think*, you little fool. He does when he's with mortals. He can't exactly wave his hand to unlock it in front of Andrew and his parents, can he? He'll come back down here, and I'll have to call Dr. Bellow to bring the key up. While he's doing that, you'll be able to get into his office."

"Won't he just send the key up here like—" She waved her hand.

"No. He doesn't think we should use any powers during the school year. He'll bring it up to Julian."

Theo tried to calculate how long it would take him to walk up the stairs and down again. "That won't leave me much time."

"No, it won't. So you'll have to think fast, won't you?" June replied coldly.

"Why can't you just *tell* me where it is?" She was perilously close to tears.

"Because I don't know. Don't you think I'd tell you, if only to get you out of my sight? This is the best I can do. Now go and hide near his office. As soon as he's gone, go in. You'll have a good seven or eight minutes. Longer, if I suggest that he stay with Julian to give them their tour. But I can't guarantee that will happen, especially if Julian thinks you're sniffing around the building again." She shooed Theo out. "Go before Julian comes down looking for the key."

Theo ran back down the corridor and down the stairs. She had reached the landing between the first and second floors when she heard the third floor stairwell door open. She cowered next to the bust of Octavian and waited as brisk footsteps came down the stairs and stopped at the second floor door. After it had swung shut she nearly fell down the rest of the stairs to the basement, and dove into an unlocked closet as she heard Dr. Bellow's voice say, from just the next door, "I'll be right up," in a long-suffering tone, followed by the click of a telephone being put back in its cradle.

I haven't used this much adrenaline in years. Theo closed her eyes and tried to calm her pounding heart as Dr. Bellow's slow tread and *sotto voce* grumbling moved past her and up the stairs. Then she slipped out of the closet and toward his office.

She and Olivia had, as a matter of course, already searched the basement and sub-basement of Hamilton Hall. In fact, it had been one of the first places they looked. But a late-night going-through of Dr. Bellow's office, down to the files in his cabinet and the panels of his large wooden desk, had revealed nothing. Nor had their search of any other place down there revealed anything.

"Don't waste your time looking where we've already searched, Fairchild," she muttered to herself, pushing the door open. "Think—and for god's sake, listen."

There was the same large desk, a little tidier now than it had been a month and a half ago now that classes were over. The ancient wood filing cabinets were shut, but she didn't spare them a glance; they'd already been thorough examined. No false doors, no hidden stairways. Not even any mirrors to climb into. Olivia had laughed at that last suggestion. "This isn't a fairy tale, Theo," she'd said.

"Too bad it isn't," Theo muttered aloud. She peered around

the back of the door. Nope, no mirror. Damn. She set the ball of June's twine in a chair and looked around her in desperation. "Open sesame!" she commanded, throwing her hands up helplessly.

A sound from behind the desk startled her. It had been a snuffling, grunting sort of noise. Then there was a rustling, and a faint clicking sound. And now, a low growl—

Theo stifled a curse. Kirby, Dr. Bellow's dog, was slinking around the edge of his desk. It was his claws that were making the clicking sound as he inched toward her. How could she have forgotten him? Dr. Bellow had said he was staying down here now because too many students had been troubled by allergies around him. He must have been asleep behind the desk, and she had woken him up with her foolish exclamation.

"Nice doggy," she said in her best coaxing-Dido-into-having-her-nails-clipped voice. "Nice..." The words died in her mouth. Kirby was still scruffy, still gray, still projected a hostility that made a rabid pit bull look like a hamster in comparison. But when had he grown two more heads? And why did he suddenly not seem so small anymore? "Kirb—" she mouthed, and then realized. She was seeing him now with immortal eyes. What else would Dr. Bellow's dog look like? And why hadn't she brought a lyre like Orpheus?

Like I could play it. Thanks for telling me, June. "Good Kirby," she whispered hoarsely, backing toward the office door. That's what you were supposed to do with aggressive dogs, wasn't it? Even three-headed ones? Not make eye contact and back away? She kept her eyes averted, staring at the floor at her feet as she shuffled backward, trying not to whimper. You weren't supposed to let an aggressive dog see that you were afraid of him, were you? But how was she supposed to do that when there was cold sweat dripping down her forehead? Dammit, where was that threshold? Surely she'd almost found it—

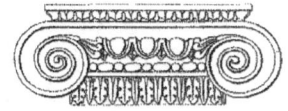

Twenty-two

ALL AT ONCE THERE was a rush of cold, damp air on her face as she stepped backward into the hallway, air that smelled old somehow, musty and dead. At the same time the worn linoleum floor at her feet started to change, the color-flecked gray tiles flowing and running like water, reforming as pitted, crumbling concrete. Kirby's low, evil growls faded into silence. What was going on?

Theo looked up.

Where the door into Dr. Bellow's office had been was a stone archway. And instead of the slightly shabby but comfortable basement office that had been beyond the doorway an instant ago there was a corridor, lit by a bare light bulb mounted in the ceiling some ten feet away. Its glow only made the damp walls look danker and drearier. Beyond the light, the corridor turned right.

"It can't be," Theo whispered. She took a few steps, then looked behind her. The archway was gone as well. Beyond her the corridor continued, dirty yellow paint flaking from its walls, at least a dozen pipes of various diameters clustered near its low ceiling. She stared and walked a few more paces backward, wrinkling her nose at the vaguely unpleasant smell of the air.

On the wall was an old-fashioned brass fire extinguisher, the kind with a large wheel-shaped valve on top. She and Olivia had seen one just like it when they had searched the sub-basement of Hamilton Hall back in late March. She looked closer and saw that the dust on its top had been brushed away— just as she had done to the one they had seen that day. But the sub-basement corridor where they had seen it had ended in a blank wall a few paces beyond that extinguisher, and she and Olivia had turned back after spending a few minutes speculating on how old it must be.

A sudden excitement gripped her. Was it possible that this *was* the sub-basement of Hamilton Hall? But why hide it? Why have this part of it only reachable through Dr. Bellow's office, unless...unless...

Unless it was because Grant was hidden here. The sub-basement must contain the labyrinth. It had to.

Now all she had to do was make her way through it, and find him. Piece of cake, right? A nervous bubble of laughter rose in her throat, and a line from a retro computer game one of her brothers used to play floated up from her memory—*You are in a maze of twisty passages, all alike.* Too bad Lucius wasn't here to guide her through the maze.

But mazes and labyrinths weren't necessarily the same thing. A maze was intended to deceive, conceal, befuddle. A labyrinth was indeed made of twisty passages, doubling back and forth on themselves, but there were no blind alleys, no dead ends, no intent to confuse: the twisting, doubling path of a labyrinth led inevitably to its center.

Would this one be a true labyrinth or a maze? And if it were truly a labyrinth, would Grant be at its center? Guarded, perhaps, by a Minotaur? She shivered again. She had no weapon, no magic sword or Gorgon-faced shield. Nor was she a Theseus, who had throttled his Minotaur with his bare hands. But at least she had her ball of—

"No!" she cried, pounding the wall with a fist. She had put the twine June had given her on a chair, just before that cursed dog had woken up and scared the daylights out of her and made her back over the threshold and find the doorway. No weapon, no ball of string to help her find her way out, no way to know what exactly lay ahead of her in this loathsome place—

And no Grant, if she gave up now.

She squared her shoulders and started down the stone passage.

She moved gingerly, trying not to brush against the peeling, flaking walls. Bits of paint and crumbling concrete crunched underfoot as she walked. The pipes in the ceiling were sweating; occasional drips of water landed on her head, making her jump, and the air still tasted musty and stale. The dim bulbs set at irregular intervals in the ceiling made creepy tentacle-like shadows through the pipes, shadows that she tried to ignore. Worst of all was where a bulb had burned out; there Theo found herself almost running from one pool of dim light to the next, able with her immortal vision to see in the dark yet fearful of seeing too much.

When she paused under a bulb to catch her breath after running through one such dark stretch with her eyes nearly closed, she heard it—a scratching, scrabbling sound, coming from somewhere overhead. She glanced up. Bright eyes peered down at her from the shadows between the pipes clustered near the ceiling. Rats! She shuddered and walked quickly away, but the scratching sound never seemed very far away. How could Grant have stood this for all these weeks?

So far the passage had had no branches or divisions, which made her feel better. Then it had to be a true labyrinth. At least she wouldn't need the string to find her way out again. Her and Grant's way, she amended. Theo remembered the intense girl, a Greek and Art double-major at her undergraduate college, who had created a labyrinth out of gravel and colored sand on one of the college greens as her senior thesis. Walking a labyrinth was a form of meditation for some, a way of reaching into oneself to discover hidden truths. If she weren't so cold and scared, she might have enjoyed walking this one.

That was a good idea, though—meditate. Relax and let her brain do the work. She slowed her pace and closed her eyes, letting her hearing guide her the way it had when she danced through Dr. Waterman's living room one afternoon with Julian. At least with her eyes closed she wouldn't have to see the mildew-stained, peeling walls and the sudden gleam of small rodent eyes peering down at her from the sweating pipes. After several minutes of just listening, keeping her breathing slow and even, she let herself start to think again.

How far would it be to the center? She had counted two turnings so far, separated by fewer paces each time. An ancient classical labyrinth usually had seven nested circles, seven layers. Two down, five to go.

But it couldn't be that easy. She doubted she would find Grant at the labyrinth's center, calmly awaiting her. Grant's state of mind when she had visited him in his sleep had been anything but calm: she had felt his confusion, his fear, his sense of being somehow imprisoned. Or was his sense of imprisonment from something else, some other type of captivity than just physical?

She shivered again.

It wasn't until the third turning that she noticed that the corridor around her had changed. The pipes had dwindled in number and finally vanished, and the flaking painted walls had changed to bare concrete, like the floor, and then something else. She paused under a light bulb and rubbed it with her fingers, realizing as she did that the corridor had widened. Where before she had shrunk from brushing against them as she walked, now she saw that three normal-sized people could walk abreast and not feel cramped or jostled. The ceiling too had risen. Now it was at least ten feet or so above her head. She stared up at it, and saw that it was rough and uneven.

"Stone," she murmured. "It's all turned to stone." She rubbed the wall again, marveling.

That light bulb was the last one. A flickering caught her attention in the corridor ahead, and she saw that it came not from a blinking, dying light bulb but a flaming torch. She paused under it and held up her hands, but the bright flames gave off no heat. She rubbed her bare arms to warm them and wished she'd worn a sweatshirt as she paused for a moment to listen and think. She had passed the third turning and must be well on her way to the fourth. More than halfway there, then. But to what?

As she had walked, she had started to reach out with her new senses to search for Grant. At first she'd felt no-thing. But lately, there had been a feeling of...of something—some *consciousness*, waiting. It had repulsed all her attempts to explore it, to identify it. Surely it couldn't be Grant, whom she'd been able to feel plainly in her dream-journeys to him. But if it wasn't Grant, then who—or what—was it?

The fourth turning came and went. The length of time between the turnings was definitely shortening, so she must be getting closer to the center. At the same time, the sense of some other presence was growing.

All right. So what if it was a Minotaur at the center of the labyrinth she was sensing? What would she do?

Sword, she demanded, holding out a hand. An enormous claymore, as tall as she was, appeared in her hand and nearly pulled her over with its weight. She'd never be able to use anything like that. Not even if it were a more reasonable size. She let it clatter to the ground and tried again. This time a small pink plastic sword-shaped cocktail pick, complete with an olive, manifested in her tense grip. That made her laugh, but the laugh sounded alarmingly like a sob.

Gun, she tried next, and found a handsome old chestnut-stock flintlock cradled in her arms. That was as bad as the claymore; she knew as much about guns as she did about particle accelerators. She set it carefully down this time, just in case it was loaded and did something un-pleasant and explosive.

What else—club? Spear? Rocket launcher? Did she honestly think she would be able to wield any weapon effectively enough to slay or disable a fearsome monster that was half bull? *Cape*, she muttered ruefully, and a red toreador's cape appeared and draped itself over her arm. She laughed again, and the torch she had just passed burned brighter for a minute.

"If I can't fight a bull with it, at least I can keep warm," she said to herself, and pulled the cape over her shoulders. Weapons were obviously not the answer. But what was?

The fifth turning came. Theo noticed it distantly, her thoughts turned inward. Would the Minotaur be able to speak? Or at least to understand? Perhaps she would be able to talk to it, to find some way to help it, in exchange for Grant's release. What would one use to bribe a Minotaur these days? Infinite grass? A private ranch in Texas? Plastic surgery?

The sixth turning came. She began to realize how tired she was. How long had she been down here? It was difficult to estimate time as she moved through these dark and featureless passages. She paused under a torch to look at her watch, and saw that it still read shortly before three—the time she had first set foot in Dr. Bellow's office. Had time stopped inside the labyrinth, or just her watch? How would she be able to tell if she were reaching Grant in time?

"You can't. So maybe you'd better get a move on, girl," she murmured aloud. "He won't get rescued if you just stand here."

She hadn't taken more than three steps, however, when a sound made her stop again. It was not loud or sudden: rather, it built in volume and then faded away, like a moan. A low, inhuman moan. She shook herself and continued walking, but she began to hear it more frequently as she continued. It reminded her of the lowing of cattle. Her mind veered from that thought.

Whatever it was, it didn't sound happy. Could it be Grant, injured or ill? Should she call out to it?

That was when she began to notice the smell—not the damp mustiness of the sub-basement that had nearly nauseated her at the start of the labyrinth. This was different: sharper and musky, like an animal's den. Like an animal's—

A louder noise made her jump. The lowing sound abruptly ceased, and a rumbling, breathy growl rolled to-ward her. She had scented whatever it was; had it scented her? In the torchlight ahead she saw a turn in the corridor. The seventh turn. So just beyond it must be the labyrinth's center, along with the labyrinth's inhabitant. The thought made her pause, the fear she had set aside before flooding back over her. But Grant had to be there, too. Theo took a deep breath and plunged ahead.

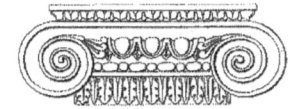

Twenty-three

THE FIRST THING THEO saw was light. At least eight or ten torches were set in iron rings around the perimeter of the circular chamber she stumbled into, making her blink at the unexpected brightness and dancing shadows. The musky animal smell was almost overpowering to her divinely sensitive nose; she opened her mouth and breathed through it instead but the smell still filled her, making her swallow hard to keep down her churning stomach.

Next to the chamber's entrance was a large pile of sour-smelling hay and a battered tin bucket. The old hay stirred memories of her horse-crazy days at age eleven and made her indignant; livestock needed fresh clean hay daily, not this moldy mess. No wonder the whatever-it-was (she avoided thinking about large bovine creatures) sounded so unhappy. *You're fixating, Fairchild. I don't think you should be worrying much about cruelty to animals just now—*

Sudden movement scattered these irrelevant thoughts. She turned to her left and opened her mouth to gasp, but the only sound that emerged was a tiny bleat. She registered its silliness even as she backed away from the hulking figure that shambled around the edge of the room. It caught sight of her and stopped.

Theo knew what a Minotaur was. She had seen artists' interpretations of them in her beloved books of mythology growing up: the sepia-toned snoring bull-headed figure lying amid a pile of human bones in her *d'Aulaires' Book of Greek Myths* had haunted her dreams for weeks after she first saw it at age nine. But no illustration, no matter how terrifying, could have prepared her for this.

It was tall—taller than a man by several inches and correspondingly broad. She stared into the glittering black eyes that were widening in surprise, the blood-shot whites visible around the dark irises. They were shockingly bright in the black-furred head or its thick muscular neck. It was not just a human with a bull's head on its shoulders but an eerie amalgam of man and animal: the snout shorter and the eyes placed further forward than was usual with a bull, the body thicker and squarer and more heavily furred than a man's. And its hands...she glanced at the useless, bifurcated stubs and looked away again.

"I—I've come to get Grant Proctor," she managed to say in a hoarse whisper. The Minotaur stared at her, and she saw the short fur on its neck and shoulders bristle like a dog's, saw the ears flatten and the long yellow horns point directly at her as it lowered its head and lumbered toward her.

She thought about what those wickedly pointed horns could do to an unprotected body, thought about ripping flesh and gouging, goring spikes driven by that powerful neck. She gasped, and suddenly found herself on the opposite side of the chamber. She had involuntarily transported herself.

The Minotaur staggered to a halt in mid-charge, looking for her. Its tail was sticking out stiff and straight behind it, and a hysterical giggle caught in her throat. *I didn't think it would have a tail—how cute.* But then it turned and spotted her again, and all irrelevant thoughts fled as it snorted angrily and charged at her again, moving awkwardly on its human feet, as if it were not quite sure how to use them.

"Stop that!" she just had time to cry out before she blinked and magically dodged once more to the other side of the room. The Minotaur paused again and bellowed in fury as it looked for her.

She tried to keep an eye on it while she looked around for some sign of Grant. She managed a kick at the hay pile before teleporting again, wondering if he were buried inside it for warmth, but her foot swished through it without touching anything solid. Then where could Grant be? There hadn't been any sign of him in the passages of the labyrinth. Had June maliciously tricked her? Could this whole labyrinth just have been a red herring of Julian's to keep her occupied until time ran out? She put that thought to one side, but her hope flickered like a dying candle.

"I need your help. I'm trying to find someone. His name is Grant Proctor. Please. Do you know where he is?" she said in a rush. The creature snorted angrily and ran at her once more. She evaded it again, its horns a mere foot from her throat. Think! If Grant wasn't here, then where was he?

"Tell me!" she panted, shouting across the chamber at the enraged half-beast. "Where is Grant? What did you do with him?"

The Minotaur roared back at her, a furious, inarticulate cry of rage. The sound of her speech seemed to antagonize it: again it stumbled clumsily toward her, broad feet slapping on the stone floor, and she noticed something just before she whisked away from its savage horns.

It was limping.

What should she remember about limping? She watched the Minotaur as it stormed at her once more, looked into the dark angry eyes, and saw something else there—a pleading, entreating spark of consciousness, all but buried beneath the bestial wildness and frenzy.

"You've hurt yourself," she said, dodging sideways this time so she could still see its eyes. "Your foot—"

It slowed, its rough panting making its sides suck in over pitifully prominent ribs with each breath, and stared at her in confusion. She felt lightheaded as she looked at it. A livid scar twisted just below its ribs, barely visible under the black hair, and then she knew. Shock twisted through her gut.

"Grant," she whispered, and took one cautious step forward. "It's you, isn't it?"

The Minotaur moaned uncertainly, head lowered as it looked at her. She saw the stiff tail slowly relax and hang still. Was it true? Had Julian put Grant into a Minotaur's form? What was it that he had said? *I can't imagine you wanting to embrace the physical Grant just now.*

"Oh yes I would. I'd embrace you in whatever form you were in," she said aloud, taking another step toward it. "I know it's you, Grant. Your scar is there. And you're limping. I could feel that you'd hurt your foot somehow, when I came to you in your dreams."

A shiver passed through its frame as she reached out a hand to close the last distance between them. "Grant," she whispered. "It's me, Theo. I know you're in there." She touched the hairy shoulder, and it quivered but didn't move. She reached out with the other hand, and slipped her arms around it, drawing it to her. "Grant," she murmured once more, resting her cheek against the furred shoulder.

The Minotaur stiffened and threw its head back. Theo gasped and nearly jumped back as the body in her arms began to shake, then to change, to *flow*. "Grant!" she cried once more.

But the figure in her arms was not Grant. A large, dirty-brown lizard was clasped in her arms, its clawed forefeet clutching at her shoulders. A long forked tongue slipped out a slash of a mouth with a sibilant hiss. Flat yellow eyes with vertical pupils stared into hers.

"Awrch!" she cried in disgust. But, like lightning, an image flashed across her mind's eye: a man on a beach gripping a strange figure, part lion, part tree trunk, and she knew. She swallowed her horror and gripped the dry scaly skin of the enormous lizard, and would not let go as it squirmed and thrashed its powerful tail. She'd experienced Theseus and the Minotaur. Now it was Proteus's turn.

"No—way—" she panted, trying to avoid the creature's fetid breath and sharp claws tearing at her shirt. "You're not—going—to make me—let go!"

The lizard hissed loudly and changed again. The scales under her hands softened and shredded into thick fur. Theo shut her eyes and dug her hands into a dense, musky-smelling pelt, gripped it for dear life, and felt long clawed paws embrace her, squeezing harder and harder—

"Go on!" she gasped at the bear. "Squeeze the breath out of me! I won't let go of you."

She clasped it even closer—and screamed in pain. The fur she had clutched so tightly had turned into countless needles driving into her hands, her arms, her torso and legs. Her eyes flew open, and she saw that she held an enormous gray-green cactus against her. She could almost have laughed at the absurd change, if it hadn't hurt so much.

"That—the best—you can do?" she said between gritted teeth as hundreds of two-inch spikes seemed to burrow into her flesh like tiny skewers. "A few—pinpricks?"

The needles vanished. She exhaled in relief as something

smooth filled her arms—something smooth but horribly foul-smelling that squirmed and nearly jerked her arms apart. She turned her face aside, screwing her eyes tightly shut to avoid the vicious, clacking beak of the great vulture that was trying to break her grip with its powerful wings.

"Go ahead, fly if you can. I'll still hold on." She grunted with the effort of keeping her arms around the slippery-feathered figure. It shrieked, sending a wave of carrion-tainted breath over her, and then the straining wings ceased pulling at her arms.

A thick streamlined column took its place, a column with strange rough skin and a thrashing tail and wide fins digging into her arms, a column with a blunt triangle of a head and cold merciless eyes glaring at her as its jaws seemed to leap out of its mouth toward her face.

Theo very nearly let go that time. One of her older brothers had made her sit and watch all the *Jaws* movies with him just before their family vacation on Nantucket the summer she was ten. She had refused to put so much as a toe in the water for the entire two weeks of their visit. There was something so inherently abhorrent about sharks, so viciously inhuman—

You guessed that one pretty well, didn't you? But it's not going to work. I won't let you get to me, she thought at it. Speech was impossible just then.

The shark's skin grated her already lacerated arms but she held on grimly, unable to shout her defiance but equally determined to overcome the repulsion that nearly choked her. She jerked away from the snapping jaws and managed to get one hand over its dorsal fin and yank it back.

All at once the savagely thrashing fish melted away in her arms, and she almost fell to her knees in relief. She had survived that metamorphosis, had survived all of them so far. What could possibly be worse than embracing a large, hungry shark?

"My dear Theodora," said a voice in her ear. Strong arms encircled her, and a gentle mouth softly kissed her. "My poor dear girl, you must be exhausted."

Theo cried out and again nearly leapt away in shock and horror. Julian stood in her arms, magnificently naked, his turquoise eyes gazing ardently into hers.

"You amaze me, beloved. I underestimated your resistance. Forgive me for scaring you like that. The shark was dreadful, wasn't it?" he said, smoothing back her hair.

"No!" Theo moaned, jerking away from his hand. No, it couldn't be Julian down here. How could he have——?

"My beautiful Theodora." He slid her shirt up, stroked her back, dropped a trail of kisses down her jaw and onto the spot on her throat that always made her sigh and writhe when it was kissed. "You cling to me. Is this the end at last? Have you chosen me?" he murmured in her ear, nibbling delicately at her lobe. "Do you long for my arms around you once again, my body in yours making you delirious with pleasure?"

She shuddered. Was this really Julian? Every instinct she possessed screamed at her to let him go, to run away, to refute his hateful words.

But no. This was another trick, another metamorphosis like the lizard and the shark, but a hundred times worse. It had to be. The last thing she should do was let go—if she did, she would be lost. *Grant* would be lost.

But was she *sure*?

"You look away from me, my dear. Do I disgust you so? Is my love so unwelcome that you would flee me?" He turned her face and covered her mouth with his. "Sweet," he murmured into her lips. "We belong together, my darling. You know that as well as I do."

She felt his hand slide over one of her breasts, pausing to cup its weight, then continue down to unbutton her jeans, and wanted to retch. It would serve him right if she threw up on him—but no, this wasn't Julian...was it?

What if he tried to make love to her? She could not—*could not*—let Julian touch her again. But if she pushed him away now, let go of him, and then found that he wasn't really Julian...

The scar. She'd seen his scar. It *had* to be Grant, chained in a terrible enchantment. But what if it weren't? She slid one hand up his side to feel if it were there.

Julian chuckled. "Ah, are you so eager for me after all?"

No scar. She stood statue-like, eyes shut tight, feeling only the trembling deep inside her and Julian's—Julian's?—warm, eager body against hers. Just because there wasn't a scar didn't mean that it wasn't Grant. Would the cactus have had his scar?

"You have to decide, Theodora," he murmured. His hand slipped into the warm space between her legs. "Mmm, you're always so warm and wet for me. Shall we assume a more horizontal posture, or shall I take you up against the wall? I do enjoy hearing you call my name in that breathy moan you use when you're about to—"

Theo jerked her hips away from his questing fingers but still kept her arms around him.

"Which will it be, darling?" he said, laughing now. "Wall or floor?"

"Neither!" she snapped. Without pausing to think, she slid first one hand, then the other, to encircle his wrists. "I won't let you make love to me but I won't let go. It's stalemate."

Julian's face darkened and he tried to yank his hands from her grasp. Theo set her jaw and held on, remembering how strong he was, how he could pick her up and carry her around like a doll. She wouldn't be able to hang on to him much longer.

But she did. Maybe it was her new powers that helped her, for no matter how he tugged and writhed, she was able to hold his wrists. New hope surged in her breast. If she could still hold him like this—if he hadn't been able to break away from her with Julian's godly strength—then maybe he wasn't a god. Maybe he was...

After a few minutes she caught a glimpse of his face. Though he scowled angrily, there was something different about his eyes. The intense turquoise was fading. Though her heart leaped with excitement, she squashed the emotion. *You haven't won yet. Don't lose your focus now.* A trickle of sweat ran down her forehead into her eyes.

Now she saw the bright silver of his hair darken, lengthen from Julian's preppy stockbroker cut to something longer and shaggier, just touching the shoulders. At the same time she could feel something else change, too. She closed her eyes to concentrate; it was the structure of the glamour that surrounded the figure in her arms. She hadn't even noticed it was there until it started to fall apart, steely gossamer threads dissolving into nothingness.

Still she held on, eyes closed, fearful of yet another horrible change, fearful of hoping too much. Julian's struggles intensified, but so did her resolve. *It's coming...you're almost there...*

With a loud cry, the figure in her arms slumped against her, panting. Theo stood still too, winded as much by the mental strain as the physical, her hands tight on—well, it *felt* like wrists. With a deep shuddering breath, she held the figure away from her and opened her eyes.

Grant stood before her.

His eyes were closed, and his breathing was ragged. She saw his pulse beat frantically in his throat as he swayed slightly, deprived of her support. She pulled him back against her and let go of his wrists to wrap her arms around his naked shivering body. He sagged against her so limply that she wondered if he hadn't lost consciousness.

"Grant?" she whispered, gently stroking his back and willing herself to stay on the ground. "It's all right, my love. You're you again." A tremor of relief ran through her. Everything would be all right, now that he was himself again. They could leave this cursed labyrinth and go back up into the sunlight together—

Then Grant's body stiffened. Slowly, painfully, he stood upright. Theo opened her eyes and looked up into his gray ones, and was chilled by what she saw there. Without a word, he pushed her from him and stumbled away.

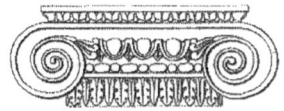

Twenty-four

THEO STARED AFTER HIM, stunned. "Grant!" she cried, following him. "What is it? Are you all right?"

He did not look round.

She went back and snatched up the cape she had summoned and lost during her struggle with the bear. Or was it the lizard? It was starting to become hazy in her mind as the shock of Grant's rejection washed over her. She ran after him and managed to slip it over his broad naked shoulders. "You'll freeze. Here," she said tentatively.

He stood still, his back to her. She waited for him to shrug it off but he didn't. "Thank you," he said in a harsh monotone and pulled it around him.

She sidled past him, trying to face him. "Grant, what is it? What's wrong?"

He did an about-face and walked back toward the chamber, keeping his face averted from her. "What do you think is wrong?"

Theo tried to run ahead to look into his face, ignoring the

sick, dizzy feeling somewhere in her chest. "I don't know! All I know is that you're yourself again, and it's time for us to get back up to the real world before Julian wins."

"Hasn't he already won?"

She looked at her watch. It still read three. "I don't know. I have no idea how long I've been down here. But if we don't hurry—"

"That's not what I'm talking about." He swayed again and caught at the wall. She tried to slip a supporting arm around him but he wrenched away from her.

"What's wrong?" she beseeched him, her throat hot and tight with unshed tears. "Don't you want—"

"What do *you* want? When I was Julian just then, I already knew exactly what your mouth would feel like under mine. I knew where to kiss you to make you shiver and squirm. I knew the softness of your—" He swallowed. "He showed me the two of you in your room, made me feel you, hear you, taste you—"

"And did he show you how he had tricked me into it?" she replied angrily. But a sick feeling had risen inside her.

"I could feel your pleasure in him, how much you enjoyed every kiss, every touch," he countered, his mouth twisting bitterly. "How do I know you care a drop for me? For all I know you and he have concocted this rescue as a charade for your own amusement and as soon as I touch you and say I love you he'll appear from the woodwork and carry you away and leave me here to rot. Can you imagine what it's been like to live as a beast? Or what it was like to take those shapes?"

"Do you really think that I'm capable of such a thing?" she demanded.

"I don't know what I think," he muttered, still averting his face. "How can I believe you love me after what I've seen and felt?"

How can I believe you love me... Theo stared up at him and remembered. She had used almost the same words to him once, had listened stonily while he begged for her understanding.

"So we're even, then," she said softly. "Once I couldn't believe in your love. Now you can't believe in mine." A thought came to her. "But don't you remember? Julian wasn't the only one to come to your mind while you were here. Do you remember me coming in your sleep? I tried to get you to tell me where you were but you couldn't. So I just held you safe in my arms so you could rest. Don't you remember?"

A long pause. "I remember," he finally said. "But I thought it was a trick of Julian's to torture me with—with losing you."

"You didn't lose me." She reached up to touch his shoulder, a quick light touch before he could pull away. "Those were true dreams, Grant. They came from the horn gate, not the ivory. You should be able to tell the difference."

He shuddered and shook his head. "No, I can't. I'm just a man now. How can I tell which dreams are true and which are false?"

"Grant," she began, then fell silent. Just as she had been conflicted and confused in March, so was Grant now. Only he didn't have a week of spring break to think things over. Theo wrapped her arms around herself and tried not to sob aloud. The Minotaur and Proteus had been nothing compared to this.

"Go back, Theo. Go back to Julian," Grant said in a low voice, his back still to her. "He's already won. I don't have anything left to give you."

"No. I won't go back without you." How could she walk the labyrinth alone again, this time without hope? Her words echoed in her mind. *Won't go back without you...go back without you...*

"That's it," she whispered. "I did the Minotaur and Proteus, but there's one picture left, isn't there? These things always happen in threes, in the old stories. I thought that the Orpheus picture was just there to show where you were hidden, but that wasn't all. This is the third picture and the third challenge. I need to be able to get you out with me."

"What are you talking about?" he asked dully.

"It's Orpheus and Eurydice, don't you see? There were clues to find you in the mosaics in the Great Room—" She knew she was babbling, knew he wouldn't understand what she was trying to tell him, but the words tumbled out anyway. "Theseus told me you were in a labyrinth, and Proteus warned me that you would change, though I didn't understand that one until now. I thought the picture of Orpheus was just telling where the entrance to the labyrinth was, but it's more than that. I need to walk out of here and trust that you'll follow me. And you—" she paused and swallowed hard. "You have to trust me enough to follow me. Otherwise, I'll lose you."

Grant was silent, his shoulders hunched under the ridiculous red cloak.

"Listen to me, Grant. It was afternoon when I entered the labyrinth, the day before Commencement. I don't know when it is now," she said, keeping her voice carefully calm. "So you don't have a lot of time to think about it. But it's not a matter for too much thought. That's the mistake I made back in March, thinking too much and not being able to trust that you loved me. I wouldn't trust you, and lost you because of it."

She took a few deep breaths, slowly rubbing her hands up and down her arms to warm them. Though there were no visible injuries left on them from her struggles with the monstrous forms Grant had been forced to take, they still felt bruised and sore. Lucky her, little Miss Immortal. She got to hug giant cactuses and horrible sharks without a scratch to show for it. Was any of it worth a damn, if she lost Grant?

She moved closer to him and briefly touched his shoulder again. "I'm going to start walking out of here. I'm going to walk and not look back, and hope that you can trust me enough to follow. I love you, but we can't share love if we don't share trust first." She took his arm and turned him to face her. The torchlight played on his hollow cheeks and haunted eyes.

"I love you," she whispered, and leaned forward to kiss him. He twisted away, his face creased with pain. She swallowed the cry of distress that rose to her lips, and reached out to touch his cheek with her fingertips. Then she turned away from him, and started walking the labyrinth once again.

"Now that I think of it, Julian made a mistake using the mosaics to choose your hiding place. He knew how much I loved them, how often I used to wander around the Great Room looking at them. I think he just assumed he was cleverer than me. Hubris, in a way. Isn't it ironic that the king of gods should fall prey to it? Maybe he'd been exposed to mankind for too long. They say that dogs and their masters start to resemble each other after a while. Maybe Julian is becoming too human for his own good. He was certainly guilty of one of man's classic sins."

Theo was babbling again. She knew it. But she had to keep talking, had to fill the silence that loomed large behind her as she walked.

"Now I know why Orpheus played his lyre all the way up the road from Hades to earth again. He didn't want to have to listen for Eurydice's footsteps behind him. I expect it would have driven him mad knowing she was behind him but not being able to look. I know it's driving me mad. At least he knew that Eurydice wanted to follow him. I don't even know if you're there. I hope you are."

She stopped speaking and started humming instead. Don't

listen. Just keep walking, one foot in front of the other. *Just keep walking, just keep walking, just keep walking, walking, walking...*she chuckled slightly.

"I was thinking about that Disney movie, about the father and son fish who get separated and have to find each other. *Finding Nemo*, I think it was called. Are all stories about quests? I suppose in a way they are. I came to school here on a quest for intellectual stimulation. At least that's what I told myself.

"Now I know that I came here looking for you. For the handsome prince to sweep me off my feet and carry me away to Neverland. But I didn't realize you were the real prince until it was too late. Oh, look. That's two turns down. They come pretty quickly, this deep in the labyrinth. But you probably know that already. Oh, god, Grant, I don't know how you stood it down here all that time. I suppose to you seven or eight weeks down here was probably nothing, compared to millennia chained to a rock on Mount Caucasus. But seven or eight weeks searching for you was—was pretty horrid. I haven't had a chance to tell you what a help Olivia was over all this time. She taught your class for you, so don't worry about that. She helped me look for you, and kept me sane in the process. I'm—I'm glad to be able to call her my friend now. I just wanted you to know that."

Was that an intake of breath behind her? Theo sternly kept her eyes focused on the floor a few feet ahead. A rat ran past her, coming from behind, and disappeared into a crack in the stones. Not Grant, then. She swallowed her disappointment and spoke again.

"So if that invitation to come to Eleusinian this summer still stands, I'd love to accept it—but I'll understand if you'd rather I didn't come. Or if I just visited for a couple of days and left. I'll need to get a pretty good job this summer, so I can pay—"

A half-laugh, half-sob shook her. "No, that's true. I won't

have to worry about paying tuition here next year, will I? I can't
stay in this department now. I'll have to find some other college
to finish my doctorate at. I'll miss Dr. Waterman, and Marlowe,
and the others. And Renee, believe it or not. Even when it was
all so strange and mystifying, I was still happy here. I'll never
forget teaching with you, no matter what happens. That was—
that was one of the best parts, having you to work and laugh
with, last fall. Do you know what being with you reminded me
of? Please don't laugh. But we reminded me of dolphins. It
sounds stupid, doesn't it? But I love to watch films of dolphins
swimming, cutting through the water so swiftly and gracefully.
You made me feel like a dolphin back in September and
October, like we were leaping effortlessly through life, keeping
pace, just glorying in moving together."

She paused to let the lump in her throat subside. "Or maybe
I'll go back to Sneed next fall. I'm sure they'd at least consider
taking me back. There aren't too many lacrosse coaches who
can teach Latin, so they may need me." Back to Sneed? She
shuddered.

"It's so strange, talking to you like this. If you're there, that
is. But I have to believe you're there. That's why I'm talking. I
need to be able to tell you what I think and feel. Of course, I
might end up driving you back into the labyrinth instead, just to
get away from me and my thoughts. That's a joke, by the way.
I'm smiling. Can you hear me smiling? You're human now, so I
expect that sort of thing will be easier for you.

"Do you like being human? I guess you haven't had much
of a chance to practice it, down in the labyrinth. But—I hate to
say this to you now, after all you've gone through—you didn't
really need to become human. You were fine the way you were.
I think *I* was the problem. I needed to learn to be human, too.
To get over being Sneed's 'poor Miss Fairchild' who no one
found attractive. To stop looking for a fairy tale prince to

worship me and heal my ego, and look for a real person instead, to be my friend. You're the most real person I've ever known. I just wish I could have seen that months ago.

"There's another turn down. The next one won't be for a bit now. I'll think I'll stop talking for a few minutes. My throat's getting sore."

It was, but not from talking. Tears streamed down Theo's face as she walked, and the effort to keep them out of her voice and not break into sobs was lacerating her throat. "I can't play the harp or sing, either, like Orpheus did," she whispered. "Guess I'll just have to cover my ears."

She kept walking, one foot after the other. Now was her chance to meditate the labyrinth, to keep her mind off who might or might not be behind her. But she felt too empty to meditate. There was nothing left within her to focus on. She felt like a husk, a cold, empty shell. She had spilled out her soul like her heart's blood as she walked and talked, for Grant. He deserved to know what was inside her, to know if he could still love her. If he was even there.

Another turn. "I hope Olivia's waiting for us when we get back," she said, when the silence surrounding her grew more painful than her throat. "She'll be able to take care of you. Make sure you're okay. I know you might not want me to—to help you. And Marlowe, too. He'll be back. Julian did something awful to him when he thought Marlowe was helping me find you. I tried to take care of him after that. At least I'll have a chance to say good-bye to him, I hope. If he doesn't hate me for Julian's turning him into a grapevine."

Will you have a chance? said a coldly reasonable voice in her mind. *What if you climb the last stairs up into the Great Room and find there's no one behind you, only Julian waiting for you with that charming crocodile smile of his? Will he let you say good-bye to any of them? Olivia? Marlowe? Will they even want to see you? Ah, not so empty after all, are you? There will always be more pain to fill you up again.*

She closed her eyes. So long as she was walking, she didn't have to know what her fate was. She was still in the realm of possibilities, not realities. Like Schrödinger's cat in the box— was it alive or dead? There was no way to know till you looked. The oblivious voice in her mind—*just keep walking, just keep walking*—started its mad refrain once more.

After a while, the crunch of rotting concrete and paint flakes under her shoes drowned out the crazed sing-song voice in her head and told her that she was approaching the labyrinth's end. Or beginning—she was too tired and drained to decide which. She didn't bother noting aloud the next turn, or the next. Only when she saw the funny old-fashioned fire extinguisher on the wall ahead did she rouse herself to speak.

"This is where I got in to the labyrinth from Dr. Bellow's office. But I don't think I can get out that way. I guess I just have to go on till I find the stairs to the basement," she mumbled. Tiredness rolled over her in waves, and she had begun to suspect that she'd been in the labyrinth longer than she'd guessed. The thought was not comforting.

Approaching footsteps pulled her from her stupor. She turned a corner and blinked. Ahead on the ceiling was a red-lit EXIT sign and an arrow pointing toward a door. Ah, the stairs. Then this was almost the end. And half-running down the hall was toward her was—

"Olivia. What are you doing here?" Theo knew she should be more surprised and pleased, but she couldn't muster the energy. Instead, she yawned hugely and stumbled as Olivia nearly ran into her and grabbed her hands.

"What do you think? Looking for you." Olivia frowned, and Theo realized she was wearing her own form. Of course. Classes were over. She didn't need to pretend to be Grant anymore.

"How did you know where to look?" She yawned again.

And then it hit her. Olivia had looked at *her*. Just her. Not beyond. Then that meant...

"You look like you're about to collapse. Here." She dropped Theo's hands, fumbled in her pocket, and held out a bottle of water. The sight of the clear blue-tinted plastic, damp with condensation, made Theo realize that her throat and mouth felt parched—and no wonder it did, between the dustiness of the labyrinth and her agonizing monologue on her outward journey. A long drink of cold water would feel so good. But there was something more important she had to do right now, something she had to remember...

Olivia's eyes were still fixed on her, concern writ plain in them. Theo stared back at her, her exhausted mind slowly spinning. She still hadn't glanced past Theo, hadn't asked if she'd found Grant. Surely if Grant were there behind her, Olivia would be making a fuss over him too. Olivia didn't know about Orpheus and Eurydice.

But if he weren't there, Olivia would want to know where Theo had been and what had happened. And she hadn't said a word about any of those things, either. Theo closed her eyes and thought furiously, fighting her weariness. There was something wrong here. But what?

Then it hit her. She straightened and put her hands behind her back. "No, thank you, Olivia. No water. Especially not from where I'll bet that water comes from. I'll keep my memory, thank you." She opened her eyes and calmly met Olivia's.

She saw them widen, saw them change from gray to something deeper and greener before Olivia vanished without another word.

"Nice try, Julian," Theo called, closing her eyes once more and leaning against the wall for a moment, careless of the dirty, peeling paint. "But not good enough." She squared her shoulders and started up the stairs.

She reached the basement. She risked a glance down the corridor toward Dr. Bellow's office, but the hall was dark.

More stairs. Each seemed higher than the last as she slowly climbed them, eyes again closed. *Don't you dare turn around, Fairchild. Don't make Orpheus's mistake now. You're almost there...*

She felt the Great Room's door handle under her fingers. Trembling, she pulled it open, walked another three paces into the room and stopped dead, unable to move any further.

If I don't turn around and open my eyes, I won't have to know, she thought childishly, even as she turned. But before she could open her eyes she felt arms close around her, holding her tight.

She collapsed against Grant's shoulder.

"Don't you even *think* about going back to Sneed," he whispered fiercely into her ear. "How can we be dolphins together if you're there?"

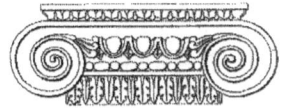

Twenty-five

IT TOOK SEVERAL MINUTES for the two of them to stop murmuring incoherently to each other. At last Theo took a deep, hiccuping breath.

"You followed me," she said, and reached up to touch his face. This time he did not shy away from the caress.

"I don't think I could have done it if I hadn't become a man. But I stood and listened to your footsteps move away from me, and turned my brain off and let my heart and feet decide. They knew far better than I did." He pulled back to look at her. "'*I offer myself to you again with a heart even more your own than when you almost broke it,*'" he said softly, in Latin, and more tears sprang to her eyes. It was one of the lines from *Persuasion* that they'd translated together, back in September when Theo realized that she was falling in love with him.

"Theo!" shouted another voice, from across the room. She turned and saw Olivia, the *real* Olivia this time, run across the mosaic floor with an ear-to-ear smile on her face, followed by another figure. With a burst of happiness Theo saw that it was

Marlowe, still trailing clods of dirt, his beard halfway to his knees, grinning hugely.

Olivia tackled both Theo and Grant, hugging them and chortling with joy. "You did it! You found him!" she crowed.

"What time is it?" Theo asked anxiously, rubbing her eyes and looking up at the sun that streamed through the high leaded windows.

"Thirty-five minutes past eleven in the morning, on the fourteenth." Olivia began to jig in place, still holding them both in her arms.

"You had twenty-five minutes to spare, Theo. Piece of cake." Marlowe's eyes twinkled with their old mischievous glint.

"Are you all right?" she asked him.

"I'm fine. You spoiled me rotten. I haven't felt this frisky in years. All that ambrosia, and the sunshine and spring water. I'd nearly overgrown the bench. It's a good thing you kept the groundskeepers off me," he replied.

Olivia had pulled back to survey Grant. "Are you all right, *magister*?" she asked, taking his hand.

"I'm tired. And hungry. Nothing that can't be easily fixed. All I want to do is take Theo back to Eleusinian and sleep and eat for a week." He rested his cheek on Theo's head.

"Then let's do that. Theo, could you be ready to leave today?"

"Give me half an hour and I will be." She had already packed over the last few days. Thank goodness she hadn't taken any of her things over to—

"Theodora!" The word filled the room like a trumpet fanfare, bouncing and echoing off the walls. They all turned.

Julian stood near the main entrance to the Great Room. He wore his academic robes, deep blue with bands of black velvet. They made him look taller and more elegantly handsome than ever. Theo remembered that the commencement ceremonies would be starting shortly.

"Julian," she acknowledged in a quiet voice that somehow filled the room even more than his had. He blinked.

She reached up and squeezed Olivia's hand before pushing it off her shoulder. "It's all right," she reassured her. "I have to talk to him."

"No!" said Grant, and pulled her back. "Don't go near him. He'll—"

"He can't do anything to me with all of you here. We won fairly, and I'm safe. I'll shout if I need you." She kissed him, then walked toward Julian, aware of her dust-smudged clothes and tangled hair. What did they matter? They showed that she'd fought well. What did she care what she looked like in front of him?

To her surprise, she realized that she *didn't* care. That it didn't matter to her what he thought of her. The thought bolstered her as she approached him.

"Theodora," he said again, when she halted before him.

"That was a shabby trick, trying to make me think you were Olivia down there just now. Clumsy, too. Definitely not up to your usual standard." Her voice sounded coolly detached, even to her own ears.

"I was desperate. Do you blame me for trying one last time?" He reached up and touched her cheek. "I want you, Theodora. I want you with me for always. Does none of the time we've spent together mean anything to you?"

Behind her, Theo could sense Grant bristle. She stepped back a pace, and Julian let his hand fall. "I can't deny that I enjoyed parts of our time together. Our dinners this spring were delightful. You can be a charming companion when you choose to be." She looked down at her scuffed sneakers. "And if I'm going to be honest, the sex was amazing too." Her voice sharpened, and she met his eyes squarely. "What I can remember of it, that is. Do you really think that I could want to be with you for always after what you've done to me—or to Grant? I may have been a pushover once, but I learn from my mistakes—as you might have noticed downstairs."

He flushed but held out his hands to her. "I did what I thought I needed to do to keep you. Doesn't that tell you how I feel?"

"No, actually, it doesn't. All it tells me is that you don't like losing. It sure as hell didn't send the message that you actually cared about me—because I've finally figured out that this never was about me, was it?"

Grant came to stand beside her and slid an arm protectively over her shoulder. "No, I don't believe it was—not really. My guess is that he'd chosen you for a dalliance, if the opportunity ever arose; Olvia says he always chooses one or two students each fall that catch his fancy."

Theo remembered that September day in Julian's office when she'd told him about Daddy's Constantine story and wanted to kick herself. She might as well have presented herself to him on a platter.

"It might have stayed a flirtation or a brief fling," Grant went on, "if I hadn't been here. Because *that's* what this has been about all along, hasn't it?"

Julian didn't speak, but seemed to swell in size, to tower over them, blocking the clear sunlight streaming down from the high windows. But all at once Olivia and Marlowe were there on either side of her and Grant, radiating menace, and Julian went back to his usual form.

"Is that such a surprise?" His voice echoed through the room as he locked eyes with Grant. "You've taken what belonged to me too many times to count. My due part of the sacrifice. My fire. My rightful place in the hearts of men. Yes, they always loved and respected you more than they did me, even if they didn't build you temples. They didn't need to, because you existed in their hearts. And you didn't care, because you were always too preoccupied with being noble and selfless."

Olivia snorted. "Pretty big tip-off there about the difference between you two that you seem to have missed, Julian."

He ignored her. "When I discovered that it was you here in my very home, I cursed you...and then I laughed. I'd found the perfect way to get back at you...through Theodora."

"Ah. So that would explain your declarations of undying devotion to me," Theo put in. "I had wondered about that part, you know. Look, Grant is tired and so am I. We want to go home. You lost." She leaned back against Grant and felt his arms encircle her. "Oh. Before I forget. I believe this is yours." She tugged at the lapis ring on her left hand. This time it slid off easily. She held it out to Julian, but it vanished from her hand with a flash of light.

"I would appreciate the return of my ring. At your earliest convenience, of course," said Grant with ironic politeness.

Theo looked up at him, then at Julian, and saw that they stared at each other as they had at the symposium, blazing turquoise confronting cool gray. She shivered; this time, Grant was no longer a god. But he stood firm, as implacable and enduring as the mountain to which he'd once been chained, and at last Julian's eyes fell before his. With a whirl of his robes, he wheeled around and stalked out of the room, just as the bell in the university's clock tower began to toll noon.

"I'll make sure you get your ring back," Olivia said, staring after him. "June will find it, if I ask her."

"Tell her it's the best way to make sure I never come back," Theo said lightly. Then all the strength deserted her legs, and she sagged against Grant.

"Are you all right, my love?" he asked, putting his arms around her.

"That was—it's just—" She shrugged and blinked back tears, then turned and buried her face against his chest.

"It's just that you two have been through a lot recently," said Olivia. "Shall we go home? Are you coming too, Marlowe?"

He patted his beard and grinned. "As soon as I can pack my SpongeBob toga. You'll love it!"

Grant slept for nearly two days after they all arrived back at the Eleusinian Institute that evening. Theo slept too, but mostly she sat at Grant's bedside, holding his hand and soothing him when he had nightmares in those first days.

"I'll bet you didn't think you'd find yourself stuck with such a useless lump," he said weakly to her on the third morning after she had woken him from a dream in which he wept as if in the grip of despair.

Which he probably had been, she reflected. "Of course you're not useless," she said aloud as she fluffed his pillows to help him sit up and gave him a cup of cocoa that Olivia had brought in a few minutes before.

"I survived thousands of years on that rock with that cursed vulture. A month or two in a nice dark, sheltered labyrinth should have seemed like a vacation in comparison," he replied lightly. But his eyes still stared into whatever horror had spawned his nightmare.

"You weren't human then, were you?" she reminded him gently.

"No. I guess I wasn't." He drank some of the rich chocolate. Theo looked at him with concern: he was still weak from his time of semi-starvation in the labyrinth. Olivia had brought Asclepius in to examine him—an Asclepius who seemed quite at home with twenty-first-century medical practices, Theo was glad to see. He'd given Grant an antibiotic injection to fight the infection in his wounded foot and pre- scribed a gentle but nutrient-rich diet to build up his strength once again.

Now Grant leaned back against his pillows and looked up at the mid-morning sun that shone in through the windows. She had tried to keep the curtains shut so he could sleep more easily but he had insisted they stay open. "I've had enough darkness for a while, Theo," he'd said with a crooked smile, one that hinted at the ghosts of dimples, and without another word she'd gone and opened the shades and curtains as far as they'd go.

The sun gleamed on the polished wood floor, scattered with intricate woven rugs. Bright tapestries covered the walls as well. Olivia and her helpers had made them from the wool of sheep raised on the institute's property. Theo gazed at them, remembering Olivia's excitement when she shyly offered up the fact that she could knit.

"But that's wonderful! I've never gotten around to learning knitting! You'll have to show us, so we can do mittens for everyone this fall."

"Gods wear mittens?" Theo had asked.

"Well, no. Not now. But they will. They'll love them," Olivia answered so confidently that Theo hadn't had the heart to laugh.

"You're quiet," said Grant, and Theo realized he was staring at her from his pillows.

"I'm sorry. I thought you'd want to sleep again," she replied and peered into his cocoa mug. "Good boy. You drank it all."

"I've slept enough for now, don't you think?" He shifted irritably and Theo, even with her limited sickbed experience, recognized his impatience as a good sign.

"If you think so," she said soothingly.

"I think so. I've never needed to spend time in bed

recovering from anything. Now that I have to..." he shook his head.

"It's true of the best and bravest of men, you know," she said. "They all need to sleep when they're tired and heal when they're ill. You're in good company. Or at least in a lot of it."

"The best of men," he mused, staring at the window again. "I've been thinking about men while I've been lying here. Not even I can sleep non-stop for three days," he said as she opened her mouth to scold him. "I've always been rather a connoisseur of humanity, you know. It was my hobby, I suppose. I watched them, learned all they're capable of, marveled at all their qualities the way racing aficionados watch horses exercising at the track. Watched and tried to understand...and now, suddenly, I've gone from being the one in the stands with the binoculars and the notepad to being the creature on the turf."

"How does it feel?" She reached out and took his hand.

"I don't know. As you said in the labyrinth, I haven't had much time to experience it yet. Frightening in a lot of ways. When I came to myself after you'd rescued me from being a Minotaur and I looked at you, it was—it was the most terrible thing I'd ever felt."

"What was?"

His gaze dropped. "Shame. Shame at what I'd just done to you when I turned into all those horrible things even though I couldn't help it. Shame at the anger I felt because I thought you'd betrayed me. Shame because I didn't know what to do or say, and a heaping side order of guilt for knowing I was the ultimate cause of all of this. I didn't realize just how crushing a weight shame can be. It makes my brother Atlas' burden look like a bag of feathers in comparison."

Theo couldn't help smiling. "A lot of humans don't seem to have the capacity to feel it, you know. At least not as much as they should, sometimes."

"But gods don't feel it all. Regret maybe, but not shame. Listen to me, Theo. When I was Prometheus, I didn't make mistakes. My name means 'forethought' if you recall. Once I met you and chose to be human, I lost that Olympian sense of omniscience. I botched things up with you quite properly, and there I was, quite as ashamed as I should have been.

"So I took refuge in an old human behavior: I blamed someone else. You. And felt ashamed of that as well. If I'd still been a god I'd have been able to see it all for the tangled web it was. I'd have seen that you were the real victim of it all. You were the one who suffered because of my trying to be human when I was a god, and then denying my human fallibility when I was human."

Theo stroked his hand. She'd emptied her pain to him in the labyrinth. He needed to have his turn now. "I'm sorry that you had to go through that. If I'd only known..."

"If you'd known, I wouldn't have made the mistakes, would I?" His smiled was crooked.

"But what about Julian? You were his victim, too."

"Julian." Grant closed his eyes. "Just another mistake on my part. I should have remembered that he has always been more human than I, and that he shares something with men that I never understood or felt—the desire for revenge. No, that's not entirely fair to men. I'm human now, and I can't say I feel an overwhelming need to avenge myself on him for what he put me—us—through. I simply never want to lay eyes on him again."

"Hear, hear," Theo agreed fervently.

"Did—did you love him?" Grant asked, after a silence.

She took a deep breath. "No. But I liked him, once. I was flattered by his attention last semester, flattered that he seemed to like me. That he seemed to find me attractive. It's hard for us imperfect humans not to like those who profess to admire us."

She squeezed his hand.

Grant shifted uncomfortably on his bed. She peered down into his face, pale against the white linen of the pillows.

"That wasn't quite the answer you were looking for, was it?" she asked. "I'm sorry, Grant, but I won't lie to you. Shame may be a terrible thing to feel, but it has its uses—it makes us try to do better next time. We humans are led astray by our secret needs so easily. I needed to be loved, to be thought desirable. Julian knew that, and played it for all he could." She shook her hair over her shoulders and smiled to herself. "One good thing came of my time with Julian. It taught me the difference between infatuation and love. That's a lesson that has to be experienced to be learned. Remember that I feel shame too, Grant. I hope we can forgive each other."

He turned his head fretfully away from her. She turned it back and saw that his eyes were bright with unshed tears.

"I don't need to forgive you for being human. It's why I fell in love with you. But now I'm the imperfect human one," he whispered, his voice rough. "I want both infatuation and love. I want to hold your love in my heart like a crystal chalice, and kiss you till your lips are swollen and your breath comes short. I want to take your body and give you my soul in return. Will you let me? Can it be both?"

This was not how I'd pictured it would happen, Theo thought as he pulled her onto the bed with him. *I thought it would be out on a mountaintop, under the stars. Or in a sunny meadow surrounded by nature. Not in a rather narrow bed in the infirmary at the unromantic hour of ten-thirty on a Wednesday morning.*

She looked up at his gray eyes, dark and serious with desire, and touched his cheek. He covered her mouth with his, sweet and demanding, a kiss such as she'd dreamed of for months. "Yes," she whispered when he finally released her lips.

"Yes what?" He was making short work of her clothes.

She helped him, then pulled his t-shirt over his head and let her hand wander down to his scarred side. "Just yes."

"Oh, Theo. My Theo." He explored her with his finger-tips until she was sure she must be glowing like a bonfire. Just when she was sure she couldn't wait another second he slid over her, and her body hummed with anticipation...and with rightness.

"I love you, Grant," she murmured, moving her legs up to cradle him.

"Theo—" His voice trailed into a soft groan as he entered her, going slowly at first, tentatively inching deeper until she gently bit his lip and moved against him, pulling him hard inside her. His breath caught, and then he buried his face against her hair and met her rhythm, hard and so sweet, so very very sweet, until the sweetness rose in a flood, immobilizing her yet carrying her along in a headlong rush. She felt Grant inside her, caught in the same flood, and held him close, rocking against him until breath and conscious thought returned.

He lifted his head and kissed her, his mouth moist and soft against hers. "Oh, Theo...oh gods, I love you!"

She returned his kiss, stroking his damp shoulders and back. "I told you it could be both," she whispered.

They went down to the Commons for the evening meal, Grant still pale but straight-backed and proud for his first foray out of the infirmary, his hands constantly straying to touch Theo's hand, her hair, her shoulder. Theo herself smiled and blushed at Marlowe's cheerful, "Hey, they're outta bed!" and accepted his loud smack on one cheek.

Others clustered around them then; Theo watched, bemused, as nine tall, handsome women, all different yet clearly related, whispered and jostled each other as they waited to greet her and Grant. She found herself exchanging pleasantries with ibis-headed Thoth and pot-bellied, elephant-headed Ganesha, whose small dark eyes twinkled wisely at her as he patted her head with his trunk.

"Are there other places like this and John Winthrop, where gods live?" she asked Olivia in a whisper over the meal.

"Oh, yes. A few. Mostly they're small prestigious liberal arts schools where one department or another isn't quite what it seems to be. And I've heard interesting rumors about why a few of the Catholic schools do so well in football," she whispered back.

Theo found her gaze traveling again to Thoth and Ganesha as she ate. After dinner she and Grant walked—Theo several inches above the ground—outside to sit on a low hillock and watch the sun set into the dark surrounding hills. "I wonder," she said softly.

"What do you wonder?" asked Grant, sliding closer to her and putting his arm over her shoulder.

"If my cat Dido could handle a little ambrosia in her tuna and liver." She glanced at him from the corner of her eye. "Seeing the animal-headed gods just made me wonder."

Grant was silent for a few moments, then said, "I keep forgetting that we've changed places. Now you're the goddess and I'm the human."

"I don't think you can call me a goddess. I can barely manage my own powers, as June Cadwallader so kindly pointed out." She pointed at a pinecone lying in the grass. To her surprise, it floated up and landed in her hand. "What do you know? It usually takes three or four tries, or else it flies up and bops me on the forehead."

"I think you'll find that you'll do better here. Less stress, for one thing."

"That's true." She set the pinecone spinning on the end of

one finger, then winced and batted it away. "Ow. Splinter. I've got a lot more to learn than just the mechanics of magic."

"Then I take it you want to stay immortal?"

"Do you want me to?" She shifted and wrapped her arms around him. "Will you take ambrosia and become immortal again, or do you want me to cast it away and be mortal with you?"

He closed his eyes. "I can't ask you to do that. Casting aside my immortality was a horrible process—I'm not sure I could endure watching you suffer the way I did. But I'm afraid to be a god again. How do I know I'll be able to remember how to love you properly?"

Theo laughed and pulled him down into the soft grass with her, weaving a curtain of light from the setting sun to set around them. He was right: using her power here *was* easier. She bent to kiss him and rejoiced at how his hands traveled hungrily over her as their lips met. "I wouldn't worry about that, my love," she whispered, breaking the kiss for a moment. "So long as we're together, I won't let you forget."

And they lived happily ever after.
Ever after.

Acknowledgements

Huge thanks and *anassa kata* to Nancy Evans, school-mate, scholar, and gentlewoman, who helped me with the bits of classical Greek scattered through *By Jove*.

Avete and *anassa kata* as well to all my teachers of Latin over eight years of study, but most of all to Mr. Paul Guy: thank you, *magister*, for the priceless gift of language you gave me.

And my love and thanks to Hal Lorin, for the recommendation of Roberto Calasso's *The Marriage of Cadmus and Harmony*. I owe you a grappa, my friend.

Thank you so much for taking the time to read *By Jove*. If you enjoyed it, please consider telling your friends or posting a review on the site where you purchased it or on your favorite social media site such as Goodreads or LibraryThing. Word of mouth is an author's best friend and much appreciated. Thank you!

Connect with me
(because I love hearing from readers!)

Website: www.marissadoyle.com
Blog: www.nineteenteen.com
Facebook: www.facebook.com/marissadoyleauthor/
Twitter: twitter.com/marissadoyle
Pinterest: www.pinterest.com/mdoyleauthor/
Book View Café: http://bookviewcafe.com/bookstore/bvc-author/marissa-doyle/

About the Author

Marissa Doyle graduated from Bryn Mawr College and went on to graduate school intending to be an archaeologist, but somehow got distracted. Eventually she figured out what she was *really* supposed to be doing and started writing. She's channeled her inner history geekiness into a successful young adult historical fantasy series (the Leland Sisters), and is now also happily writing contemporary romantic fantasy. She lives in her native Massachusetts with her family, including a bossy but adorable pet rabbit, and loves quilting, gardening, and collecting antiques. Oh, and coffee.

Read a sample of another
contemporary romantic fantasy by
Marissa Doyle

Skin Deep

Chapter 1

COLD MARCH SATURDAY MORNINGS were made for sleeping late. Garland Durrell knew that. But here she was, snuggled under her down quilt, eyes resolutely shut against the coronas of light around her windows—and wide awake.

She would have been happily snoozing if it hadn't been for a freak storm that no one had predicted blowing in off the Atlantic during the night. She'd never heard the wind make sounds like that, shrieking and howling so fiercely that she'd half-dreamed it was trying to smash her windows and seize her. Not the best way to spend the first night of the rest of her life in Mattaquason on Cape Cod's outer arm. If she believed in omens—but she didn't. Not anymore. Her wedding day had been gloriously sunny, and look how her marriage had ended up.

Though the storm had screamed back out to sea some time before dawn, she'd only been able to doze fitfully since then...and now, not at all. Well, if she couldn't sleep, then she might as well be up and about doing something about unpacking all the boxes stacked around the house.

She threw aside the quilt and went to the bank of windows to open the curtains. Past the grass and a long, low dune the beach's creamy white sand spread enticingly before her. Maybe a walk before she began excavating her life out of moving boxes and reassembling it into its new form would be a good idea?

Garland yanked off her nightshirt and dressed quickly in jeans and a turtleneck sweater and a heavy, violet-colored flannel shirt on which she'd appliquéd a Compass Rose quilt square, along with a down vest. She almost ran down the stairs and through the garage where her little sailing dinghy sat on its trailer. Bigger sailboats were handsomer, but this one was so much closer to the wind and water, so much closer to what really mattered about sailing. Derek had always called it "Garland's toy boat." His own tastes ran to motorboats with more horsepower than was decent—and damn it, why did everything have to remind her of Derek? Had moving to this house been a mistake? Should she have sold it and gone someplace where memories wouldn't leap out at her unexpectedly like ugly Halloween spooks?

She slammed the garage door behind her and strode across the terrace to the back lawn. Once away from the protection of the house, the wind hit her like a fist to the stomach. But the sky was a soft, milky blue and the sunshine was so bright that instead of scooting back inside she paused to breathe deeply, expanding her chest as far as it would go.

Past the lawn the beach was still damp and smooth from the receding tide. Off to her left, the long, narrow finger of Monomoyick Island poked into the ocean off the end of Cape Cod, pointing south toward Nantucket. The water was deep blue and choppy this morning but sparkling in the sun, making her squint as she stepped onto the sand.

Beachcombing after a storm was fun. Smashed lobster pots weren't uncommon, or broken oars, or other detritus tossed or lost off fishing boats. But sometimes the oddest things washed up. Once she'd found a waterlogged, two-foot long Winnie-the-Pooh half-buried in the sand, its red shirt faded to rose pink. And after another storm, a lacy, bright fuchsia bra from Victoria's Secret, size 46 DD. That find had sent her best friend in Mattaquason, Kathy Hayes, into gales of laughter, speculating whether any of the local fishermen had a secret lingerie fetish.

The memory made Garland smile. Kathy hadn't been home when she called last night. Out on a date, perhaps? Kathy often lamented the dearth of eligible men—whom she defined as "over six feet and without a substance abuse problem"—who lived year-round on the Cape, but maybe she'd found someone new. Hopefully she'd be in later, just in case Garland found the panties to match the bra.

Kathy had been delighted when she'd called to tell her that she'd be moving to the Cape. "Without Derek, I'm assuming," she'd said in the dry tone she always used when talking about Garland's husband. "It's about damn time. He was smothering you, Garland. Every year when you came down for the summer, you looked a little paler and flatter. No, don't laugh. It was true. He was a mistake, and it was time you cut your losses and started over. So when are you going to start quilting again? I told you, I'm keeping a space in the gallery for you, and Mrs. Feinberg asked again last summer if you'd made anything new."

Starting quilting again. She thought of the boxes of fabric and threads and the new long-arm quilting machine waiting for her at the house. She was free to create with cloth again—free of Derek's disapproval and his feigned dust allergies. She could festoon the house with fat quarters and leave pads of graph paper and piles of colored pencils in every room, and no one would care. It would be *wonderful*.

A sharp, barking call made her shade her eyes and stare out at the water. Was that a seal? Sometimes in summer she would see them a little way off the beach, lounging on the sandbar at low tide. Yes, there they were—three, no, four seals swimming parallel to the shore and looking at her with their liquid brown eyes. She'd always loved to watch them with their whiskery, inquiring faces, so at home in the water.

A houseguest had once given her a fancifully illustrated children's book about seals who could take off their skins and dance on the beach on moonlit nights in the form of beautiful men and women. Selkies, they were called. She often thought about them on the full moon nights in July and August, but Derek had never wanted to use them as a pretext for a romantic walk on to the beach. How well she remembered the patronizing smile he would give her as he told her to 'run along and enjoy herself' while he logged into his portfolio account.

One of the seals barked again. A gull, handsome in its sober gray and white feathers, cackled as it landed a few dozen yards up the beach before her. Something edible must have been tossed up in the storm, for another gull was already there.

Garland blinked away the tears in her eyes brought by the wind and squinted at the sand. There was something on the beach ahead—something large and pale, almost blending into the sand itself. The two gulls regarded it quizzically, as if wondering if it were tasty or not. She took three more steps, then froze.

The something was a naked body sprawled on its stomach, partly buried in the sand.

Skin Deep is available at all your favorite online retailers in both e-book and print formats.

ABOUT BOOK VIEW CAFÉ

Book View Café Publishing Cooperative is an author-owned cooperative of over fifty professional writers, publishing in a variety of genres such as fantasy, romance, mystery, and science fiction.

BVC authors include *New York Times* and *USA Today* bestsellers; Nebula, Hugo, and Philip K. Dick Award winners; World Fantasy Award, Campbell Award, and RITA Award nominees; and winners and nominees of many other publishing awards.

Since its debut in 2008, BVC has gained a reputation for producing high-quality e-books, and is now bringing that same quality to its print editions.